USER

A NOVEL

BLAKE NELSON

USER

A NOVEL

BLAKE NELSON

Versus Press
San Francisco

USER
by Blake Nelson

Versus Press, LLC.
First Printing

The Author would like to thank Don Waters, John DeWitt, Cat Tyc, Casey Kait, Dave Dunton, Richard Parks, Gary Hustwit, Lizzie Simon, Julia Schwadron, Frieda Duggan and especially John Fahs.

ISBN 0-9704817-1-3
Library of Congress Control Number: 2001092200

Cover Photo of Beth Lisick by Peter Ellenby
Book Layout by Don Waters

Versus Press
Literary Pushers and Avant-Anomicists
PO Box 170187
San Francisco CA 94117

For more information about this title and others, get your stats checked at: www.versuspress.com.

Printed in Canada

For Sally Cohen

ONE

Mitch Smith pushes out the heavy side door of Quest nightclub. For a moment the pulsing dance beat follows him onto the sidewalk, it fills the entire block. Then the door shuts behind him and everything is quiet again. Mitch walks to the corner. He reaches into his Stussy racing jacket for his cigarettes. It's mid-November: cold, damp. And it's rained. The streets are shiny black. He lights a cigarette and crosses the street.

"Hey, Mitch!" calls a voice. A Toyota Celica is stopped at the intersection. He bends slightly to see inside. It's Amy Peterson. A girl he knows. A girl he made out with once.

Amy rolls down her window. "Hey," she says.

"Hey, what's up?" says Mitch.

"Nothing. What's up with you?"

Mitch shrugs. "I was just at Quest." He moves closer to the car. He made out with her at a party. She was a good kisser. And she was into it. But he blew her off.

"Where are you going?" says Amy.

"Home."

"Wanna ride?"

"Sure," says Mitch. He throws down his cigarette and gets in the car.

"So, what was going on at Quest?" asks Amy, accelerating when the light turns green.

"The usual," says Mitch. He watches the street ahead of them. Then he looks around at the interior of the car. "Is this yours?"

"Yeah," says Amy.

"I didn't know you had a car."

"It's not much of one."

"Hey, if it runs."

Amy smiles. She drives. "So what are you doing these days," she asks. "I haven't seen you in a while."

"Not much," says Mitch. "I got fired from Quest."

"Oh no."

"Not fired really. I got laid off."

"But you were just there."

"Yeah. I still go there. I get in free."

Amy stops at a red light.

"What are you doing?" asks Mitch.

"Working at Borders."

"How's that?"

"They're redoing the computers," says Amy. "So we're just typing stuff all day. It sucks."

Mitch nods. "Yeah, I got this new job driving a delivery truck," he says. "It's pretty lame."

Amy nods. When the light turns green she drives. "Where do you live again?"

"Across the river. Take the Hawthorne Bridge."

She does. Mitch cracks his window and lights a cigarette. He looks over at Amy. She's wearing a beige overcoat, a plain dress underneath. But she has a cute face. And he can see the soft white skin of her neck and shoulders. He remembers it from when they made out.

"Hey, you wanna go get a drink or something?" says Mitch.

Amy glances over at him. "Where?"

"I don't know. The Monte Carlo?"

"I sort of have to get up early."

"Yeah?"

"What time is it?"

"Not that late, twelve?"

Amy thinks about it. "I guess I could have one drink. I haven't done anything all week."

"Turn right up there," says Mitch.

Mitch directs her to the Monte Carlo. It's a colorful dive bar. The booths are bright red vinyl. They take one near the back. "So what do you want?" says Mitch.

"Vodka tonic?"

Mitch goes to the bar. He orders two vodka tonics. He lights a cigarette while he waits. He looks back at the booth where Amy is smoothing her hair. Then she straightens her coat. She sees him and smiles. He smiles tightly back.

The drinks come. He pays. He takes them to the table.

"Here you go," says Mitch, sliding in across from her.

"Thanks," says Amy. She takes the drink. She stirs it.

Mitch stirs his. "So..." he says. But he can't think of what to say next.

Amy tastes her drink.

"So what else have you been doing?" asks Mitch.

"Well, I moved."

"Where to?"

"A house in Southeast. With this girl Tracy and another girl."

"Tracy? Not Tracy Richards?"

"Yeah, do you know her?"

"Sure. Who doesn't?"

"I know," says Amy, frowning. "It seems like everybody knows her."

"How did you end up there?"

"I answered an ad. For a roommate. And it was her and the other girl."

"No shit?" says Mitch. "That house in Southeast? Where they had all those parties last summer?"

"I know. That's what everyone says. Everyone wants to know when the next one is."

"Those were great parties," says Mitch.

Amy puts down her drink and takes off her coat. She looks good in the dress: her neck, her shoulders, her creamy white skin.

"That's a cute dress," says Mitch.

"Oh, this?" she says, bashfully. "It's just for work."

"I sort of forgot how cute you were," says Mitch.

Amy smiles. She pokes at her drink. Without looking up she says: "I forgot how cute *you* were."

Mitch smokes. He watches her. "So how's your love life?"

"Terrible," says Amy.

"Why's that?"

"I broke up with Andy."

"Who's Andy?"

"Andy White? That really tall guy? He used to play drums in The Miserables."

"Oh, right," says Mitch.

"Yeah. He went back with his old girlfriend."

"That sucks."

"What about you?" asks Amy. "Are you seeing anyone?"

Mitch shrugs. He drinks his drink. "I got this delivery job. At like five in the morning. It kind of makes things difficult."

"I can't imagine anything slowing *you* down," says Amy. This is her first reference to the night they made out. Mitch waits to see what else she'll say. But that's it. She stirs her drink.

"There must be a lot of guys around your house," says Mitch. "With Tracy Richards living there."

"I know. When I first moved there this one guy kept coming over. He was so in love with her. He'd try to break in and stuff. We finally had to call the police."

"Jesus."

"I mean, what is it about her? That's what I want to know."

"She's cute."

"But she's so mean. At least to boys."

"She can afford to be."

"Why?"

Mitch shrugs. "She's the coolest girl in Portland."

Amy frowns. "How can someone be *the coolest girl*?"

"Well, in her case," says Mitch. "I mean, I'm not saying I think so. But if you asked people."

"She's okay as a roommate. But these *men*, they're just so...they get so...*obsessed*."

Mitch now remembers why he blew off Amy. She's kind of slow.

"I don't know," says Amy. She looks at Mitch. "Did you ever like her?"

"Tracy? Nah. She's not my type."

"But you noticed her."

"Yeah, sure," says Mitch. He smokes. He drinks more of his vodka. Then he looks at his glass, it's two thirds gone. "The drinks here are too small."

"Get another one," says Amy.

"I'm kinda broke."

"I'll pay for it," says Amy. She digs into her purse. She hands him a five.

Mitch takes the bill but doesn't get up. He watches Amy put her wallet back into her purse.

"You know what?" says Mitch.

"What?"

"Take this." He gives Amy back her five. "Let's go to my place. I got vodka. Fuck these overpriced drinks."

Amy takes the five. She stuffs it in her purse. She grabs her coat and hurries to catch up to Mitch, who is already striding toward the door.

TWO

Mitch lives in a house off Hawthorne Boulevard. It's dark when they arrive. His housemates are all asleep. Mitch leads Amy up the stairs to his room. He turns on the light. It's a mess. The radio is on, it's playing static. He steps through the dishes and the dirty clothes to turn it off.

"Sorry about the mess," he says.

"It's okay."

"Take your coat?"

"Sure," says Amy. She slips it off. Mitch takes it. He throws it over the chair in the corner. Amy crosses her arms over her chest.

"Okay," says Mitch. "I think I have a couple of beers downstairs. Or do you want a real drink?"

"Do you have any juice?" asks Amy.

"I might."

"Or maybe some tea?"

"I can look," says Mitch.

"It doesn't matter. Whatever," says Amy. She looks around the room. The only place to sit is the bed. She sits on it.

Mitch goes downstairs. In the dark kitchen he gets himself a beer and pours Amy a small glass of his housemate's grapefruit juice. Then he goes into the living room and unplugs the small TV. He grips it in his free hand and carries everything up the stairs. He nudges his door open with his foot.

Amy is sitting on the bed, flipping through an old *Bikini* magazine. Mitch hands her the drinks and puts the TV on the chair. He plugs it in and faces it toward the bed. He turns it on. He turns off the lights.

Mitch sits on the bed. Amy hands him his beer. But the TV picture is jagged and blurred. Mitch gets up and moves the antenna.

Amy watches him. The picture clears, and then blurs again.

"This TV sucks," says Mitch, changing the channel. He finally gets something that looks like a movie. He adjusts the antenna until it's watchable. He sits back on the bed. Amy is leaning forward slightly. Her shoulders look even whiter and softer in the blue TV light.

"It's cold in here," says Amy.

"Grab those covers," says Mitch. He's a little nervous now. But happy. He positions a pillow so Amy can sit back against the wall. He throws blankets over her, tossing away a dirty sock that appears among the covers.

He leans back against the wall with Amy. He watches the TV and kicks off his shoes. Amy pulls the covers up to her chest.

"You wanna take off your shoes?" asks Mitch.

Amy looks at her Doc Martens where they stick out from under the blankets.

"I'll do it," says Mitch. He leans forward and unties Amy's left shoe. He loosens the tongue and slips it off. He squeezes her foot once in his hand. The sock is slightly damp.

"My feet get sweaty," says Amy.

"It's all right," says Mitch. He unties her right shoe.

"So you aren't dating anyone?" asks Amy, watching him.

"Nah. I don't go on dates." Mitch slips off the right shoe. He squeezes her foot, massages it for a second. But the TV isn't working. He gets up and adjusts the antenna. When the picture clears he sits down again, a little closer to Amy this time. He can smell her now. She smells sweet, feminine.

Mitch pulls the covers close. They are shoulder to shoulder, knee to knee. He looks at her.

"What?" says Amy, grinning.

"Nothing," says Mitch. He slides his leg under Amy's.

"What are you doing?" says Amy.

"Trying to keep warm."

"*Mitch,*" says Amy, slyly.

"Why don't you sit in front of me?"

"Why?"

"It'll be warmer," says Mitch, patting the place in front of him.

Amy does it. Mitch spreads his legs to let her lean back against him. She rearranges the blankets to keep them both covered.

"How's that?" says Amy, looking at him over her shoulder.

"That's nice," says Mitch. He slips his hands around Amy's front and cups her breasts with both hands.

"*Mitch,*" says Amy again.

Mitch ignores her. He squeezes her breasts and kisses the back of her neck.

Amy puts her arms around his arms, snuggles back against him. She sighs. But Mitch continues to kiss her. And fondle her. Finally, she twists herself around enough to kiss him.

She's a good kisser, wet and warm. And she's into it. Mitch finds the zipper of her dress and pulls it down. He slides the straps off her shoulders, exposing her collarbones, her chest, her bra. Mitch unhooks the bra. It falls away. Her tits spring free. Mitch touches them while he kisses her, he touches the nipples.

"Mitch?" says Amy. She pulls away. She turns until she is completely facing him.

"Yeah?" he says.

"What are we doing?"

Mitch looks at her bare breasts. They're round and firm. He touches them. He holds them from underneath. He squeezes the nipples. He kisses her.

"*Mitch*?" breathes Amy, her lips still touching his.

"What?"

"What are we doing?"

"We're making out."

"Are we going to have sex?"

Mitch says nothing. He grips her breasts more firmly. Then he eases her onto her back.

After that they don't talk. Her dress comes off. Her panties come off. Mitch eases her legs apart and guides his dick inside her. Amy remains cautiously still beneath him. Like she doesn't want to make a mistake. Mitch isn't going for anything fancy. He fucks her for a while. It feels good. He comes.

Afterward, he rolls off her onto his back. In the cold room he can see his breath in the TV light. He pulls the covers over the two of them. Then he curls up next to Amy. He is already dreaming when he hears her voice: "Do you want me to turn off the TV?"

THREE

In the morning, Amy is still there. Mitch was hoping she might be gone. She said she had to work early. And she has her car.

"Mmmmm," says Amy, sleepily gripping Mitch. She appears to be asleep. Mitch pretends he is. He tries to slide away from her but his bed isn't big enough. And she's lying in the middle of it. Mitch is pressed against the wall. Amy shifts toward him and drapes her arm clumsily over his shoulder.

There's no escape. So Mitch turns toward her. He thinks she closes her eyes as he does this. But Mitch enjoys her warm softness despite himself. One of her legs is resting against his. He touches her hip. He shifts. His leg slides between hers.

"Mmmmm," says Amy, still asleep. Mitch glides his hand along the curve of her waist. He scoots closer. She presses against his leg.

Mitch pulls her toward him. They are both still "asleep" but he pulls and she rolls and then she's on top of him. She's heavier than she looks. Mitch's breath is constricted. But it's nice. It's warm. Her soft hair falls in his face, falls across his neck and shoulders. It feels heavenly. Mitch reaches through her legs and finds his dick, which is rigid, almost painfully so.

But it feels better inside her. Mitch closes his eyes and savors the sensation. Amy meanwhile does nothing. She just lays there. Mitch wants her to move, to do something. She doesn't. At first. But then slowly, almost imperceptibly, she presses down against him. She presses and releases. Mitch breathes. She presses again, releases. Mitch reaches down and lightly caresses the small of her back. This makes her press harder, she holds it longer. Then the release. But this is driving Mitch crazy. He wants more. He begins to push back against her, to fuck her from below. But once he's got a rhythm going, he becomes even more impatient. He rolls her over, gets her legs open, gets all the way inside her. He fucks her in this position, long and steady, hoping she'll come. Or at least get into it. Which she does. Mitch increases his rhythm. She wraps her legs around his back. He rocks the bed hard and for a second time empties himself inside her.

Afterward, he curls up under the covers. He goes back to sleep. When he opens his eyes she's still there. She's lying on her back, staring at the ceiling, waiting for him.

"You can take a shower if you want," says Mitch, a few minutes later. He's completely awake now. He's sitting against the wall, naked except for a blanket over his lap. He's lit a cigarette and is dropping the ashes into the beer can on the floor beside him.

Amy is sitting on the edge of the mattress gathering her things. "Where are your housemates?"

"They're at work. Go for it. It's across the hall. Use that towel right there."

"Okay," says Amy. She walks naked across the room to the towel hanging on his closet doorknob. Mitch watches her. He smokes.

When the shower comes on, Mitch gets up, stretches, drops the cigarette into the beer can where it sizzles and dies. He digs through the covers for his underwear. He finds his favorite Adidas sweat pants in his laundry box. He slips on his suede Vans and laces them tight.

But once he's dressed he doesn't know what to do. The shower is still on. What's he going to do with Amy?

• • •

He's reading *Bikini* when she comes back into the room. She's got the towel wrapped around her middle. "I just noticed it's almost ten," he says. "Don't you have to work?"

"I don't think I'll go in today. I don't really feel like it."

"I thought you said you had to?"

"We can go in whenever we want. As long as we finish by next week."

"But I thought..."

"They don't care when we do it," says Amy. She gets her underwear and her dress. She goes back into the bathroom. His housemate's blowdryer comes on.

Mitch flips the pages of the magazine. Not only is he stuck with her, he's stuck waiting for her. He drops the magazine and crosses the room to his CD player. He puts on the new DJ Slider CD. It begins with a slow growling bass line. He turns it up. He sits back on the bed. He picks up the *Bikini*. He flips the pages.

Amy returns. She's dressed. She puts on her socks and then looks for her Doc Martens, one of which is right beneath her. Mitch neglects to point this out. Amy starts digging through the blankets.

"What band is this?" asks Amy.

"It's a DJ," says Mitch. He stops flipping and pretends to read something.

"This sounds like Pearl Jam."

"*Pearl Jam*?" scoffs Mitch.

"Well, I don't know."

"It's DJ Slider," says Mitch. "He's from England."

"Do you know that band Baxter?" asks Amy.

"No."

Amy finds her shoes. She sits on the bed and puts them on. "They're from Olympia."

What's that got to do with anything? thinks Mitch. But he should try to be nice. "Is Baxter the name of the guy or the name of the band?"

"The name of the band. The guy's name is Fritz."

"Then why is his band called Baxter?" says Mitch, more to the magazine than to Amy.

"Tracy's after him," says Amy. "Her and Erica and everyone are going to see them."

Mitch thinks about Tracy Richards. There's someone he could have a one night stand with. But he's got Amy to deal with. She's going to want to get something to eat. She'll probably want to hang out all day. Christ. This is why he blew her off that other time.

"So!" says Amy when she's got all her clothes on.

"So," says Mitch, staring into the magazine.

"Feel like some breakfast?"

FOUR

Mitch works a compromise. They'll go to breakfast. But then Amy will leave, so he can run some errands. Once this is decided, Mitch feels better. He actually enjoys the walk along Hawthorne, the main drag of his neighborhood. Amy looks good outside. There's a healthy bounce to her step. Also, other guys seem to notice her. They watch her. Mitch likes this. He likes the power of it. They want her. He's got her.

They go to Rafferty's, a small diner at the end of the strip. It's crowded. They have to wait for a table to open up. Mitch doesn't like waiting but he doesn't want to think of another place to go either. He picks up the sports section of an abandoned newspaper. He leans against a post and reads. Amy stands straight, both hands gripping the straps of her purse in front of her.

Mitch is happy again when they finally sit. Now he's glad they came. Hot coffee and a filling meal is exactly what he wants. The waiter comes. He pours coffee. Amy smiles at Mitch.

When the food comes Mitch digs in: scrambled eggs, sausage, home fried potatoes, two slices of sourdough toast. He gulps his coffee.

Amy eats more slowly. She seems to be thinking. "So there's something I've been meaning to ask you," she says. "About that time. At Rachel's party."

Mitch chews his food. "Rachel..."

"That girl who had the party in Northeast. You were with that guy Stuart." She means the party where they made out.

"Huh," says Mitch. "What about it?"

"Don't you remember?"

Mitch chews and swallows. "You mean like...when we–" He makes a rolling hand gesture.

"Well, yeah," says Amy, shyly.

"What about it?" says Mitch. He's actually enjoying this. He's eating. He's drinking. He just got laid. Twice.

"When we made out," says Amy.

"We made out?"

"*Yes*. God, Mitch."

"Oh, yeah. I remember. That was fun."

"It was *fun*?"

Mitch cuts a slice of sausage in half with the side of his fork. He stuffs one half in his mouth. "Didn't you think it was fun?"

"Of course I did," says Amy. "It's just that, well, what happened?"

"What do you mean?"

"I mean, you got up for a second and then you never came back."

"I did?"

"Yes."

Mitch thinks about it. He eats more sausage. "I don't remember."

"And you said to wait for you. And I did. And I thought you were going to give me a ride home."

"You didn't have your car?"

"I didn't have a car then. I told you that."

"That was a weird party," says Mitch. "I think Stuart got in a fight."

"I mean, I know when a guy says he'll call, sometimes they're just saying that but you just got up *for a second*."

Mitch wipes his face with his napkin. He's full and he wants to smoke. But you can't smoke inside Rafferty's.

"Were you drunk?" says Amy.

"Probably," says Mitch. "Fuck, you know what? You can't smoke in here."

"You want to smoke?"

"I go crazy in the morning, you know," he makes the same rolling hand gesture. "I gotta have a cigarette."

"We can go," says Amy. "I'm done."

"No, you're not," says Mitch. He spears one of her sausages and eats it.

Amy wipes her mouth with her napkin. "I waited for you Mitch. I stayed and waited for you and then I had to get Bill Watson to take me home and you know how Bill is."

"No, I don't."

"Well, if you do anything to encourage him he thinks you like him. He wanted to come up to my apartment. He wanted to kiss me."

"Bill Watson? Wanted to kiss you?"

"He always does."

"What's wrong with that guy's face? He's got zits on top of zits."

"Well, he can't help it."

"It's fucking disgusting."

"I know. That's why I was so mad. I have to tell you something Mitch. I was going to call you and tell you off. But I didn't."

"Thanks," says Mitch. But he's not really listening. He needs to smoke. Now. He gets out his wallet and waves at the waiter. "Check!"

FIVE

Outside, Mitch lights a cigarette. He smokes as they walk. Amy doesn't speak. Mitch avoids looking at her. They walk down Hawthorne and turn onto Mitch's street. They arrive at Amy's Celica.

"Well, I'll leave you to your errands," says Amy.

Mitch nods.

Amy gets out her keys. She turns to Mitch. "So will you give me a call sometime?"

Mitch nods. He smokes.

"Will you really though?"

Mitch shrugs. "Yeah, sure."

"When?"

"I don't know."

Amy unlocks her door. But she doesn't get in. She turns back to Mitch. "Are you going to see Baxter?"

"When are they playing?"

"Tonight. At Club UFO."

Mitch looks down. "Yeah, maybe."

"I'm sure Tracy and those people will be going."

"Are you going?"

"Yeah. I might be a little late," she looks at her watch. "I'll have to go work on the computer for a while."

Mitch nods. He sucks in the last drag of his cigarette. He drops it on the ground and steps on it. When he looks up Amy is leaning against her car. Her arms are crossed against her chest. She's staring at him.

"What?" says Mitch.

Amy looks at the ground. Her hair falls into her face. She pulls it back over one ear. "I mean, if you don't want to," she says.

"What? Call you? Sure I want to," says Mitch.

"But you won't. I know you won't."

"If you're going to make a big deal out of it." He finds himself focusing on her eyebrows as he says this: how straight they are, how slight.

"This is going to be just like Rachel's party."

Mitch shrugs. He looks at the ground. "I don't know what I'm going to do. I never know what I'm going to do." He moves forward. He touches her shoulder.

Amy doesn't respond.

"I'm sorry about Rachel's party," says Mitch as he leans forward and kisses her smooth forehead.

Amy's head lifts slightly. Mitch finds her lips. He kisses her. He unhooks her hands which she reluctantly slips around his waist. He kisses her more. He presses against her.

Amy stops. She makes her hands into fists, which she presses into his chest.

Mitch steps back.

"I can't make you do something you don't want to do," says Amy. She turns and starts to get in her car.

"Wait a minute," says Mitch.

"I'm going."

"Just come here a second."

"What?"

This time Mitch just hugs her. He doesn't kiss her or rub against her. He just holds her. He smells her. He feels her soft breasts against his chest. Then he lets her go.

"What," says Amy. "What was that for?"

"Nothing," says Mitch. He steps back and feels around in his coat for his cigarettes. "I'll see you."

"Okay," she says, hopefully.

"Have fun at work," says Mitch.

Amy opens her door. Mitch walks backward away from her. He puts a cigarette in his mouth. Then he turns and walks away.

But back in his house Mitch is angry with himself. That last bit: now he really will have to call her. Or maybe he won't. He doesn't know. He goes into the bathroom and strips off his clothes. He turns on the shower. He tests the water with his hand and gets in. It feels good under the hot water. The heat relaxes the tight muscles in his shoulders. There's no need to be tense. Whatever else happens, he just got laid. Twice. And he has to admit, Amy had a great body. It was heaven to be inside her. Mitch lets the thought of it fill his brain. His dick begins to swell and soon he is holding himself. He imagines Amy beneath him the way she was last night. Then above him the way she was this morning. And then, as he begins to stroke himself, in new positions, right there in the shower. Amy kissing him. Amy touching him. Amy down on her knees, sucking his cock. Then with Tracy Richards in the bathroom. Tracy, who he barely knows. But he knows what she looks like. And he can imagine her naked, in the shower, with the two of them. Tracy watching while Mitch takes Amy from behind, Tracy commenting on Mitch's prowess, his size, and then kissing him while he continues with Amy. The ending is some such mingling of the two women and then Mitch comes, the water mixing with the milky liquid as it dribbles off the end of his dick into the water swirling at his feet.

Mitch takes a nap and wakes up just as the sun is going down. He's going to see Baxter, he knows it as soon as his eyes are open. He wants to see Tracy Richards for one thing. And her cute friends. And if nothing else, he could always have sex with Amy again.

He calls his friend Stuart. But Stuart wants to go to Quest.

"We always go to Quest," Mitch says. "Let's go to UFO for once."

"UFO sucks. And *Baxter.* What is that? That's the stupidest name I ever heard."

"They're from Olympia. Girls will be there."

"Fuck Olympia. There'll be girls at Quest."

"Tracy Richards will be there. And Erica. And lots of other girls."

"I hate that fucking geek rock shit."

"It'll be fun. That girl Amy Peterson will be there."

"So?"

"She's sort of cute."

"I think Dieter fucked her."

"Really?"

"Why? Are you after her?"

"Sort of."

"Sort of what?"

"I sort of already got her," says Mitch.

"What, you nailed her?"

"Kind of."

"Well, you did or you didn't."

"I did."

"When?"

"Last night."

"Are you serious?"

"Uh-huh."

"How was it?"

"Okay."

"Just okay?"

"It was good."

"Did she go down on you?"

"No."

"She went down on Dieter."

"She did?"

"Yup."

"How do you know?"

"He told me."

"I'm sure she would have," says Mitch. "It didn't come up. We weren't in that position."

"Well, you should get yourself in that position, my man."

"Jesus," says Mitch. "What happened when she fucked Dieter?"

"Nothing."

"I mean, did he go out with her?"

"Not that I know of. Are *you* going out with her?"

"Nah. She wants to though. She's already bugging me to call her."

"She's got a nice body."

"Well, fuck. Let's go to this show."

"Oh, *man*," whines Stuart.

"C'mon. Tracy Richards? Erica? It'll be rad."

SIX

Mitch waits for Stuart on the front porch of his house. He smokes a cigarette and watches the rain fall in the streetlight across the street. When Stuart's Dodge Charger pulls up he runs down the steps and gets in.

Stuart's stereo is cranked. "Hey," shouts Mitch, over a pounding techno beat.

"Hey," shouts Stuart.

Since UFO is an all-ages club they stop at a liquor store on the way. It's bright inside. The old people at the counter stop talking when they walk in. Mitch and Stuart cruise along the back aisle. "What do we want?" whispers Stuart.

"Rum...tequila..." says Mitch.

"We need something small," says Stuart. "Something we can sneak in."

They go to the front counter, where the pint bottles are. The old woman eyes them warily. Stuart especially. He's six two, two hundred pounds. He's wearing a black sweat shirt, a Fuct baseball cap. Part of a large dragon tattoo shows on his neck.

"Pint of Cuervo," says Stuart.

"Can I see some ID?" says the woman, not moving. Stuart and Mitch both get out their wallets. Stuart's twenty-one. Mitch is twenty-two. The woman rings them up.

Back in the car, Stuart cracks the bottle and takes a long swig. He hands the bottle to Mitch who does the same. They drive. At

UFO, they park in the back. Stuart gets out his pipe and some pot. They get stoned. They go inside.

UFO is one large room in the back of a warehouse. It has cinder block walls, a cement floor. At one end of the room is a stage. Off to the side is a juice bar. Scattered elsewhere are old couches, chairs. Except for some musicians and a few others, the place is empty.

"I told you this place sucks," says Stuart.

"It's early. C'mon, let's get something to mix."

They get two cups of orange juice and take them to a couch in the back of the room. Stuart pulls the tequila out of his pants and spikes the drinks. Mitch lights a cigarette.

"So you fucked Amy Peterson," says Stuart, stirring his drink with his finger.

Mitch shrugs. He watches two girls come in. "So what else did Dieter say about her?" he asks.

"Not much."

"He must have said something."

"Why? Are you thinking of going out with her?"

"No," says Mitch.

"Why not?"

"I don't know," says Mitch, watching more people come in.

Stuart watches too. "So where's Tracy Richards?"

"Good question."

"Who's she fucking these days?"

"One of the Baxter guys, I guess."

"Yeah? Who told you that?"

"Amy."

"How does she know?"

"They live together."

Stuart nods. "Ahhh. So that's it. You're using Amy to get to Tracy."

"I wish."

"You better watch yourself."

Mitch smokes. "Why?"

"That Tracy's a fucking cunt, that's why."

"Yeah? What's she done to you?"

"Nothing. I'm just saying."

Mitch flicks his cigarette into the middle of the floor. He watches it burn a black spot on the cement.

More people come in. The room is filling up. Mitch and Stuart drink their drinks. After a while the lights go down. Baxter comes on. Stuart was right. They're geeks: they wear sweaters, slacks, big black shoes. But their first song is tight and fast and the lead singer screams and flails around. The crowd moves forward toward the stage. People are getting into it.

"See? They're not that bad," says Mitch.

"They suck," says Stuart, drinking his tequila.

"I'm going up front," says Mitch. He takes his drink and walks to the side of the stage. He watches Baxter begin their next song. The guitar sound is wanky but the drummer is good. Mitch watches the crowd. It's mostly girls in front. Cute girly types in short skirts and barrettes. The Olympia scene. The riot grrrl thing. Then there's a commotion on the opposite side. It's Tracy Richards, he knows it even before he sees her. She's pushing her way to the front. When she gets there she begins to dance. The people in front stop watching the band and watch her.

Mitch lights a cigarette. He watches her too. She's wearing sunglasses and some sort of fake fur coat which she stops to take off. She lays it on the stage. Erica is squishing up to the front also. And another girl. But Tracy is the most interesting to watch. She does a little go-go dance that doesn't quite work but is all the sexier for its gawkiness.

Some boys start moshing in the back. Everyone gets pushed forward and Tracy and her friends fall over the stage. Mitch watches to see if they'll get pissed. They don't. They laugh. Tracy rights herself and yells at the singer. He doesn't hear her though. He jumps in the air and lurches across the stage in his big black shoes.

Mitch goes back to find Stuart. He's standing near the door with another guy.

"What's up?" says Mitch.

"We're going to Quest."

"Yeah?" says Mitch.

"Yeah, come on," says Stuart. "You saw a couple songs."

"Tracy Richards is here," says Mitch.

"So?"

"So, I wanna hang out."

Stuart looks at him. "You're not seriously going to try for her."

"Not *try for her*," says Mitch. "I might *talk* to her."

"Yeah, but will she talk to you back? That's the question."

Mitch looks into the crowd at the front of the room.

"Well, whatever," says Stuart. "I'll be at Quest."

SEVEN

After Stuart's gone, Mitch sits on the couch. He sips his drink. He lights a cigarette. Baxter plays. Mitch finds himself staring at the girl behind the juice bar. She used to work at the X-Ray, the old all-ages club. Her name is Catherine? Kathleen? Something like that. She's cute. And there's nothing else to look at. Mitch flicks ashes and stares at her. She's giving someone a juice but as she takes the money she looks up, right at Mitch. Their eyes meet. She pretends she doesn't notice and looks away. Mitch smokes.

Baxter is almost done. Mitch gets up and walks to the front. Tracy's sitting on the stage with Erica and her other friend. They look bored. Baxter plays their last song and quickly return for a short encore. The other cute girls in the front have moved away. A bunch of suburban guys have taken their place. The show is losing momentum. And Amy isn't here. He should have gone with Stuart. It's a long walk back to Quest.

When Baxter finishes, the crowd disperses. Tracy and Erica wander back toward the juice bar. Mitch watches the suburban guys talk to the singer while his bandmates clear the stage. Mitch checks out the Baxter guys. Most of them are preppie mod types. But the drummer is wearing Reeboks. Mitch wonders about that: guys in bands who dress stupid. Why doesn't one of the other guys just tell him? For the good of the band?

When the gear is moved, the Baxter guys mill around. The singer continues to chat with his suburban fans. Then Tracy comes running up. She grabs the singer and hugs him, spilling half her juice down his back. He squirms when he feels the liquid soak through his shirt. Everybody laughs. Mitch laughs too. He moves closer to the group, so he is right behind Tracy. He'll ask her if Amy is here. He'll introduce himself. Erica approaches. She sees Mitch and smiles at him. She must remember him from the parties last summer. This gives Mitch confidence. Tracy will remember him too. Mitch starts to say something but is interrupted by Tracy laughing. She's now mad at the singer for something. She's pretending to be mad. Everyone is laughing. The drummer comes over in his Reeboks. He's not laughing. He pulls the singer aside and for a moment they confer about something. Mitch makes his move. He reaches out to Tracy, touches her arm. "Hey, Tracy, do you know if Amy is here?" But somewhere in the middle of the sentence his voice tightens, it strains and breaks. He barely gets the words out.

Tracy, who was not aware of Mitch, turns and looks at him. But there's no recognition in her face, no acknowledgement at all. She walks over to the singer and grabs him. "What are you guys talking about? Tell me! Go away *you*!" She pushes the drummer. She's trying to separate the singer from him. Mitch stands where he is. He looks at Erica but she's talking to someone else. Mitch fucked up. He tried to talk to Tracy and he fucked it up.

He retreats. He walks back toward the juice bar but when he sees Kathleen he shies off in the other direction. Fuck. He downs the rest of his drink. He drops the cup on the floor and pushes out through the door.

Outside, it's cold and overcast. He pulls his Stussy racing jacket tight around him and heads toward Quest. He's been walking for fifteen minutes when Amy's Celica drives by going the other way. Mitch's head is down, he sees it too late, he shouts, waves his hand. But he's missed her. Or maybe not. Her brake lights come on. Mitch watches while her car turns into a parking lot and turns around.

She's coming back. Mitch blows into his frozen hand as Amy pulls up beside him. She rolls down the passenger window. "Hey, Mitch."

"Hey," he says.

"What are you doing out here?"

"Going to Quest," says Mitch.

"Why are you walking?"

"Stuart went ahead."

"It's kind of a long way isn't it?"

Mitch shrugs.

"Do you want a ride?"

Mitch hesitates. He does want a ride but he doesn't want to hang out with her.

"Come on," says Amy. "I can drive you over there."

Mitch gets in.

"Is the Baxter show over?" asks Amy, as she pulls into the street.

Mitch nods.

"Was Tracy there?"

Mitch doesn't answer.

"You didn't see her?"

"She might have been," says Mitch. "There were a lot of people."

"Was Baxter good?"

"They were all right."

Amy drives. "I think they're staying with us," she says. "Their van was in front of our house today."

Mitch stares straight ahead.

"Well, I should go check it out. I told Tracy I would."

"Yeah, I think I saw Erica," says Mitch. "I'm sure Tracy was there somewhere."

"Quest might be fun though," hints Amy. "Do you like, dance and all that?"

"Nah. I just hang out. In the DJ booth. You can't really go up there. Unless you work there or you're helping the DJ."

"Is that what you do?"

"More or less."

They get to Quest. Amy slows down at the corner. "Well, I should go back to UFO."

"Okay."

She stops at the corner. Mitch opens his door and gets out. But then he hesitates. He leans back into the car. "I mean, you can come in if you want. It's just that I gotta talk to this guy about maybe getting my job back..."

"That's all right Mitch."

"I can get you in, if you just want to come in."

"That's all right."

"Okay," says Mitch. He stands up. But then he thinks for a moment. He leans back down. "What are you doing later?"

"Later, when?"

"Tonight."

"Going to bed probably."

"Maybe I should come by."

"I'll probably be asleep. Why don't you call me tomorrow?"

"Yeah, okay. Whatever," he says. He shuts the door. Amy drives away.

EIGHT

Mitch goes into Quest. He nods his way past the doorman, the money taker, the hand stamper. Inside, it's dark and loud. Mitch weaves his way across the dance floor to the DJ platform. Stuart is sitting on the steps. Dieter is sitting above him. Dieter is the DJ tonight but he's taking a break. DJ Troy is at the turntables, he's gyrating in place to the beat.

"Hey," says Mitch. He slaps hands with Stuart. "Hey," he says to Dieter but Dieter can't hear him. Mitch sits on the step below Stuart.

"Hey, check it out," Stuart shouts into his ear. "There was this girl here before. She had this tiny skirt. No underpants."

Mitch frowns. "So?"

"So?" says Stuart. "Fuck man, what do you want?"

Mitch stares into the crowd on the dance floor. There's an extremely cute girl right in front of them.

"Man!" says Stuart, nudging him.

Mitch stares at her. He finds his cigarettes and puts one in his mouth.

"And check out Jeanelle," shouts Stuart. He points into the crowd. Mitch can't see her. "She's wearing this plastic jacket thing with nothing beneath it."

Mitch stares at the closer girl. She's got a tiny backpack. "I hate those tiny backpacks," he says to Stuart.

"What?" shouts Stuart.

Mitch shouts back: "I said I hate those tiny...nevermind..." Then he shouts into Stuart's ear. "I tried to talk to Tracy."

"And let me guess," shouts Stuart. "She shut you down. Ha ha. I told you."

Mitch shakes his head. He lights his cigarette. He smokes. Then he looks up at Dieter. Dieter is wearing yellow sweat pants with a glittery silver strip down the side. Mitch climbs over Stuart to talk to him. "Where'd you get those pants?" shouts Mitch.

"L.A.," Dieter shouts back.

Mitch touches the silver stripe. "Those are slick," he says. He's now on the top step of the platform. From here he can see the whole room. "Jeanelle is wearing some sort of–" he shouts to Dieter.

"–Plastic coat. I know. You can see her tits." Dieter shrugs.

"That's what I thought, but you know," says Mitch. He smokes his cigarette and watches the crowd. Then he leans into Dieter's ear: "Stuart says you went out with Amy Peterson."

Dieter shrugs. "Not really."

"She gave you a blow job or something?" asks Mitch.

"We messed around."

"I sort of went home with her the other night."

"Yeah?"

Mitch nods. He watches the dance floor. "She doesn't have any diseases or anything does she?"

Dieter looks at him. "Not that I know of."

"How come you didn't go out with her?"

"No reason."

"She dresses sort of yuppie," volunteers Mitch.

Dieter says nothing.

"And she doesn't know shit about music," says Mitch.

"She's just not into the scene that much," says Dieter. "But that's cool. She seems like a good person."

"Yeah, she's all right," says Mitch. He watches the dance floor. Jeanelle has moved into view. Dieter, Stuart and Mitch all watch. She's wearing a plastic jacket with a transparent strip across her chest. You can see her tits.

"You ever talk to Tracy Richards?" Mitch asks Dieter.

"Sometimes."

"What did you talk about?"

"To Tracy?" Dieter looks at him strangely. "I don't know. Nothing."

Mitch is going to ask another question but there's a commotion on the dance floor. Some guy has been bumping up against Jeanelle. Now there's a confrontation. Stuart jumps off the stairs. "Jesus Christ," says Dieter.

"Stuart!" yells Mitch. But the bouncers get there first. They break it up. They drag the guy away. Stuart reluctantly returns to the platform steps. Peace is restored.

Later, Stuart and Mitch retreat to the back room where Stuart plays video games. Mitch drinks a rum and coke and tries to catch the eye of a girl playing pinball.

"Fuck, now what do we do?" says Stuart, when he's out of change.

"I should have gone home with Amy," grumbles Mitch.

"Why didn't you?" says Stuart.

Mitch doesn't know. He lights a cigarette. The girl he was watching leaves with her friend.

"We gotta find some girls," says Stuart. "Or at least get fucked up."

Mitch says nothing.

"What about Baxter?" says Stuart.

"What about them?"

"Where are they? They're probably hanging out."

"They're at Tracy's."

"Let's go there."

"Nah."

"Why not?" asks Stuart. "Amy'll be there."

"I don't want to see Amy."

"And Tracy."

Mitch smokes. "I don't want to see her either."

"What did she say to you exactly?"

"Nothing. She didn't even see me."

"Then what are you worried about?"

"I don't know."

"Come on, let's just drive over there. We'll get stoned. We'll go to Hurley's if no one's there."

They drive to Tracy and Amy's. They smoke pot on the way. Stuart cranks the stereo. When they get there, Stuart stops across the street. He turns down the music. They both look at the house. "What do you think?" says Stuart.

Mitch looks. There's a van with Washington plates outside. Most of the lights in the house are on.

"I think I hear music," says Stuart.

Mitch hears it too.

"C'mon, man, let's go for it."

Mitch hesitates.

"What else is there to do?" says Stuart.

"Go to Hurley's?"

"Fuck Hurley's."

"Let's go back to Quest."

"Fuck Quest, let's go in here. Those guys are geeks anyway, if they give us any shit, we'll kick their ass."

Mitch looks again at the house. "What time is it?"

"It's one. C'mon. All the lights are on."

"Fuck," says Mitch. He pops his door and pushes it open.

NINE

They approach the house. They climb the stairs. Mitch stops Stuart before he knocks. "Listen, if Tracy's here you do the talking. Just say you heard there was a party here."

Stuart nods. He knocks. It's cold out and he's wearing only his sweatshirt. He bounces on the balls of his feet to keep warm.

Mitch is also cold. He hunches his shoulders and waits for the door to open.

It doesn't. Stuart moves across the porch and looks in the window. "There are people in there," he reports.

"Yeah, but they're not answering."

"Fuck it," says Stuart. He tries the door. It opens. He goes in. Mitch follows.

The door leads into the living room. Tracy is sitting on the couch. There are about eight other people. One of the Baxter guys is sitting with Tracy. The drummer is sitting in a chair, reading a magazine. Now, not only is he wearing Reeboks, he's wearing a button-down shirt as well. On the floor is Erica and another girl. The Baxter singer appears just as they walk in. There are voices in the kitchen.

Tracy turns as Mitch and Stuart walk in. "Hel-lo?" she says. She does not look like she was expecting company.

"Hello," says Stuart. Mitch says nothing.

"Can I help you?"

The room grows silent. Stuart looks back at Mitch. "We heard this was where the party was."

Tracy smiles a fake, polite smile. "And what party would that be?"

"The Baxter party," says Stuart.

Tracy turns to the Baxter singer. "Did you invite these guys?"

The Baxter singer shrugs.

"We got pot," says Stuart. "Do you guys got anything to drink?"

"There's beer in the fridge," says the drummer, not looking up from his magazine.

"Cool," says Stuart. He walks around the couch to the kitchen.

"Uh, just a second," says Tracy, stopping everyone where they are. "Who invited you here?"

"We heard this was where the party was," says Stuart.

"Yeah, but *who* told you that?"

Stuart looks to Mitch.

"Amy," says Mitch.

Stuart continues into the kitchen.

"Because this isn't a party," says Tracy. She stands up. "And Amy's asleep and these guys have to get up tomorrow."

"No we don't," says the drummer, not looking up from his magazine.

"That's okay," says the singer. "If they got pot."

The half dozen people sitting on the floor go back to their conversation. The Baxter singer says something to Erica and she laughs. Tracy is not going to be able to keep them out. She focuses on Mitch. "And who are you?"

"I'm a friend of Amy's."

There's laughter from the kitchen. Stuart reappears with a beer and sits on the floor with Erica and some of the Baxter guys.

Tracy steps closer to Mitch. "How do you know Amy?"

"Just around."

She studies him. "Are you Mitch?"

"Yeah."

"You were at the show tonight."

Mitch doesn't answer.

"Weren't you?"

"No."

"No?" says Tracy. "I think you were there. I think I saw you there."

"Where's Amy's room?"

"Upstairs."

"Where upstairs?"

Tracy steps back. She looks him up and down. Mitch doesn't move. "So you're Mitch," she says, smiling a new, more complicated smile. "Amy said you were cute. And you are."

"You're kind of cute yourself," says Mitch. He gets out a cigarette and lights it. He walks around Tracy to drop the match in an ashtray on the coffee table. Tracy watches him for a moment, then goes into the kitchen.

"Hey, Mitch, you want a hit of this?" says Stuart.

Mitch does. He sits on the floor beside Stuart. He takes a hit off the pipe. He hands it to the Baxter bass player.

"So you guys are from Olympia?" says Stuart.

The bass player answers. "Well, Jason is, but Ben is from North Carolina and Steve..."

As the guy talks, Stuart puts his beer to his lips, tips it up, and drains the entire bottle.

As the guy finishes his explanation, Stuart lowers the empty bottle and burps in his face.

Mitch smokes his cigarette. He doesn't feel like goofing on the Baxter guys. Maybe he should go upstairs. That's why Tracy thinks he's here. And Amy would probably be into it. But then he looks over at Erica. She's totally hot. She's wearing a tight sweater with a leather miniskirt. Her ass is amazing. Why is he even thinking about Amy when there're girls like Tracy and Erica around? Because Amy will fuck him, that's why.

Mitch casually stands and goes up the stairs. The second floor hallway is dark. He tries a door. It's a bedroom. He turns on the light. There's a futon, some clothes, a boom box. He shuts the door. He tries the room at the end of the hall. It's another bedroom, but much larger. He flicks the light switch, but instead of an overhead light, a red tinted light comes on at the bedside table. In the faint light Mitch sees a large double bed. Against one wall is a vanity covered with necklaces, jewelry, a wig. On the window sill is an uneven row of candles. The closet to his left is overflowing with shoes.

This is Tracy's room.

There's a noise on the stairs. Mitch shuts the door. There's only one door left to try. Mitch opens it silently, steps inside, closes it again. It's pitch dark inside but Mitch knows he's in the right room. He can smell Amy. He can hear her breathing. He focuses on a clock radio and waits for his eyes to adjust to the darkness. Slowly he begins to see the bed, the lumpy form of Amy. She's fast asleep.

Mitch unzips his Stussy racing jacket and drops it on the floor. But he should keep his clothes together, to facilitate leaving. He rolls up his jacket and throws it in the near corner of the room. He pulls off his shoes and socks and puts them there too. Then he takes off his Adidas sweat pants, removing a condom from his wallet. He steps forward, finds the bed with his hand, and carefully eases his weight onto it.

TEN

Amy wakes up with a start. She's facing away from him and when she turns over, her arm whips around and hits Mitch in the head.

"Ouch!" says Mitch.

"Oh!" she says.

"Shhhh! It's okay, it's me," whispers Mitch, holding his hand up to protect himself.

"What? Who is it?"

"It's me. It's Mitch."

"What?" says Amy. She's asleep, she's confused. Mitch immediately slides his arms around her. In the dark, he can see her eyes open. She sees him. "Mitch!" she says.

He kisses her.

"Mmmmmmm," she says, pulling away. "What are you doing here? What time is it?"

Mitch pulls the covers down. Amy's wearing a flannel pajama top. It's soft and warm. It smells delicious. Mitch buries his face in her chest.

"Oh," says Amy.

Mitch moves upward and begins to nuzzle her neck. Her hands come up and grip his shoulders. He finds her mouth and kisses her long and deep. He begins to pull the covers away from her. He unbuttons the front of her pajamas.

"Mitch?" says Amy.

He pulls open her pajama top. Her white skin seems to glow in the darkness. Her round breasts jiggle slightly. He begins to lick and suck them. Then he pulls the rest of the covers away. He kisses her belly. He pulls her panties down a few inches and kisses the edge of her pubic hair.

There's a noise in the hall. Mitch freezes for a moment. Someone is coming up the stairs. Footsteps pass in the hall. The door at the end of the hall opens. It's Tracy. She's in her room. She's right through the wall. Mitch enjoys the thought of it. He pulls Amy's panties further down and gets his face between her legs. He opens the folds of her cunt with his tongue.

"Ohhhh," says Amy.

Tracy's door shuts. The footsteps go back down the stairs. Mitch sits up and tugs Amy's panties all the way off. He spreads her legs and slides his dick inside her.

"Mmm," she sighs. She grips him. She seems more into it than the other time.

Mitch begins to move back and forth.

"Oh, *Mitch*," breathes Amy.

Mitch thinks about Dieter fucking Amy. He thinks about Andy fucking Amy. He props himself up so he can watch himself fuck Amy.

"Oh," says Amy.

Mitch gets a nice rhythm going. But then he lifts his head. In the dark he sees a Counting Crows poster, right above the bed. Mitch hates the Counting Crows. The band members are standing on a city street, their hands in their pockets. They look thoughtful and artistic, like the pretentious dweebs they are. Mitch looks down at Amy.

She's got her legs up now. She's as wide open as she can get. He looks down at her face. Her eyes are closed. Her mouth is open. She's gasping, straining to come.

Mitch keeps the exact same rhythm. The bed is helping. It rocks just enough, not too much.

"Oh, yes," says Amy.

Mitch stares down at her. He tightens the muscles in his chest, in his legs and butt. She begins to flail beneath him. He continues to rock her. The exact same amount. The exact same rhythm. Great techno does that. Just pounds on you. Never quits.

"Oh," she repeats. "Oh *yeah*!"

Mitch grabs a fistful of her hair and pulls her head to one side. He kisses her wildly, mashing his face into hers. At the same time he begins to rock the bed harder. He pounds into her.

"—Where? This door?" he hears a voice say. And then Amy's door opens. The room fills with light. "Oops, oh shit."

Mitch stops fucking. He turns his sweaty face toward the door, which is now closed again. Almost. It's open just a crack. "What?" demands Mitch.

"It's me, Stuart."

"What do you want?"

"I want to go."

"Jesus Christ," hisses Mitch. He looks down at Amy. He looks at the door. "Well, hang on a second."

Amy grabs Mitch's arm. "You can stay if you want. You can stay here."

"I can't."

"Yes you can. Why can't you? I can give you a ride."

"Wait for you?" says Stuart, from the hall.

"Yeah," says Mitch. The door closes.

"But Mitch!" says Amy.

"What? I can't. I have to work." In the dark he kisses her. But her face is cold now. Damp and wet and cold. He begins to work her again, but she's not into it.

"I said I could drive you," says Amy.

Mitch doesn't answer. He's trying to get it going again. Eventually he does. They get their rhythm back and Mitch finally comes. He pulls out immediately. He sits up on the bed. Amy rolls onto her side and curls up in the blankets. Mitch leans forward and kisses her temple. "I gotta go, I really do."

He gets off the bed. He goes to the corner. His clothes are all there, in reverse order. His underwear, his pants, socks, shoes, jacket. When he's dressed he goes back to the bed. He kisses Amy's face. "You are so hot," he whispers to her. "But I gotta be at work in like three hours." He kisses her again and then goes to the door.

"Mitch?"

"What?"

She doesn't say anything.

"What?" he says again, his hand on the doorknob.

"Can you come here for a second?"

He goes back to the bed. He sits. He strokes her hair. "What?"

"Do you want to do something this week?"

"Like what?"

"Go to a movie or something?"

"Sure," he says. He doesn't know what to do so he kisses her again on the side of the head. "Now go to sleep."

"Mitch?"

"What?"

She pulls some hair out of her face. Her face is wet. Is she crying? "I really like having sex with you."

Mitch nods. "Me too."

She touches his hand.

He takes it in his own and squeezes it. "You know what?" he says.

"What?"

"You should get rid of that Counting Crows poster."

"Why?"

"Because they really suck."

"My sister gave it to me. I don't really like them."

"They're like, the worst band in the world."

"I know."

"And I don't like them watching me."

Amy doesn't answer.

"Now go to sleep," says Mitch. He kisses her again and this time makes it out the door. He hurries down the stairs. Tracy is in the living room with the others.

Mitch heads for the door. But Tracy's waiting for him. "So Mitch," she says. "Will we be seeing more of you?"

Mitch hesitates long enough to zip up his racing jacket. Then he turns, smiles at her once and goes out.

ELEVEN

Mitch gets home at three. He sets his alarm and sleeps for a couple hours before it goes off. Then he takes a shower and rides his bike through the dark to the Natural Bakery Company.

Mitch punches in at 5:27. Janet and Rob are both there, kneading dough in their white bakery outfits. They're earnest, hippy types. They greet Mitch when he comes in. It's obvious Mitch hasn't slept much. But the previous delivery driver did the same thing: stay out all night and then do the deliveries last thing before he went to bed.

Janet helps Mitch load the trays into the truck. Janet is overweight. She sweats a lot. But she's nice. While they're waiting for Rob to finish the last couple trays, Mitch walks around to the front, to the cafe part of the bakery. They open at six but the coffee's on and Carmen is there. She's a little hipper than Janet and Rob. And cute. But Mitch is always too late, too frazzled, sometimes too drunk or stoned to really chat her up. He smiles at her now though, with the tingle of sex still in his system.

"Hey," he says as he pours himself some coffee.

Carmen smiles. She has a boyfriend. She mentions it every time he talks to her.

"Where'd you get those shoes?" asks Mitch, looking down at her platform loafers.

"Karmic Kosmic."

"Those are slick," says Mitch.

"They're kind of hard to work in," says Carmen.

Mitch puts a lid on his coffee. He takes a tiny sip. It's too hot. "You ever go to Quest?"

"I've been there."

Mitch drinks his coffee. "We should go there some time."

Carmen smiles. "I don't think my boyfriend would like that."

"No no. Just to hang out. I used to work there. I could get you in for free."

"I don't go out that much anymore."

The coffee's too hot. Mitch blows into the little hole in the lid. "Yeah, you're *so old,*" he says, sarcastically. Carmen smiles again, more deeply this time. She really is cute.

When the truck is finally loaded Mitch starts it up. It's an old Nissan. The clutch is fucked up. As happens every morning, the Nissan dies a couple times before Mitch is out of the parking lot. But he gets it going. He turns on the radio and begins his run.

The first stops are several expensive restaurants across the river in Northwest, the rich part of town. Mitch likes it there. It's where the cutest girls are. And also, except for Zell's, the people are pretty cool. But at Zell's, his first stop, they're already pissed that he's late. Also they think they were overcharged. Mitch has only been doing this a couple of weeks. He doesn't know how the billing works. Also the manager at Zell's is gay. Mitch doesn't mind that, half the people at Quest are queer. But this guy is impossible. His name is Henry and he's all over Mitch from the moment he pulls in.

"I asked you on Thursday to talk to Fred about this," says Henry.

"And I told you I never see Fred," said Mitch. "I don't even know what he looks like."

"Well, somebody is going to have to straighten out what happened last week because we're not paying for something we didn't get."

"Call Fred," says Mitch. "That's all I can tell you. Call Fred." Mitch is tired. "And can you move please?"

Henry moves. Mitch slides the tray onto the counter. The kitchen guys at Zell's are all gay. But the coolest one of them, Marcus, knows Mitch from Quest. And so they're all nice to him.

"Hey, Mitch," says Marcus, as he hurries by.

"Mr. Mitch," says someone else.

"Hey, you guys," says Mitch.

But Henry is still following Mitch around. He's counting the trays as Mitch brings them in. When he gets in the way, Mitch has to stop. "Would you mind–?"

Henry glares at him.

"You want me to drop it?"

"I'm calling Fred," threatens Henry.

"Call him. *Please* call him."

Henry leaves. Mitch slides the last tray onto the counter. He gives Marcus and the others a mock salute and hops in the truck.

At a restaurant called Westwood there are just two girls in the kitchen. They let Mitch in and go about their prep work. They're talking about their boyfriends. They aren't just cute, they're beautiful. Rich kid beautiful. Beautiful hair, beautiful skin, beautiful clothes. Mitch tries to hear what they're saying. He can't imagine why girls like that are working in a restaurant at six in the morning. But there they are. Mitch says goodbye to them but they barely notice.

Mitch finishes his deliveries in Northwest and heads back to Southeast. This is where he lives, where most everyone he knows lives. Mitch's first stop is the Three Sisters cafe. This is a lesbian, feminist hangout. But the people are nice. They're listening to folk music in the kitchen. The stereo is turned up, Mitch has to pound on the door. They finally hear him and let him in. Mitch brings in his three trays. They offer him an oatmeal muffin when he's done.

He takes it, eats some of it, throws it out the window on his way to the next place.

He hits two other cafes and then goes to Java Jones which is the scenester hangout of the area. Mitch doesn't know the guy's name who opens the door, even though he sees him every morning. The guy is tall, heavy, he wears all black, his hair is dyed black, he wears a faded Pixies T-shirt. He lets Mitch in. He doesn't speak and then disappears into some back room. Mitch hauls in his load and steals a cinnamon raisin bagel out of the wire baskets.

After Southeast, Mitch drives into Northeast. This is the poorest section of town. This is where Stuart grew up, where he still lives with his dad. But mostly it's black people. Mitch goes first to the Irvington neighborhood, a pocket of white people in the center of it. There's a cafe restaurant here called Soup and Saucer. It's kind of hippyish. The owners are older, in their forties. They are weirdly skinny, weirdly nice. They offer Mitch food, coffee, one of their macrobiotic tofu concoctions. He takes some coffee and is happy to be gone.

From there he stops at the Buckner Community Center. Mitch has never understood what this place is exactly. Some sort of social services center. The black woman inside has the door propped open for him. Mitch drops his one tray there. The woman says good morning. Mitch says the same.

After that, it's the long forty-five minute drive to Salem. This is a smaller town about forty miles down the interstate. Mitch leaves fifteen trays with the store manager of Healthmart. Then it's back to Portland. Mitch gets the truck back by 10:20. He rides his bike home and is asleep in his bed by eleven.

TWELVE

Mitch works the rest of the week. On Thursday night Stuart calls. Does Mitch want to hang out? Of course. An hour later the Dodge Charger pulls up in front of his house. Mitch runs down the steps and gets in.

"Whazzup?" says Stuart, handing Mitch a pint bottle of tequila.

Mitch waves it off. "I just got up."

"So?"

Mitch takes the bottle. He takes a swig. He hands it back. "My job sucks."

"All jobs suck man, what do you want?"

Mitch reaches for his cigarettes. "So where are we going?"

"Magic Gardens. To play pool."

"Shit man, that place costs too much."

"There's strippers there," says Stuart.

"*Strippers,*" scoffs Mitch, he lights his cigarette.

"I told Dieter we'd meet him there."

"Dieter doesn't need strippers. He's a DJ."

"Nobody *needs* strippers."

"It's just stupid to play pool in a strip club. You're playing pool. You're looking at the table. What's the point?"

"There is no point."

"Go play pool in a cheap place and then go to a strip bar and watch the strippers when you're already drunk."

"Jesus," says Stuart. "You do need a new job."

• • •

At Magic Gardens, Mitch and Stuart move slowly through the door and into the club. It's dark. The jukebox plays a low thumping beat. They work their way through the tables to the pool table which is dimly lit and shrouded in cigarette smoke. Mitch checks out the woman on stage. It's the older woman. She's always here. Her tits are fake.

Dieter is playing pool with a rough-looking kid.

"We need girls to play pool with," Mitch tells Stuart.

"There's your girl," says Stuart, pointing behind him without looking. "Bought and paid for."

Mitch looks back at the woman on stage. She's bent over, wagging her butt to the crowd. She spreads her pussy lips so the men in front can look inside.

"Jesus," mutters Mitch. "That's disgusting."

Stuart isn't watching. He's concentrating on the pool game. Dieter, who never loses at pool, is behind. But he's coming back. Mitch finds himself watching too. There's something going on here. They're really playing. He sees the kid has some friends sitting along the far wall. They're all watching the game. Dieter is lining up a shot. He is very focused. "Are you guys betting?" asks Mitch.

No one answers. Dieter tries for the seven in the side pocket. It's a tough angle but Dieter kisses it just right. The seven, just barely moving, rolls one complete rotation and drops in the side pocket. Dieter chalks his cue. He walks around the table very quickly. He drives the two into the corner. It's now even, two balls apiece. He tries for the one but he rushes the shot. He misses. He breathes deeply, and sips his cocktail.

"Are they betting?" Mitch whispers to Stuart.

Stuart doesn't know. He stops a waitress and orders a drink.

The kid hits the nine in. But he's left himself a tough shot. Mitch watches his friends. They look like the kids that hang outside the runaway youth shelter: ugly, fucked up, dangerous. He looks back at the woman on stage. She's finished her dance. She's picking up bills off the stage. She's got a slinky nighty thing on now. Her fake tits look better semi-concealed.

The kid misses. Dieter studies the table. He needs to finish it now, because the kid's last ball is in the middle of the table. His will be an easy shot, no matter what the leave. But Dieter misses.

"That's not like you," Stuart says to him. The kid immediately punches in the fifteen. The cue ball rolls slightly to the left, leaving him in perfect position to hit the eight ball. Which he does. Quickly, confidently. It drops in, the game is over.

"He didn't call it," says Stuart, loudly.

No one says anything.

"Did he?" says Stuart to Dieter.

"Yeah, he called it," says Dieter.

"No, he didn't, I didn't hear anything," says Stuart.

One of the kid's friends puts new quarters in and racks up a new game.

Dieter hands over his stick and stands next to Mitch.

"Did he call it?" says Stuart.

"He pointed," says Dieter.

"I didn't see him point."

"With his eyes."

"That doesn't matter. You have to say it. With your mouth."

Dieter shakes his head. The new player breaks.

"You wanna put more quarters up?" says Stuart.

"Nah."

"Fuck pool," says Mitch. "Let's sit down."

They find a table away from the pool table and sit. A new dancer comes onto the stage. Mitch stares at her. "Hey," he says. He nudges Stuart. "I know that girl."

Stuart is drinking his drink. But he sets it down quickly. "*Yeah.*"

"She used to hang out at Quest," says Mitch.

"Fuck. What's her name?"

"She was friends with Jeanelle," says Mitch. "And that other girl."

"Check it out."

"Ask Dieter," says Mitch. "He probably knows her."

Stuart nudges Dieter. "Who is that?"

"Beats me," says Dieter.

"She was friends with Jeanelle," Mitch tells Stuart.

"She was friends with Jeanelle," Stuart tells Dieter.

"Don't know her," says Dieter.

"Fuck, man," says Mitch. He lights a cigarette and leans back in his chair.

"Look at her," murmurs Stuart.

They all watch the new girl dance.

"Man," Mitch whispers to Stuart. "You know how sometimes at Quest you see some chick and you think how cool it would be if she just started taking off her clothes?"

"Fuck, yes. And here it is!"

"And fucking here it is!" says Mitch.

"We gotta figure out her name."

"We'll ask Jeanelle."

"Fuck, we gotta buy her a drink or something."

"What for?" says Mitch.

"To see what's up. See what she's doing."

"What she's doing? She's *stripping*."

"Well, obviously."

"You're going to ask her why she's stripping?"

"Nah," says Stuart. "But just, you know. See what's up. See if she wants to party later."

Mitch scoffs. "You can't ask a stripper if she wants to party later."

"Why not? She's friends with Jeanelle. She's fucking hot. You just said so."

Mitch looks around the room. "Every guy in this place wants to *party later.*"

"But she used to hang out at Quest," says Stuart.

"This ain't Quest my man. This is the Gardens."

Stuart looks around. He watches the girl on stage. "Well, so what? I don't care. I'll do it anyway."

"Go ahead," says Mitch. "See what happens."

THIRTEEN

But Dieter has to go back to Quest. So they do that instead. There's a line in the front, so they go around to the back entrance. Fortunately, they're with Dieter because it's a new guy in the back. Dieter, an official Quest DJ, gets them in for free.

They go inside. They come out behind the DJ platform. There's a bunch of girls sitting on the steps. Dieter climbs up through them. Mitch and Stuart start to follow but there's no room. They proceed to the bar.

"Who's that DJ?" Stuart asks Mitch.

Mitch doesn't know.

"Whoever he is, he's bringing in the chicks."

"Fuck," says Mitch, staring into the girl-packed dance floor.

"Hey, look, there's Jeanelle," says Stuart. Mitch follows him through the crowd.

Jeanelle is sitting in one of the prized circular booths along the back wall. She's got two girls with her and two guys who look like they're trying to pick them up.

"Hey, Jeanelle," says Stuart.

Mitch is worried Jeanelle might blow them off but it's just the opposite. She waves the two guys out of the booth. "These are my friends I was telling you about," she says. The two guys grumble and leave. Stuart slides in next to Jeanelle. Mitch slides in on the other side, beside her two friends.

Stuart talks to Jeanelle. Mitch looks at the two girls he's sitting next to. The nearest one is putting on lipstick. She's cute. Mitch smiles at her.

"So yeah," Stuart says to Jeanelle. "Me and Mitch, we gotta ask you something."

Jeanelle lights a cigarette.

"This girl's name. We just saw this girl," he looks to Mitch for confirmation. "She used to hang out here. She's sort of..."

"What?" says Jeanelle.

"Well, she's..."

"She's stripping at Magic Gardens," says Mitch.

"She's sort of blonde," says Stuart.

"Beth," says Jeanelle.

"Beth," says Stuart, nodding.

"What about her?"

"Well, just like, what's she doing? Does she have a boyfriend?"

"She's a junky."

Stuart nods some more.

Mitch smiles again at the girl putting on lipstick. This time she smiles back.

"What do you want to know about her?" asks Jeanelle.

Stuart shrugs. "Nothing. We just thought she was kinda rad."

"Oh, she's rad all right," says Jeanelle. She takes a deep drag of her cigarette.

"But she's like, a junky?"

Jeanelle shrugs. "Not full on. Not yet."

"She didn't look like a junky," says Stuart.

Jeanelle smokes.

"She sounds depressing," says the girl sitting next to Mitch.

"What's your name?" Mitch asks her.

"Belinda."

But just then Dieter comes by. He squats down so his head is just over the table top. He motions for Mitch to lean forward. "That DJ?"

"Yeah?" says Mitch.

"That's DJ Westy."

"Yeah?"

"From L.A."

"Yeah? So?"

"He's only like the biggest DJ on the West Coast."

"Huh."

"Listen to that drone in the back. And that phase wash. Nobody does that kind of stuff around here."

Mitch listens.

"This guy's the shit."

"Huh," says Mitch, listening.

"I wonder what he's doing here. Do you think George might have hired him?"

"Fuck George," says Mitch, George being the guy who fired him.

"Oh yeah," says Dieter. "And Amy's here."

"Amy?" says Mitch.

"Yeah, she's over there." Dieter points toward the stage, off to the left.

Mitch looks. It's so crowded. But then he sees them: Erica, Amy, Tracy Richards. "Fuck," says Mitch.

Dieter leaves. Mitch lights a cigarette. Belinda smiles at Mitch who smiles tightly back.

"I think I met Beth here once," Stuart is telling Jeanelle. "I almost asked her out."

"Buy her some heroin. She'll go out with you."

Stuart seems to think about it. "Is that why she strips?"

"What do you think?" says Jeanelle.

"I don't know."

"Why are you even talking about this?" Mitch says to Stuart. "You heard her. She's a fucking junky."

Stuart gives Mitch a pained look.

"Junkies are gross," says Belinda.

"I hate needles," says her friend.

"I like Xanax," says Belinda, smiling at Mitch.

"Me too," says her friend.

A waitress comes by. Stuart orders a rum and coke. Mitch gets the same.

But then Belinda and her friend want to leave. Mitch lets them out. Jeanelle leaves too. Mitch and Stuart sit by themselves. The waitress brings their drinks.

"Fuck," says Stuart.

Mitch stirs his rum and coke.

"You ever done heroin?" Stuart asks Mitch.

Mitch shakes his head.

"Ever thought about it?"

"Not really," says Mitch.

"Man," says Stuart, shaking his head.

"Seems like a lot of people are getting into it," says Mitch, but he's not looking at Stuart. He's staring at Amy. And Erica. And Tracy. They're all walking straight toward him.

FOURTEEN

Amy hesitates when she reaches the booth. But Tracy pushes her in. "Hi, Mitch," says Amy. Tracy keeps pushing her around until Amy's right next to him.

"Hey," says Mitch. He smiles at her, then at Tracy as she scoots in. Erica sits on the end. She stares into the dance floor.

"Who's your friend?" says Amy.

"Oh, Stuart," says Mitch. Stuart is also staring into space. "Amy, Stuart, Stuart, Amy."

"Hi," says Amy.

Stuart nods to her. He goes back to staring at the dance floor.

"So what's up?" says Mitch. In a way he's glad to see her. He can't say why exactly. The familiarity of her maybe. Or the possibility of sex later.

"Nothing," says Amy. "What's up with you?"

"Nothing," says Mitch, reaching for his cigarettes.

Amy nods and then weaves her head with the music.

Mitch doesn't like her doing this. Part of doing the Quest scene is never being affected by the music, at least not to the point of weaving your head.

"Mitch?" says Tracy. "Could you spare another cigarette?"

Mitch gives her one and lights them both. "You should have told me you were coming," he tells Amy quietly. "I could have got you in for free."

"It's only five bucks," says Amy.

Mitch shrugs.

All five of them stare into the swarm of dancers.

Stuart gets up and walks toward the bar.

Mitch again speaks quietly to Amy: "Poor Stuart. He finally met the girl of his dreams and she's a junky."

"Wow," says Amy.

"She's at Magic Gardens. She's a stripper."

Amy's eyes widen more.

Mitch nods. He smokes. That's one nice thing about Amy: she's easily impressed.

Erica and Tracy are talking. They get up. They leave. But they've left their stuff.

When they're alone Amy unexpectedly leans over and pecks Mitch on the cheek. He shies away.

"*Mitch,*" says Amy, grinning and bumping her leg into his.

"What?"

"You're so funny."

"Why?"

"You don't want me to kiss you in public."

"Well, *yeah.*"

"Don't worry, nobody saw."

But it affected him. The kiss. The warm wetness of her lips. He wants to feel those lips again. "No, it's not that."

"What is it then?" says Amy.

"Just you know, I used to work here."

Amy sighs. Under the table her hand crawls into his. "I had three drinks tonight," she tells him. "That's a lot. For me."

Mitch nods. She's now got both hands under the table. She's holding his hand open and lightly caressing his open palm. It's sending shivers down Mitch's spine. It's making his dick strain in his pants.

"Do you want to come over later?" Amy asks him.

Mitch glances over at her. She touches his leg. She caresses it. Her hand touches his dick where it's poking to one side. "Oh, is that–" she says. She giggles. "Sorry."

Mitch looks down at the table.

"Or..." she stops laughing. She scoots closer. She whispers: "Should I touch it?"

Mitch says nothing.

Amy reaches under the table and finds his dick again. She begins to caress it. She grips it through his pants. She squeezes.

"Oh, *man*," says Mitch.

"I was hoping I'd see you tonight. That's why I came here."

Mitch has forgotten the cigarette he's holding. Now he takes a hurried drag of it. "Maybe we should go," he whispers to Amy.

"Where's Tracy?" says Amy.

"Jesus Christ," says Mitch. He's squirming in his seat now. "Let's go somewhere."

"Wait a minute. I've got to use the rest room."

Amy scoots out of the booth. Mitch waits until she's gone. Then, under the table, he rearranges his hard-on into a more comfortable position. He's just got himself straightened out when Tracy appears. She's sweating. She's been dancing.

"Uh, you better take your coat. I think we're leaving," he tells Tracy.

"Where are you going?"

"I'm not sure."

Tracy smiles knowingly. She slides into the booth, "Can I have another cigarette before you go?"

Mitch gives her one.

"Amy said you used to work here," says Tracy.

"Yeah."

"Did you like it?"

"Yeah, it was all right."

"If you like to dance you should have come to the parties me and Erica had last summer."

Mitch looks at her. "I went to those parties."

"You did?"

"Yeah. With Dieter Holtz."

"Oh, Dieter. He had a different name then, DJ Crack or something? I just love how all the DJs have their little names. It's so cute."

Mitch finishes his drink. He chews on an ice cube.

Tracy smokes. Then she scoots around, to get closer to Mitch. "I have to tell you something."

"What?"

"Amy talks about you constantly."

"Yeah?"

"She really likes you."

"So?"

"Do you like her?"

Mitch shrugs.

Tracy stares at him.

"What?"

"You *don't* like her?" says Tracy.

Mitch shrugs again. "I don't know her that well."

"I *see*," says Tracy, raising her eyebrows.

"What's wrong with that?" says Mitch forcefully. "We just started hanging out. Besides," he says, his voice lowering, "there's other girls I like."

Tracy stares at him. "In that case. I just wanted to say. I consider Amy a friend."

"So?" says Mitch.

"I don't want to see anything happen–" but she sees this is not going to work on Mitch. She stares at him for a moment. Then she scoots away.

Mitch watches her. She's actually flustered. "I'm going to find Erica," she says. But as she's leaving, she stares back at him. There's a strange look on her face. It suggests that something has begun between them. Something that will be continued later.

Then she's gone. And Mitch is alone. Until Amy comes back.

FIFTEEN

Outside, Mitch holds Amy up when she slips drunkenly on the wet pavement. It's raining. They hurry to her car. Mitch is thinking they can drive somewhere and fuck in the back seat. Or maybe she can give him a blow job. But when they get in the little Celica Amy can't get the key in the ignition.

"Maybe I should drive," says Mitch.

"Do you want to?" says Amy. She drops the keys onto the floor and starts reaching around for them.

"I'll get them," says Mitch. He gets out and Amy crawls over to the passenger side.

Mitch finds the keys. He starts the car but can't figure out where the windshield wipers are. Amy reaches over and turns them on. Then she kisses him on the neck. She starts nuzzling him. She's drunk. She smells drunk. But she's warm. And her tongue and mouth are wet. Mitch kisses her back. He guides her hand to his dick. But that just slows things down. He moves her back into her seat and shifts the Celica into drive.

Mitch drives toward his own house. Amy will sober up after sex and then she can drive herself home. He crosses the bridge and speeds up Hawthorne. As he drives he lights a cigarette. He looks over at Amy. She's snuggled sideways in the seat, her face toward him, her eyes closed, a strange half-smile on her face.

Mitch parks outside his house. "We're here," he whispers to her. Without speaking she opens her door. Mitch helps her up the front steps. He guides her quietly up the stairs to his room. There's a phone message taped to the door. He ignores it.

Amy collapses onto his bed. She finds the pillow and curls up into a ball. Mitch takes off his jacket and looks down at her. He doesn't feel so horny now. But he will when he gets in bed with her. He walks around the bed and leans over her. "You'll be more comfortable if you take off your coat," he says.

She's half-asleep or pretending she is. Mitch rolls her from side to side and gets her coat off. She's wearing a T-shirt and vest beneath her coat. Mitch gets the vest off. He undoes her belt, her jeans. She lifts up enough to help him pull them off her. Now she's in her underpants, her socks, her T-shirt. Mitch throws the covers over her. He takes off his own shirt. He undoes his pants and kicks off his shoes. He looks for a condom in his bureau but the Trojan box is empty. He stops to think: maybe in the bathroom.

In the bathroom, each housemate has their own drawer. There's nothing in Mitch's. He looks in Gillian's. He digs through her prescription drugs, her tampons, her rubbing alcohol. No condoms. He looks in David's. He's got nothing, aspirin, band-aids, an old asthma inhaler. Mitch looks behind the mirror. Assorted junk. No condoms. He creeps down the hall to David's room. David spends most nights at his girlfriend's. Mitch knocks lightly. There's no answer. Mitch opens the door and creeps into the room. He looks around the bed, around the dresser, in the desk. Nothing.

He'll just have to risk it. He goes back to his room. Amy is really asleep now. Mitch pulls off his underwear. He gets into the bed and curls up behind Amy.

"Hey," he whispers. He pulls some of her hair around, so her neck is exposed. He kisses it. Amy sighs. He gently pulls at her shoulder until she rolls onto her back. He slides his leg over her thigh and presses his dick against her.

"Mmmm," says Amy. She's waking up. Mitch touches her breasts through her T-shirt. She's not wearing a bra. He finds her nipples and squeezes them lightly. He scoots down and sucks on the nearest one through her T-shirt. The nipple gets hard. The T-shirt material slowly soaks through. He moves his knee into her crotch.

"Mmmm," says Amy again. Mitch slides one hand into her panties. Her pubic hair is scratchy dry but her cunt lips are warm and moist. He eases a finger inside. He watches her face as he does.

After that Mitch sits up and pulls off her panties. He turns himself around sixty-nine style. Amy sees what he's doing. She suddenly comes to life. She finds his dick and gets it in her mouth. Mitch was going to give her head but Amy's so fast with her own actions he finds himself just watching while she grips and sucks his cock. She's totally into it. Mitch has never seen anything like it. She bobs and strokes and licks and sucks. This is what Dieter got. And Mitch isn't even a DJ.

He lays back and enjoys it. He strokes her hair, moving his head from side to side to get the best view. Within a few minutes he comes. It's an easy, smooth orgasm. Mitch isn't breathing heavy, his heart isn't pounding. He just pours his own warm liquid into her warm liquid mouth.

Afterward, they lie together, both of them half asleep. Then they begin to wake up. They kiss. They touch each other. Amy starts caressing his dick but Mitch wants to go down on her this time. He does. He goes slow. He gets into it. He licks her cunt, all the way around to her asshole. She somehow turns herself around so she can suck him again. They are using the entire surface of the bed now. They do sixty-nine with Mitch on his back and Amy spread over him. Then they do it with Amy on her back and Mitch's tongue as deep inside her as it will go. They finish by fucking. Mitch is totally primed by now. He fucks her so hard they fall off the mattress. He fucks her across the floor and keeps going until they're pressed against the far wall, crushed into his cardboard laundry box. When Mitch comes his entire body trembles and shakes. He bucks and grunts and finally collapses onto Amy, who strokes his hair long after he's passed out.

• • •

It's light out when Mitch wakes up. He and Amy are still on the floor. There are dirty clothes beneath them. The covers from his bed are on top of them. Amy must have pulled them over. She's nestled comfortably under his arm. So comfortably that Mitch doesn't want to move. He finally shifts enough to lift his head and look at his clock. It's 8:11 a.m. "Fuck," he says. He's supposed to be at work. He's three hours late.

Amy wakes up. "What is it?"

"I was supposed to work today."

"What time?"

"Five."

"What time is it now?"

"Eight."

Amy sits up and looks around. She sees the daylight in the window. "You should have told me you had to get up."

"It doesn't matter," says Mitch, lowering his head.

"I could have woken you up."

"It's too late now," says Mitch. He rubs his eyes.

"Should you call them?"

"Nah, it wasn't working out anyway."

"You're going to quit?"

"I probably won't have to."

"Oh, Mitch, it's my fault. I'm sorry." She squeezes against him.

"It's all right," says Mitch, his dick swelling again amidst the chaos of covers and dirty clothes.

SIXTEEN

An hour later they get up. On his way to the bathroom, Mitch sees the phone message taped to the door. He reads it, standing in the doorway. "Ah, shit," he says.

"What is it?" says Amy.

"Thanksgiving. Fuck." He wads up the paper. "My grandparents are coming up from San Diego."

Amy is snapping on her bra. "Don't you like your grandparents?"

"I just don't want to deal with it."

Amy gets dressed. She has to work. When she's gone, Mitch calls The Natural Bakery Co. Rob is straightforward. Mitch has worked there for three weeks. He's been late three times and now he didn't show up at all. They're going to have to let him go. Mitch can pick up his check this afternoon.

Mitch hangs up. He drags himself back upstairs and sleeps for a couple of hours. Then he rides his bike to the bakery.

He goes in the front, into the cafe part. Carmen is working the counter. He sees Janet briefly as he walks in the door. She disappears into the back.

"Hey," Mitch says to Carmen.

"Hi Mitch," she says.

He looks around. He's not sure who he's supposed to talk to.

"Coffee?" says Carmen.

"Sure," says Mitch, scratching his mussed hair. "Thanks."

She pours him a cup. "I heard," she says. "Sorry."

"It's all right."

Janet reappears. "Hi, Mitch," she says.

"Hi, Janet."

She's got his check. "Here you go," she says.

"Thanks," he says sheepishly. "Sorry about this morning."

"It's all right," says Janet. "Good luck." She goes into the back.

Mitch opens the envelope. His expression improves when he reads the figures. "Well, that's not too bad."

"Severance pay?" says Carmen.

"A little bit," he says. "It'll cover the rent." He looks at Carmen. She's smiling at him. Her face is full of warmth and sympathy. "You know, I get off in ten minutes," she says. "Do you want to go get something to eat?"

Mitch focuses on her. "Uhm..."

"I'll treat. You know, since..." She looks at the envelope in his hand.

Mitch looks at it too. "All right. Yeah. Sure."

"Maybe I can just leave now. Let me check." She goes into the back. She returns with her hat and coat.

They sit by the window at the Three Sisters Cafe. It's not the place Mitch would have chosen. But Carmen's buying. The feminist lesbian waitress comes. She brings water and menus. Mitch wants sausage, syrup, bacon, pancakes. But they don't have stuff like that here. He orders an omelette.

"Are you bummed out? About the job?" Carmen asks him when the waitress is gone.

"Nah, it wasn't really working out anyway. And that stupid truck..."

Carmen smiles at this. Mitch smiles too. The day hasn't turned out so bad. Sex. A big check. And now lunch with Carmen. He just wishes she wasn't wearing her third world hat, or whatever it is.

Nepalese probably, or Guatemalan. He could also live without the moaning folk singer that's playing on the stereo.

Carmen drinks her water. "So I wanted to tell you. That guy I was seeing, that *idiot,*" she glances up at Mitch. "He's decided he wants to see other people."

Mitch nods sympathetically. "I hate that," he says.

"It's such a lame thing to say. It's so typical."

Mitch continues to nod. The front door opens. Three women come in. Erica is one of them. Mitch looks out the window.

"And he was so wimpy about it," continues Carmen. "I can't stand when men start whining about needing their *space.*"

Mitch nods. He drinks his water. Erica didn't see him. And now she's sitting at a table, facing away from him. And so what? He's not going out with Amy. And even if he was, he can have lunch with someone else.

"So anyway, and then when Rob said he was going to let you go," says Carmen. "I just thought. Because before. You know, we worked together and I was seeing someone. And now we *don't* work together and I'm *not* seeing anyone."

"Oh," says Mitch, suddenly realizing what she's talking about.

"I should warn you, though, I'm really only interested in committed relationships."

"Sure, sure," says Mitch. But he doesn't like this forwardness. Probably in bed, Carmen tells you exactly what to do. And then you have to do it until she comes. It's the whole hippy feminist world. Mitch has never understood it.

"I mean, I don't–" says Carmen, pulling back. "I guess I'm getting ahead of myself. What I meant was just, you know, your idea that we should hang out..."

"No, no–" says Mitch. But then he can't think of what else to say. He thinks about Amy. That's how a girl should be in bed. Open and into everything. If you do everything, and you do it all night, everyone's going to get what they want eventually, right?

The food comes. Mitch eats. He drinks his coffee and keeps his head down. Neither of them talks for a while. Then Carmen asks him what he might do now for a job.

"I don't know," says Mitch. "I wish I could get back in at Quest."

"You're really into the club thing aren't you?" says Carmen.

"Yeah, I guess I am," says Mitch.

"I just think it's sort of pretentious, all those people, trying to act so cool all the time. Don't you?"

"What do you mean?"

"Well, it's not like this is New York or San Francisco."

"It's still fun," says Mitch

"Yeah but who do they think they are? Nobody dresses like that here. They just look stupid."

Mitch doesn't know what to say to that.

Carmen picks up the check when it comes. She studies the amount. "Would you mind leaving the tip?" she asks him.

"How much?"

"Two bucks. Or three if you got it."

Mitch reluctantly gets out his wallet. Two bucks is exactly how much he's got. He puts the two bills on the table. Then he sees Tracy. She's standing over the table where Erica is eating. She sees Mitch and waves.

Carmen stands up. Mitch stands up. Carmen goes to the counter to pay. Mitch has no choice but to say hi to Tracy and Erica.

"Hey, Tracy."

"Hey, Mitch, who's your friend?"

"Just somebody from work."

"What's her name?"

"Hi, Erica," says Mitch, looking past Tracy.

"Hi, Mitch," says Erica.

Mitch looks over to see how Carmen is doing. She's paid. She's ready to leave. "I gotta go," Mitch tells Tracy.

Outside, Mitch and Carmen walk back to the bakery. "So that sucks about your boyfriend," he says.

"I'm glad," says Carmen. "He was a waste of my time."

Mitch says nothing. They walk in silence. When they get to the bakery, Mitch separates from Carmen and goes to his bike. "Thanks for lunch," he tells her, looking at his keys, so he won't have to look at her face. When he gets to his bike she's already inside. He unfastens his lock and rides away.

SEVENTEEN

On Wednesday, Stuart comes by in his Dodge Charger. He's got a pint of rum. Mitch takes a long drag of it and lights a cigarette. They drive around. They go by Quest but there's a promotion tonight with KRRC, the local alternative rock station. There's a line halfway down the block. It's an ugly crowd: bland, suburban, alternative. Stuart suggests Magic Gardens. Mitch agrees.

They sit at the bar. It's the same middle-aged woman dancing, the one with the fake tits.

Stuart scans the room. He checks up and down the bar.

"Looking for Beth?" Mitch asks.

Stuart shrugs.

"What about you, where's Amy?" asks Stuart.

"Haven't seen her."

"Why not?"

"I don't know."

"I thought she looked pretty good the other night."

Mitch shrugs. "She's got a fucking Counting Crows poster over her bed."

"Ouch."

"I know," says Mitch. "I mean, I like fucking her. But Jesus, what am I supposed to talk to her about?"

"Take her to a movie. You don't have to talk at a movie."

"Yeah, I guess."

Stuart looks around again. He drinks his drink.

"What've you been doing?" asks Mitch.

"I came here last night."

"Yeah?"

Stuart nods a couple of times.

"Did you see Beth?"

Stuart nods more.

"Really?" says Mitch. "What happened?"

"I bought her a drink."

"You fucking bought her a drink? And then what?"

"Nothing. We talked a little bit."

"Did she remember you from Quest?"

"Yeah, I guess so. She didn't really say much. I did most of the talking."

"Was she still like, in her robe and all that?"

Stuart nods and drinks.

"With the lingerie and the garters?"

"Yep."

"You know what they do, don't you?" says Mitch.

"No. What?"

Mitch moves closer, so the bartender won't hear: "They get you to buy them a drink but it's not real. It's just water or juice or whatever. And then they keep the money. It's like a deal they do with the bartender."

"No way."

"They can't drink when they're working. So they get you to buy them a drink. But it's got no alcohol in it. And they keep the money."

"What the fuck are you talking about?"

"That's what I heard," says Mitch.

"What the fuck?" says Stuart, sneering at him.

"Hey, it makes sense."

"Fuck you man."

"I'm just telling you..."

"Fuck you."

Mitch shrugs. "I didn't mean..."

"Whatever."

Mitch goes back to his own drink.

Stuart chews on an ice cube.

"Check out this one," says Mitch. They both watch the new dancer. She's young, hispanic. She's got a thick bush of pubic hair.

"Too hairy," says Stuart.

"So with Beth," says Mitch, cautiously. "Like, could you tell if she was on heroin?"

"No."

"Not at all?"

"She didn't really talk. She just sat there," Stuart chews more ice. "Now that I think about it, maybe it was a scam. There was something weird about it."

"She's just checking you out," says Mitch. "I mean, every guy in the place is checking *her* out."

"Maybe," says Stuart. "But man, you should have seen her. She was...I mean, when you got up close to her. She just had this way about her. Just cute and quiet and sort of...graceful like."

Mitch nods.

"I asked her if she had a boyfriend."

"What'd she say?"

"Nothing."

"What did she say about Quest?"

"Not much."

"What about Jeanelle?"

"She just smiled."

"Fuck."

"That's what I said."

"Well, she's a fucking stripper," says Mitch. "What do you want?"

"I want her," says Stuart, chewing his ice. "That's what I want."

They go back to Quest. It's later now but the KRRC thing is still going. There's still a line. There's also now a limo parked across the street, with several radio station types standing around it. Stuart rolls the Dodge Charger past the crowd. "Look at these idiots," says Mitch.

"Fucking KRRC," mutters Stuart, taking a drag off his rum. He tries to spit on a teenager in a Luscious Jackson T-shirt. But it's too far. The kid doesn't even see it.

They try UFO. There's a show going on. They pull into the back parking lot. As they walk around to the front they see Tracy, Erica, and local musicians Brendon and Pete. They're huddled in the cold outside the entrance.

Mitch lets Tracy decide to say hi or not. She does. So Mitch and Stuart stop and talk.

"Who's playing?" Mitch asks her.

"The Miserables."

"How is it?"

"Noisy," says Tracy.

"Too much feedback," says Brendon.

"What are you guys doing?" asks Tracy.

"Getting drunk," says Stuart. He pulls the pint of rum out of his pants and takes a swig.

"You better be careful, they're searching people," says Pete.

"They won't find it," says Stuart, sliding it down the front of his pants.

"They're totally busting people," says Pete. "If they catch you, they'll eighty-six you forever."

"So? What do I care about UFO?" says Stuart. But now he sounds stupid. He pulls the bottle out of his pants and takes another swig.

Mitch, meanwhile, is watching Tracy. She's wearing her fake fur coat, a mini-skirt and white go-go boots. She shivers when the wind blows. She pulls her coat close around her.

Stuart is also cold. "Maybe we should go back to the car," he says. "And get stoned."

Everyone agrees. They walk to the car. Mitch gets in back. Pete starts to follow but Tracy stops him. "I want to sit next to Mitch," she says.

Mitch scoots over to the far window. Tracy sits beside him. Pete squeezes in. Tracy scoots closer. Mitch can smell her. He can feel the warmth of her against his shoulder. She settles in beside him. Mitch can feel his heart beat faster. He starts to look at her but finds he can't. He looks out the window instead.

EIGHTEEN

"These boots are killing my feet," says Tracy, once everyone's in. Stuart is in front with Erica and Brendon. He's loading his pipe. Brendon is telling Stuart about a new dance club that's just opened in Northeast.

"Could you help me with my boot?" Tracy asks Mitch.

Mitch looks down at it.

"Can you unzip it?" she asks.

Mitch reaches down and unzips the closest go-go boot. It gets stuck a couple times but he gets it. He sits back.

"Good," says Tracy. "Do the other one."

It made sense to have Mitch do the first one. It was on his side. It was easier for him to reach. But to reach the other one, he has to lean over Tracy's lap. He looks at her. But she's looking down at her boot. Pointing. She even shifts her knees to make it easier.

Mitch leans over and pulls down the zipper. It moves three inches and stops.

"See," says Tracy. "They get stuck."

Mitch tugs on it. He can smell Tracy's lap. It's a deep musky smell.

"Can you get it?" she says.

Mitch can't. He can't really grip it. He leans his forearm on Tracy's thigh.

"Ow," she says.

He takes his weight off her leg. "I can't get it," he says, straightening up.

"Yes, you can. You got the other one."

Mitch leans over and tries again. This time, on the very first try, the zipper goes all the way down to her ankle.

"Perfect," says Tracy.

Mitch sits up. The smell of Tracy is everywhere. Also he can't help but glance at her thighs, at her lap, her skirt has bunched up, he can see her underwear.

"They're awful, these boots," says Tracy. "They're so uncomfortable."

Mitch looks at them. He looks at Tracy. The car is filling with pot smoke. Brendon hands back the pipe. Mitch takes a hit. He gives it to Tracy. Tracy takes a hit. She gives it to Pete. The rum comes around. Everyone is now talking about the new dance club across the river.

Tracy leans over to Mitch. "So where's Amy tonight," she asks him.

"I wish people would stop asking me that."

"You haven't called her?"

"No."

"Don't you like her?"

"I told you. She's just a friend."

"A friend who you have sex with occasionally but never call or talk to?"

Mitch takes a swig of rum. "Yeah. I guess she is."

Tracy shakes her head. She gets her cigarettes out.

"Can I bum one of those," Mitch asks. She gives him one. She lights his, hers.

"What about you?" asks Mitch.

"What about me?"

"Who are you going out with?"

"None of your business," says Tracy.

"That guy from Baxter?"

"Maybe."

"But you just asked me."

"This isn't about my boyfriends," says Tracy. "This is about you and Amy."

"Yeah, but why can't I ask you the same question?"

"Because it's none of your business."

Mitch smokes. He looks at the window beside him. It's fogged. He draws a box on it.

"So who was that girl in Three Sisters?" says Tracy.

"Nobody."

"You were sitting at a small table."

"She's nobody. She's a hippy."

"I hate those hats."

"Me too," says Mitch, making the box into a house. "She was saying how she thought the Quest scene was pretentious."

"Wearing South American peasant hats is pretentious."

Mitch draws. "So you have several boyfriends?" he tries.

"I might."

"That Baxter guy was sort of cool."

"He's stuck on some film student girl up in Olympia."

Mitch is enjoying this conversation more than he knows. Because when he hears the familiar click of Stuart's door opening, his heart drops like a stone in his chest.

Stuart gets out. Brendon gets out. Stuart lifts the seat to let Pete out of the back.

Mitch prepares to follow. But Tracy doesn't move. "Stuart?" she says.

Stuart's head pokes in the door.

"Mitch and I are going to need a little more time. Can we stay?"

"Sure," says Stuart. He throws Mitch the keys. Everyone else is out. The doors shut. It's suddenly very quiet in the Dodge Charger.

"I gotta get these boots back on," says Tracy. Alone with Tracy, Mitch is suddenly so nervous he can't talk. He watches Tracy slip the boots on and then struggle to zip them up.

"These stupid things," says Tracy. Mitch watches the back of her fur coat.

"All right, there," says Tracy, sitting up. "Now a quick lipstick fix."

Mitch remains speechless. He swallows a dry hard swallow, made worse by the pot he just smoked.

"Do you mind sitting here with me?" asks Tracy, as she digs through her purse.

"No."

Tracy finds her lipstick. She unscrews the top and twists the dark head out of its sheath. She's got a compact out too, which she opens and watches herself in. She runs the lipstick across her lower lip.

Mitch watches in silence.

"I have to admit that I'm a little jealous of Amy," says Tracy, watching herself. "For finding you and everything. She's very good at finding guys you wouldn't normally notice."

Mitch stares at her. Tracy does her upper lip. She goes one way, then the other. She studies herself in the tiny mirror.

"Okay, how's that?" she says, turning suddenly toward him.

Mitch is startled by it. "What?"

"My lipstick dumbhead. Is it straight?"

Mitch looks. "Yeah, I guess so."

"What about my teeth?" She grits her teeth for him.

"What about them?"

"Do they have lipstick on them?"

Mitch looks. "No."

"All right then," she says. Mitch watches her put her compact away. But her breath, the smell of her, it's everywhere again. He wants to touch her. He wants to inhale her.

"Wait a minute," he says. "I think your hair's stuck."

"Where?" says Tracy, reaching behind her head.

"Don't move," says Mitch. He reaches back and pretends to unhook her hair from some obstacle. Mostly he touches it. He avoids looking at her face and concentrates on the back of her head. He smooths her black hair. It feels coarse to the touch. Too much hair dye. But the smell of it. And the fact that Mitch is handling it.

He's handling *her*. He glances at her face. She's watching him intently.

"You have nice hair," he says.

"I like you, Mitch," says Tracy without blinking. "But I don't know if I trust you."

"Trust me about what?"

"I'm not sure exactly." She reaches up and grips his arm. The one that's stroking her hair. She pulls it away, places it on his lap, holds it a little longer than she has to. She smiles sweetly at him. "I think it's time to go."

NINETEEN

Stuart is waiting for Mitch at the entrance. As he and Tracy approach, Stuart pulls Mitch aside. "Fuck this man, I don't want to go in here."

"Why not?" says Mitch. He was enjoying the sensation of walking beside Tracy, of approaching the door as if they were together.

"It's like six bucks. I ain't paying six bucks to see some noise band."

Tracy, who has already been stamped, continues forward. Mitch and Stuart both watch her disappear inside.

"What's up with her?" says Stuart.

"Fucking nothing now," says Mitch. "Thanks to you."

"Well, you wanna hang out? Cause I don't."

"Well, fuck," says Mitch. Other people go by. Two guys in glasses and gas station jackets go by.

"Look at these fucking geeks," says Stuart.

One of them turns and looks at him.

"Whassup dude?" Stuart says. He gives him the peace sign.

Mitch grabs Stuart. "What the fuck are you doing? We got bigger problems here."

"What's that?"

"What you just saw. Fucking Tracy. She's fucking hitting on me."

"No way. What did she do?"

"Nothing, but she's working me."

"She's fucking with your head."

"She made me unzip her go-go boots."

Stuart gives him a skeptical look. "That chick is the biggest fucking cunt in this town. She's just fucking with you. You're fucking Amy so now she's going to fuck with you."

"Who cares why? If I can fuck her..."

"You're never going to fuck her," says Stuart.

This statement stops Mitch cold.

"You wanna go or what?" says Stuart.

Mitch stares at him.

Stuart ignores the stare. He looks around. He looks everywhere but back at Mitch. "What? You want me to tell you something different?" Stuart jams his hands in his pockets. "She's fucking with your head. She fucked with you when we went to her house that time and she's fucking with you now. C'mon man, let's go to Hurley's and drink some beer."

They go back to the gravel parking lot. When they get to Stuart's car, there's a car load of guys getting out of an old station wagon. There are four of them. They're all wearing suits.

Stuart is unlocking his door when he sees them. "Hey, Mitch, check it out," he says loudly. "It's those assholes who always wear suits."

Mitch looks over at them. They heard Stuart.

Mitch turns back to the car door. He waits for Stuart to unlock his door.

But Stuart doesn't get in the car. "Hey, assholes who always wear suits. Whazzup? How's the suit business? You get laid wearing that shit? Or do you do each other?"

"What the fuck are you doing?" says Mitch.

"Hey, it's Mr. Rave," says one of the suits.

"Fuck yes," says Stuart loudly. And then in a lower voice: "Rave on your fucking head."

"Jesus Christ," says Mitch.

The suits are talking among themselves. They're being cool but they don't leave their car. They're waiting for Stuart to leave.

"Would you get in the car?" says Mitch.

"Look at theses fucking losers," whispers Stuart.

Mitch doesn't look. "Would you get in the *fucking car*?"

Stuart watches the suits for a few seconds more. Then he unlocks his door and gets in. He lets Mitch in. He starts the car and backs out of his space. Then he keeps backing up, until he's directly behind the station wagon.

"All right, suit-boys. Enjoy the show," says Stuart. He floors it. Gravel sprays the stationwagon. The Charger rockets forward. It bounces wildly out of the parking lot. Stuart turns hard to the right. They squeal around the corner, run the stop sign and fishtail down the street.

Mitch tries to keep his balance as the car pitches around. He's got a cigarette out but he can't get it in his mouth. Stuart finally lets up when a red light appears. He slows, stops. Mitch lights his cigarette.

They go to Hurley's. They drink. They play pool with some bar girls. Mitch isn't into the bar girls. He's got Tracy on the brain. He's finding the Tracy situation to be so interesting and complicated he can turn it over endlessly in his head. And the three minutes they just spent in the back seat...he could replay that all night. In fact, that's exactly what he's going to do. He tells Stuart he'll walk home.

But outside, his thoughts seem to dissolve in the damp night air. His brain loses focus. It doesn't matter. Tracy's impact has been so profound that he can run on the physical residuals. Like the time he and Stuart crashed Cindy Green's car into a tree. Mitch could feel the impact in his chest for months. And so it is with Tracy. He walks through downtown. She is there. He walks across the Hawthorne bridge. She is there. He walks along the busy streets, the quiet streets, his own street and she is there. In his room he puts on headphones, closes his eyes, loses himself in music. And still she is there.

But then someone is really there. Someone is shaking him. Mitch wakes up with a start. He's still got the headphones on but it's daytime. It's the next morning. The person touching him is Richard, his older brother. How did he get here? *Why* is he here? But then Mitch remembers. Today is Thursday. Today is Thanksgiving.

TWENTY

Mitch sits in the passenger seat of his brother's Ford Fiesta. He hasn't seen Richard since last Christmas. Richard is a school teacher in Tacoma. He's six years older than Mitch and this year he looks it. There's flecks of grey around his temples. His face looks flabby and pale.

"Mom's been trying to call you all morning," says Richard.

"Jesus," says Mitch, rubbing his eyes.

"What happened?"

"I don't know. I forgot."

"How can you forget Thanksgiving?"

"I fucked up."

"You're lucky your front door was open," says Richard.

Mitch feels around for his cigarettes. "Do you mind if I smoke?"

Richard looks crossways at him. "If you have to."

Mitch has to. He lights a cigarette and cracks the window.

"Mom said you're not working at the nightclub anymore," says Richard.

"No."

"How do you feel about that?"

Mitch shrugs. "Not very good."

"So you're not over your nightclub phase yet?"

"My nightclub phase?"

"You're not thinking about doing something else?"

"Not really."

Richard signals for a right turn. He looks to make sure it's clear and carefully moves his car into the right lane. "I know that Mom and Dad are wondering about it."

"Let 'em wonder," says Mitch.

"I mean they're not necessarily critical of what you're doing now. You're working at a bakery? But I think they're wondering what direction you're ultimately going to go."

"Down," says Mitch. He laughs at his own joke.

Richard can't help it. He laughs too.

Richard steers the Fiesta through the west side suburbs to the Smith residence. He pulls into the familiar cul-de-sac and up their driveway. He shuts off the engine.

"Well," says Richard. "It's nice to see you anyway."

Mitch gets out. Richard follows him into the house.

"Mitchell!" says his grandmother the minute he's inside.

"Hi, Grandma," he says. The old woman approaches him, hugs him, kisses him. "Hi, Grandpa," he says, when she withdraws and her husband approaches. Mitch shakes his hand.

"Mitchell?" comes a feminine voice from the kitchen. "Is that you?"

Mitch grimaces.

"Now don't be like that," says his grandmother. "Go in and say hello to your mother."

Mitch pushes through the swinging door to the kitchen. His mother is there. She smiles when he first comes in. But when the door swings shut the smile vanishes.

"What happened to you?" she snaps. "Why weren't you here last night?"

"I didn't know. I didn't have a ride."

"I *told you* I would come get you."

"I didn't get the message," says Mitch. "What difference does it make?"

"Your grandparents haven't seen you in a year and a half. *That's* what difference it makes. And they're leaving tonight. Why didn't you call this morning?"

"I didn't know I was supposed to."

"Now it's almost two o'clock. Your grandparents have to leave for the airport *in three hours*!"

"So they'll see me for three hours. How much time do they need?"

His mother glares at him then opens the oven. A turkey is cooking.

Suddenly the door swings open. It's Mitch's dad. "Where the hell have you been?" says the older man.

"I screwed up."

"You can't answer your phone?"

Mitch looks at the floor.

"You can't return a simple phone message from your own mother? On Thanksgiving?"

"It's my housemates," says Mitch. "I never get my messages."

Mitch's father shakes his head.

"Could you help me with this," Mitch's mom asks his dad.

"Here, let me help," offers Mitch. But they both glare at him. His father lifts the turkey out of the oven. Mitch is only in the way. He backs out of the kitchen.

He goes back to the living room. There's a woman there, sitting next to Richard on the living room sofa. She's older. She's dressed up. "Hello," she says to Mitch.

"Oh," says Richard. "This is Ellen. You two haven't met."

"Hi, Ellen," says Mitch, he goes to her, shakes her hand.

"Hello, Mitch."

Richard looks at the two of them. "Ellen and I work together. At the school."

Mitch nods his understanding. He smiles at Ellen. She's bigboned, pale, hard-looking in her face.

Mitch moves so his grandfather can see the football game. Mitch sits on the couch beside Richard and Ellen. They all watch the big screen TV. The Dallas Cowboys are playing the Detroit Lions.

The Smith's two dogs, Brandy and Jake, are working the room. Mitch pets them. Richard pets them. Grandma and Grandpa pet them.

"So you playing any ball these days?" asks Grandpa Smith, who for some reason has never forgotten that Mitch was a guard on his highschool basketball team.

"Not really," says Mitch, as he watches the TV. But he should try to say more. He should try to make conversation. "There's no place to play. And it's always raining and everything."

"What about a gym? Couldn't you play in a gym?" says his grandfather.

The old man is speaking loudly so Mitch does the same. "Yeah, I guess I could play in a gym."

"How about those Lakers?" Richard says to his grandfather. "They'll be pretty good this year. With Shaq."

But his Grandfather frowns. He doesn't seem to hear.

"The Los Angeles Lakers dear," says his grandmother.

But his grandfather just frowns more. "Shaq," he says. "He's just a thug. That isn't basketball."

Richard laughs patronizingly at this observation. Ellen slips her hand into Richard's as he does. Mitch watches the TV. He needs a cigarette. He excuses himself and walks down the hall toward the bathroom. He ducks into his old room. The bed is still under the window. Mitch steps on it and slides the window open. He crawls out and jumps into the backyard. He's practically lighting his cigarette as he hits the ground.

He takes several deep drags. He looks around at the backyard. It's depressing. The brown fence has faded to a dull grey. The lawn is sparse and yellowish, in some places it's just mud. Beyond the back fence Mitch can see the second story of the Collins' house across the way. It's the only two story house in the neighborhood. Mitch used to play with Brenda Collins. In third grade they used to tie each other to the jungle gym and pull down each other's pants.

Mitch smiles at the thought of that. He sucks hard on his cigarette. He looks up at the heavy grey overcast. A single black crow flies by. Mitch finishes his cigarette. He drops it, steps on it, and crawls back in his bedroom window.

TWENTY ONE

At half-time of the football game, dinner is served. Mitch sits at the far end of the table, away from his parents. Mitch hasn't eaten all day and waits hungrily while the various dishes are passed around. Then he has to wait for grace. His father says it. His grandparents, Mitch notices, take it quite seriously. But that would make sense. They're old. They're hedging their bets.

Finally they eat. Mitch digs in. He eats turkey, mashed potatoes, gravy, cranberry sauce, pumpkin pie, a fruit salad, some other vegetable dish, rolls, butter, jam. In between bites he watches the Cowboys stomp the Detroit Lions, or at least he does until his mother sees everyone watching TV and turns it off. After that a strained silence spreads over the table.

"So Mitch, Richard says you're working at a health food store," Grandma Smith finally says.

Mitch nods. His mouth is full of food. And then when he swallows he has to decide if he should lie or not. He decides it'll be easier to lie. "It's a bakery," he says.

"It's a health food bakery? How interesting," says his grandmother.

Mitch nods. He eats.

"What sort of ingredients do they use?" Ellen asks Mitch.

Mitch thinks about this. He chews. "I'm not sure. Healthy stuff I guess."

"Isn't it more of a health food store that also sells bread?" asks Richard, helpfully.

"It's more of a bakery," says Mitch. "It just has 'Natural' in the name."

"And what do you do for them?" asks his grandfather.

"I deliver it," says Mitch. "I used to."

"You used to?"

"I uh, I used to help them make it. But now I deliver it. That's why I have such weird hours. Which I wanted to apologize to you guys for. I mean, for falling asleep and not coming earlier."

"That's all right Mitchell," says his grandmother. "We understand."

"So no more of this nightclub business for you then?" says his grandfather.

"Actually, I'd like to get back into that. I mean, the music part of it. I know this guy Dieter who's a DJ. I'd sort of like to do that if I could."

"Don't those people get shot?" says Ellen.

"The DJs? Nah."

"In Seattle they're always having these rap things and the people are always getting shot," Ellen tells Mitch's mother. "It's usually, you know, more urban people."

"Knowing Mitch he'd forget to show up," says Mitch's dad. "You can't get shot if you're not there."

"If I was doing that, I'd show up," says Mitch, quietly.

"What do these people do at these nightclubs?" says Mitch's grandmother.

Mitch shrugs. "Nothing much."

"No, really, Mitchell," says his grandmother.

Mitch looks up from his plate. His grandmother's eyes are intent with curiosity.

"I really want to know," she says. "What did you do at that place? What was it called?"

"Quest?"

"Yes."

Mitch shrugs. "I worked the door. I bussed."

"But what do people do there?"

"Dance. Take drugs."

"Mitchell!" says his mother.

His grandmother continues to stare at him. "I'm serious. What's it like there?"

Mitchell remembers now that Grandma Smith was the one that gave him his first Beastie Boys record for Christmas. When he was in eighth grade. She bought him *License to Ill*. She had read about it in *Time* magazine and she bought it for him and then she actually sat there and listened to it with him.

"I remember nightclubs when I was a little girl," she continues. "Reading about them at least. Everyone dressing up and dancing...is that what it's like?"

"Yeah," says Mitch. He looks into her intent face. "Yeah. That kind of *is* what it's like. Except different. The music is electronic. And the lights are really fancy. There are lasers and fog machines and stuff."

"Fog machines," she says.

"It's like a dream, Grandma," says Mitch. Everyone is listening to him. "It's like a dream you can go in and escape from everything."

"And get shot," says his dad. Everyone chuckles at this. But Mitch's grandmother doesn't laugh with the others. She looks at Mitch. "Thank you for telling me that," she says. "No one ever wants to tell me anything. And I want to know."

Mitch is alarmed by the expression on her face as she says this.

"People think you're so old you can't understand anything," she continues. "But I understand. I was young once." Her lip starts to tremble. She looks like she's going to cry.

Mitch watches her. Then he looks into his plate.

"Could you pass the potatoes?" Ellen asks Richard.

Then, as if things weren't weird enough, the doorbell rings, the front door opens and in walks Brenda Collins, the girl Mitch used to tie to the jungle gym. She's carrying a baby. And her mother, Irene, is behind her.

"Irene!" says Mitch's mother. "Brenda!"

"We just wanted to stop by. And wish everyone a happy Thanksgiving," says Mrs. Collins.

"And you've brought the baby!" says Mitch's mother. She brings them into the dining room. Mitch's dad stands to greet them. Richard gets up and begins clearing the table.

"You're not finished eating," says Mrs. Collins.

"Oh, don't be silly," says Mitch's mother. "We're just having coffee. Would you like some dessert?"

"Oh, we couldn't."

"Of course you could."

Throughout all this, Mitch watches Brenda. She's holding the baby. She talks to it, bounces it. It's apparently hers. Mitch also notices that Brenda–who was not very cute when they were tying each other up–is still not very cute. She's wearing a stonewashed denim jacket and her plain face is now partially hidden beneath a bad Supercuts perm.

Richard picks up Mitch's plate. Mitch should help. He does. When he's alone with his brother in the kitchen he asks about Brenda. "Does she have a husband for that thing?"

Richard shrugs. "I don't know anything about it."

Mitch gets coffee and goes back to his place at the table. Brenda is sitting beside her mother. She looks up as he walks by. "Mitch! I didn't even see you there," she says.

"Hey," he says, forcing a smile.

"Look, I'm a mommy now," she says. She flashes a self deprecating smile that reminds him that Brenda, though not popular when they were growing up, was always pretty cool about things.

"Wow," says Mitch. "What's its name?"

"It's a he. His name is William."

"All right," says Mitch. "Who's the daddy?"

Brenda's smile fades slightly. "His daddy is a man who's not here right now," she says, more to the baby than to Mitch.

"Well, he sure is uh. . .big."

"He sure is," says Brenda, bouncing William and making a funny face.

Mitch sips his coffee. The baby, he notices, isn't amused.

TWENTY TWO

Later, Mitch gets stuck riding with his grandparents to the airport with Richard and Ellen. He makes sure to get Ellen between him and his grandfather in the back seat. But even by the window, Mitch feels suffocated. He needs a cigarette. Also, the conversation in the front seat, between his grandmother and Richard: it's mind numbing.

"So how's the weather been in San Diego?" says Richard.

"It's been a bit cool," says his grandmother.

Mitch stares out the window and tries to think about something else. Tracy. Amy giving him head. What it would be like to suck on Brenda's breasts. Would milk come out? But none of these thoughts provide escape. He looks over at Ellen, at her hands where they rest in her lap.

"How are those Trailblazers doing this year?" Grandpa Smith asks Mitch across Ellen's front.

Mitch looks past Ellen to tell him not very good. "They got a new coach," says Mitch.

"Shaq. He's a thug," says Grandpa Smith. Mitch waits for him to say something else. But the old man looks lost. Like he's forgotten what he's talking about.

Mitch looks back out the window. They're winding their way through the old neighborhood. He sees the Seven Eleven where during junior high he asked an off duty cop to buy him beer and got busted. Further on they pass the Chevron station where he worked his first two years out of high school. At the final intersection before the freeway, two girls are waiting for the bus into the city. Mitch remembers doing that. Friday nights, a pint in his pocket, cigarettes, sitting on that bench, staring down the street waiting for the 44 bus to get him the fuck out of here.

Richard accelerates onto the freeway entrance ramp and merges into traffic. A cute girl in a Volkswagen Jetta passes them. Mitch tries to see her face but she passes too quickly. He looks for other girls in other cars. But there aren't many. The few he spots are suburbanites. Dull, plain, bland. Brenda Collinses.

When they get to the airport, Mitch is so bored he barely knows where he is. Richard has to ask him twice to get the bags out of the trunk. Mitch finally does. It's just a shoulder bag and Grandpa Smith's little suitcase.

Mitch carries the bags. He follows the others across the parking lot to the terminal. There's two cute girls waiting outside for their rides. He finds himself veering toward them. One girl's wearing a corduroy coat. She has long blonde hair, a ring in her eyebrow. She and her friend see Mitch coming. They check him out. He's wearing his racing jacket, his suede Vans. There's some eye contact, some looks.

"Mitch, over here," says Richard. Mitch shifts his direction and follows his relatives inside and onto the escalator. Here too there are women to look at. Right in front of him is a middle-aged platinum blond with tight black synthetic pants. Mitch studies her heavy ass, the lines of her panties. When they reach the top he checks out her face. She's ugly. She's wearing tons of make-up. But her full tits project nicely from under her tight blouse.

Again he must adjust his direction to follow his grandparents. Richard is talking to them. Ellen is lagging behind. Mitch falls in beside her.

"How are you doing with that stuff," she asks him.

"It's all right," says Mitch. He sees another girl coming his way. She's by herself. She's wearing Pumas, baggy overalls, a fluffy sweater. She's short, wispy thin. Her skin is milky smooth.

"Hi," Mitch says to her.

She looks up, startled. Mitch smiles at her. Who could she be? There's nobody around that dresses as cool as that, at least no one that he wouldn't know about.

She doesn't answer him. They pass. She must be visiting. She's probably from Vancouver or Seattle. Or maybe she's just really young. That happens sometimes. You see some rad girl who's got the perfect look and then you talk to her and she doesn't know anything. She's just copied a magazine or something. She's never heard of Quest. She doesn't know the music or the DJs or the scene.

Mitch turns for one last look at her. She's even got the walk, that lazy droopiness. She's probably just young. She'll end up at Quest. Or else she'll go off somewhere. To Seattle. California. The smart ones always do that. They leave.

"Friend of yours?" asks Ellen.

"Nah," says Mitch. "I just thought I recognized her from somewhere."

The scene at the gate is pathetic: Richard getting all mushy and weird, Ellen with her forced smile, Mitch trying one last time to talk basketball with Grandpa Smith. Mitch's grandmother seems distant now. Maybe she's embarrassed about her little breakdown at dinner. When she goes around and kisses everyone, Mitch is shocked by how cold her lips are. What if she dies? What if Mitch never sees her again? He tries to talk to her. "It's great to see you, Grandma," he says. "Sometime I'll tell you more about the club scene."

She warms. "I would love to hear about it."

"All right," says Mitch.

"And you be nice to your mom and dad now. They love you."

"I will," says Mitch. He smiles at her as she takes her shoulder bag. Grandpa Smith takes his suitcase.

Smiles, waves, and then it's over. They're gone. Mitch, Richard and Ellen begin the walk back. It's awkward at first, the three of them. But Richard and Ellen talk among themselves. Mitch looks at girls, spaces out.

In the car, Mitch sits by himself in the backseat. He sits back and imagines he's a star DJ somewhere, in the back of a limo. The freshly paved airport road, the futuristic lights: he's in some foreign city, on his way to a huge outdoor rave where he'll play to a crowd of thousands.

But when they're away from the airport the highway is dark and full of pot holes. It's begun to rain now too. Mitch wonders what he's going to do for real work. He's got to start looking for a job.

Richard drops Mitch off at his house in Southeast. Richard turns and tells Mitch goodbye. Ellen makes a great effort to smile as she wishes him well. But behind their formal goodbyes they seemed pissed at him. Perpetually disappointed. Fuck 'em, thinks Mitch. *Fuck 'em all.* He slams the door shut and walks up the stairs to his house.

TWENTY THREE

Back at his house, there's a phone message stuck to his door. "Wondered how Thanksgiving went," it says. Beneath that is "Amy" and her phone number. Mitch has nothing better to do. He goes back downstairs. He grabs a beer from the fridge. He sprawls on the couch and picks up the phone. He dials Amy's number. He drinks as it rings.

Amy answers. "Hello?"

"Hello?" says Mitch, lowering the bottle. "Amy?"

"Mitch? Is that you? Wow."

"What's up?"

"Nothing. What are you doing?"

"Nothing," says Mitch. "Drinking a beer."

"How was Thanksgiving?"

"It sucked."

"How come?"

"It just did. How was yours?"

"Okay. Just the usual."

"Huh," says Mitch. He scrapes at the beer label with his fingernail. "So what are you doing now?"

"Nothing. Tracy and Erica and I were playing Scrabble earlier."

"Huh."

"Tracy is so good at it. It's scary."

"Why is she good at it?"

"I don't know. She knows a lot of words."

"Does she cheat?"

"No. I don't think so."

Mitch drinks his beer. "So you feel like coming over?" he says. It feels weird asking her. It puts the pressure on him.

"Over to your house?"

"Yeah."

"I kind of have to work in the morning."

"You wouldn't have to stay."

"I'd like to."

"Yeah?"

"But I better not."

"Maybe we should have phone sex," says Mitch, quietly.

"What?"

"Nothing."

"Did you say you wanted to have phone sex?"

"I was just kidding."

"Are you into that?"

"No," says Mitch. "I don't know. I've never done it before."

"That's so weird because Erica was just talking about that earlier."

"Really? What did she say?"

"Just that she used to do it with her old boyfriend."

"Did she like it?"

"She said it was weird. But I guess she liked it. She kept doing it."

"It just seems sort of...like something married people do," says Mitch. He sits up. He doesn't think anyone is here but he looks around to make sure. He covers the phone and listens. The house is perfectly still.

He slouches back down on the couch. "I'm sorry, what were you saying?"

"About phone sex?"

"Yeah."

"Just that Erica did it with her boyfriend."

"How do you do it?" says Mitch. He pulls open his belt buckle.

"I don't know. I mean, I guess you just do yourself. While you're talking to the person."

"And you talk about it."

"I guess."

"On TV they always say: 'What are you wearing?'"

"I know," says Amy. "Erica was laughing about that."

"What if you just say: 'I'm naked.'"

"You can. But I think it's better if you have your clothes on. At least at the beginning. Don't you think?"

"Sure," says Mitch. He takes a last chug of beer and puts the bottle on the floor. "So what are you wearing?"

"What do you want me to be wearing?"

"I want you to be sucking my cock," says Mitch.

"Wow," says Amy.

"Do you want to?"

There's a settling sound on Amy's end. "...Okay."

"So you like sucking it?" says Mitch, his voice dropping suddenly.

"Uh-huh," says Amy, she too has dropped her voice to a low whisper.

Mitch gets his fly undone. He gets his dick out. "I like the taste of your pussy," he says, stroking himself.

"I like sucking your cock."

Mitch increases his rhythm.

"Mmmmmmmmmm," breathes Amy.

"And you know what?"

"What?"

"I love fucking your pussy."

"I love it when you fuck me."

"Me too."

"Ohhhh, mmmmmmm, oh yeah..."

There's a noise on the outside porch. The front lock makes a noise. The front door opens.

Mitch sits up. He yanks the front of his racing jacket over his erect cock. It's Gillian, Mitch's housemate. "Oh, hi Mitch," she says.

She's got an umbrella, a shopping bag, several dishes covered with tin foil.

"Hey, what's up?" he says to her. The phone is sliding off his shoulder. He repositions it, being careful to keep his jacket front over his dick.

"Did you have a nice Thanksgiving?" says Gillian.

"Yeah, it was great," he says. Then he gestures to her that he's on the phone. He talks into the receiver: "Amy?"

"What happened?"

"Nothing," he says. He watches Gillian go into the kitchen. "My housemate just got home," he whispers.

"Oh, no," says Amy.

Mitch feels through his coat for his dick. He's hoping Gillian will go into her room. But she's arranging stuff in the refrigerator. Sorting stuff. She's staying in the kitchen. "Shit," says Mitch into the phone. "She's hanging out. Why don't you come over?"

"I can't Mitch," says Amy. "I have to get up."

"I'll come over there."

"I don't think you better."

"Why not?"

"I have to work."

"Just go to bed. Go to sleep. I'll sneak in and visit you. Like the other night."

She doesn't answer.

"Okay?" says Mitch.

"I didn't like that, the other night."

"You didn't?"

She doesn't answer.

"Why not?" asks Mitch.

"It made me feel...I don't know. Why can't we go to a movie or something? Why can't we hang out some time?"

"We can. We can hang out right now."

"It just seems like the only time you want to see me is when you want sex."

Mitch frowns. He finds the beer beneath him and takes a sip.

"How do you think that makes me feel?" asks Amy.

Now it's Mitch who doesn't answer.

"Mitch?"

"What?"

"How do you think that makes me feel?"

"I don't know," he says. He drinks. "It's just that, like, Thanksgiving really sucked. And now I'm all horny and everything."

"I'm sorry Mitch."

"Well, I'm sorry too."

"If you would call me sometime–"

"–but I just called you right now!"

"You know what I mean."

"No," says Mitch. "I *don't* know what you mean."

"I'm going to go now."

"Tell me what you mean."

"I'm sorry you didn't have a nice Thanksgiving."

"Jesus Christ."

"Goodbye, Mitch."

"Fuck."

She hangs up.

"Fuck."

TWENTY FOUR

On Saturday, Mitch and Stuart meet Dieter at Magic Gardens. They play pool. Mitch plays Dieter. Stuart sits at a table and watches the stage. Beth is here tonight. She's about to go on.

Dieter breaks. Two solids drop in. Mitch watches while he hits a third ball in. Then a fourth.

Stuart's leg is bouncing in place. He's drinking, waiting for Beth.

"Is he okay?" Dieter asks Mitch as he circles behind him to line up a shot.

Mitch shrugs. The dancer who is on finishes her final dance. She kneels in her high heels to scoop up the ones and fives that are scattered across the stage. She disappears behind the curtain. A moment later Beth comes out. She's carrying a drink with a stir straw which she sucks from as she studies the on-stage jukebox. She's wearing a silver vinyl miniskirt, fishnet stockings, a tight 70's disco top which shows the shape of her medium-sized tits. Mitch and Dieter stop playing to watch her pick her music. The first song is "Queerest of the Queer." She lets it play a moment before she puts down her drink.

"See?" says Stuart, pointing at her. "What's that she's drinking?"

"A drink?" says Dieter.

"A drink, exactly!" says Stuart. "Mitch says they don't drink real drinks."

"Hey, that's just what somebody told me," says Mitch. He considers his next shot.

"Fuck man, look at her," says Stuart, in awe.

Mitch shoots, misses.

Dieter shoots. A ball drops in.

"She's *amazing,*" says Stuart.

Dieter shoots again. Another ball drops in. Mitch sits down next to Stuart.

"Look at those tits," says Stuart. "That's no fucking silicone there. That's the real fucking deal."

But Mitch isn't looking at her tits. He's looking at her arms. He thinks he sees something. "Check out her forearms," he tells Stuart. "On the inside."

"What? Why?"

"Track marks."

"What the fuck are you talking about?" Stuart says, sneering at him. "You wouldn't know a fucking track mark if it hit you in the head."

"I just thought I saw—"

"—I sat right next to her and there's no fucking *track marks*. Go play your fucking pool game."

It's true. Mitch isn't sure what a track mark would look like. He goes back to his pool game, which he has just lost, Dieter has sunk the eight ball.

When Beth is done, she leaves the stage. "Now what happens?" Mitch asks Stuart. He's sitting beside him. Dieter is playing a Mexican guy.

"She comes out that door, and she goes to the bar."

A minute passes and then Beth appears. She comes out the door and goes to the bar.

"And now I go buy her a drink," says Stuart, getting up.

Mitch says nothing. He watches Stuart approach the bar. Stuart says something to Beth. They talk. Beth sits on a bar stool. She crosses her legs while Stuart lights her cigarette. She says something to the bartender. He brings her a drink. Stuart pays.

Mitch looks back at the pool table. The Mexican guy is not very good. It takes Dieter five minutes to clear the table and sink the eight ball.

Dieter sits next to Mitch. "What's going on?"

"Stuart's buying Beth a drink," Mitch tells him.

"No shit?" says Dieter, watching.

"Wanna go over there?"

"And do what?"

"Nothing. Say hi."

"Nah. Better leave him alone."

"C'mon," says Mitch. "I want to see if that drink is real."

"Go ahead," says Dieter. "I got another game."

Mitch goes. He walks across the room and casually approaches the bar.

"Hey," Mitch says to Stuart.

"What do you want?" says Stuart.

"Nothing," says Mitch. "I just wanted to say hi."

Stuart scowls. Beth smiles pleasantly at Mitch.

"Hi," Mitch says to Beth. "My name's Mitch."

She smiles at him. "Wanna buy me a drink?"

Mitch laughs. He grins at Stuart. "You already have a drink."

"But it's almost gone," says Beth. She sucks on the straw. "Now it is gone."

"Those must not be very strong drinks," says Mitch.

"What the fuck are you doing?" says Stuart, suddenly.

"I'm just–"

"–Why don't you both buy me a drink?" says Beth.

"No," says Stuart. "I have an idea. Why doesn't my asswipe friend here go back to his fucking pool game."

"Okay, okay," says Mitch, raising his hands in a peacemaking gesture. He smiles once at Beth and then walks back to the pool table.

"How'd it go?" asks Dieter, as Mitch takes a seat.

"Fucking Stuart," laughs Mitch. Stuart's beer is still sitting on the table in front of him. Mitch takes a long drink from it.

Meanwhile a new dancer is on stage. Mitch focuses on that. She's not very cute. And she has no sense of rhythm. She twirls around. She does a few cheerleader moves. She bends over and flashes her cunt.

Then Stuart's back. He grabs Mitch by the coat. "Where's my fucking beer?" he demands. He sees the empty glass. "You fucking drank my beer!"

"No, I–" says Mitch.

"You little fuck!" Stuart's hand is suddenly under Mitch's chin. Mitch feels himself being driven back in his chair. The chair tips, the table tips...everything falls. Mitch lands on his back on the floor. Stuart continues to press down on him. He's got Mitch by the throat. Mitch tries to twist free. He tries to pry Stuart's thumb loose. But Stuart is bigger, stronger. Mitch is pinned to the floor, Stuart's red, enraged face over him.

A waitress appears. "Out!" she barks. "All of you, out! Now!"

Stuart releases him. He storms out, knocking people out of his way. Mitch struggles to stand. Dieter helps him up.

"You! Both of you, out!" says the waitress. Dieter starts to leave.

"I *slipped,*" protests Mitch. But now there's a bouncer, a huge guy with a mustache, he grips Mitch's upper arm and starts to push him toward the door.

"I'm going, I'm going," says Mitch. Dieter is in front of him, hurrying toward the door. Mitch is being pushed faster than he can walk, he knocks into a chair, he almost falls. As they pass the bar, he sees Beth. She's still on her stool, her bare legs crossed. Some new guy is trying to talk to her.

The bouncer keeps pushing Mitch forward. Someone is holding the door open. Dieter is not moving fast enough. The bouncer gives Mitch one final shove out the door and his face collides with the back of Dieter's head. Their two skulls *thock* like pool balls. Mitch sees stars, he staggers onto the sidewalk. Dieter veers off to the right. He's swearing, holding the back of his head. Mitch follows, also swearing, holding his face. But the two of them keep moving, down the sidewalk, away from the club, in the general direction of Quest.

TWENTY FIVE

A few blocks later Mitch's head is clear. He catches up with Dieter who is walking very fast.

"Jesus, slow down," he says.

Dieter looks back at Mitch. Dieter is visibly shaken. He continues his fast march.

"It's all right man, chill out," says Mitch.

"Why'd that guy have to push you? We were *leaving*."

"It's okay," says Mitch, but he's rushing on adrenaline too. "Fuck, are you all right?"

"I don't know," says Dieter, he reaches back and touches his head. "I better be."

"Where are we going?"

"What a dick!"

"If we go to Quest, Stuart might be there."

Dieter isn't hearing what Mitch is saying. He's walking so fast, Mitch has to run to catch up.

"Dieter, chill!" says Mitch.

"What?"

"Look at my face."

"What?"

"My lip, is it bleeding?"

Dieter stops. He looks. "No."

"It's swelling up though, I can feel it."

Dieter walks.

"Dieter, wait a sec! What if Stuart's at Quest?"

"So what if he is?"

"What if he's still pissed?"

"What do I care if he's pissed or not?" says Dieter, turning on Mitch.

Mitch recoils from Dieter's glare. "What are you yelling at me for? It's not *my* fault."

"I kind of think it is," says Dieter. "I told you to leave him alone!" He turns the corner. They're at Quest.

There's a line in front. They go around to the back entrance. Dieter nods at the burly security guard and goes in. Mitch follows but the guy grabs him.

"What?"

"DJs only," says the guard.

"I'm with him."

"DJs only."

"I *am* a DJ. I used to work here."

"I've never seen you."

Dieter comes back. "He's with me."

"You're not a DJ," the guard says to Mitch.

"He's with me," says Dieter. "He helps me."

"I used to *work here*," says Mitch.

The guard is not convinced. But he releases Mitch's arm. Mitch follows Dieter inside.

"If you lie to the guy he won't let you in at all," Dieter tells Mitch.

"Fuck that piece of shit," says Mitch. But he's distracted now by the crowded main room of Quest. He looks around for Stuart.

Dieter heads toward the DJ platform. At first Mitch follows, but he can tell Dieter doesn't want him to. So he goes to the bar instead. He's still watching for Stuart. It's not that he's afraid of him physically. Mitch has lost lots of fights. There's no great disgrace in it. He just doesn't know what he should say to Stuart if they don't fight. He decides to get drunk. That'll help either way.

He orders a double whiskey and a pint of beer. Mitch puts a ten on the bar. The bartender brings him back a single dollar bill. Mitch leaves it as a tip. He drinks half the whiskey and lights a cigarette. A cool trip-hop groove is playing, over it DJ Troy is sampling The Butthole Surfers' "Hurdy Gurdy Man." Mitch tries to get into it but his nerves are still jangled. He downs the rest of the whiskey. The alcohol warms his spine, calms his heartbeat. He stubs his cigarette out, grabs his beer and walks around the club.

Jeanelle is in the big booth with two girls Mitch doesn't know. Mitch might hesitate to sit with them normally, he's never actually talked to Jeanelle himself. But he's drunk, adrenalized, and still a little fogged in the brain from getting his head banged. He slides into the far side and scoots around a little ways. One of the girls is talking to Jeanelle. The closer girl is just sitting there, smoking.

"Hey," Mitch says to her.

She smiles tightly.

Mitch sips his beer. He gets out his Marlboros. "Cigarette?" he offers.

"I'm smoking one," she says, holding her lit cigarette up to his face.

"Oh," says Mitch. He lights his own. He feels his lip. "Hey," he says to the girl. "Is my lip swelled up?"

The girl looks. "No."

Mitch touches his lip and looks at his finger. "I got thrown out of Magic Gardens," Mitch explains. "And the bouncer smashed my head into my friend's head."

The girl flicks an ash into the ashtray.

"It kinda hurt," says Mitch.

"I bet," she says.

Mitch smokes.

The girl smokes.

"So what's your name?" asks Mitch.

"Gretchen."

"Huh," says Mitch. He looks more closely at her. She's skinny. She has a sharp, pointy nose. She wears plastic barrettes in her hair, which is short and expensively cut.

Erica appears. She nods to Jeanelle and then slides into the booth. She's got a guy with her. A dark swarthy guy in a black leather trench coat. She doesn't see Mitch until she's sitting right next to him. "Oh, hi Mitch."

"Hey," he says to her.

Erica lights a cigarette and starts talking to the guy. Mitch sits back in his place. If Erica is here maybe Tracy or Amy are around. He scans the dance floor.

Meanwhile Gretchen has noticed that Mitch and Erica know each other. That's one advantage to sleeping with Amy. The connection to Tracy and Erica gives Mitch all sorts of social credibility.

"So what's your name again?" asks Gretchen.

"Mitch."

Gretchen nods. And then quietly: "How do you know Erica?"

Mitch shrugs. "Just around."

"Oh, that reminds me," says Gretchen. "There's a party next weekend. It's a friend of mine's birthday." She pulls a flier out of her purse.

"And tell Erica too."

Mitch takes the flier. She's given him several copies.

"Give one to Erica," says Gretchen.

Mitch taps Erica's shoulder and hands her a flier. Erica takes it, glances at it, leaves it on the table in front of her.

Mitch is more careful with his. He folds it, slips it in his pocket. "How do you know Jeanelle?" he asks Gretchen.

"Oh, just around," she answers.

Mitch nods. He smiles. He kind of likes this Gretchen girl. He drinks more beer and watches the dance floor.

TWENTY SIX

Mitch gives Stuart most of the week to cool off. On Thursday, he's downtown anyway, so he ventures into the parking garage where Stuart works. He's nervous as he enters the low-ceilinged cement structure. He approaches the little booth. Stuart is inside. Stuart sees him and slouches down in his chair. He's got the mini-TV on.

"Hey," says Mitch.

Stuart stares at the TV.

"Whassup?" says Mitch.

"What do you want?"

Mitch looks around the parking garage. "Nothing. I was just checking out a temp place. Thought I'd stop by. See if you were still pissed."

Stuart says nothing.

"I went to that temp place on Broadway. Excel. Didn't you work there once?"

"I don't remember."

Mitch nods. It's cold in the parking garage. Mitch blows into his hand. "So you're still pissed?"

Stuart doesn't answer.

Mitch nods. He looks around the parking garage. He blows into his hand.

Stuart has a Starbuck's coffee. He drinks from it.

"Also, I wanted to say," continues Mitch. "I mean, that stuff I said to Beth. At the bar. That was out of line."

"Fuck yes it was out of line," says Stuart quietly.

Mitch nods. He gets a cigarette out of his coat. "You sure got out of Magic Gardens fast."

"I'm smart."

"That bouncer nearly cost me some teeth."

Stuart says nothing.

Mitch lights his cigarette. He smokes. "But anyway, like I said, I was out of line. But the thing is. I met this girl at Quest. And she's friends with Jeanelle. And maybe with Beth too, but I didn't ask. Anyway, she's having a party. And I thought maybe you'd want to go. In case Beth shows up."

"How do you know she'll be there?"

"I don't," says Mitch. He looks at the ground. "That's the thing. I don't at all. It's just a possibility. I was just thinking if she was, you'd want to be there."

Stuart looks at him. "Who was the girl at Quest? The one you met?"

"She was just some girl. I don't know."

"You met a girl. You want to go to her party. You want me to drive. So you come here."

Mitch looks around the parking garage. He smokes. "My thinking was more, here's a chance for both of us to possibly get laid."

Stuart nods at the logic of that.

"And the thing is, I may have got 86'd from Magic Gardens for good. And I got my face smashed. So, you know, it wasn't like that night was so great for me either."

"You caused it yourself."

"Yeah, I know. But still."

Stuart drinks his coffee.

"Yeah, well, if you don't want to go that's cool," says Mitch. "But I thought I should at least tell you about it."

"What's Dieter doing that night?"

"I don't know."

"We should call him."

Mitch nods. "He was kind of freaked out actually. About getting bounced."

Stuart smiles at the mini-TV. "That's probably the first time he's ever been thrown out of a place."

Mitch smiles at the ground. "Probably."

But then Stuart's face turns serious. "But if it's Jeanelle's friends we should bring him."

"Definitely," says Mitch.

"Jeanelle likes him."

Mitch nods.

"All those girls like him."

Mitch drops his cigarette and steps on it. "I'll call him."

But Dieter is DJing that night. At the new club across the river. It's called Pulsar. Mitch and Stuart decide to check it out before they go to Gretchen's.

Pulsar is in Northeast, in the industrial section. They find the address. They find the parking lot. As they pull in, Stuart almost hits a black kid running out from behind a van. "Whoa," says Stuart. "Watch yourself there homey."

Inside there are more black people. Stuart and Mitch walk around the outside of the dance floor. The crowd is about half black, half white. "The brothers are in the house," says Stuart.

Mitch follows him to the bar. They order rum and cokes. A beautiful Asian woman serves them. "Man," says Stuart. "Check her out."

"Check out Dieter," says Mitch. He points to Dieter in the DJ booth. He's got a pumping beat going. He's listening to his headphones, digging through his records.

"This is what a hip hop club is supposed to be," Stuart says to Mitch.

"But are there going to be girls?" says Mitch.

"No, but fuck 'em."

They both look around. There aren't any booths. Nobody's really dancing. Two black guys walk past and stare a little too long at Stuart and Mitch.

"Well, fuck," says Stuart. He drinks his rum and coke.

"Maybe we should get going," says Mitch.

They finish their drinks and leave, almost getting run over at the entrance by some tough looking white guys in basketball jerseys. In the parking lot a group of black teenagers are leaning on Stuart's car. They're leaning on the passenger side. They look at Mitch as he waits for Stuart to unlock his door. "Yo," says one of them. "Whaddup?"

"Not much," says Mitch.

"This yo car?"

"It's my friend's."

"This car's a bitch," says a different voice.

Stuart unlocks Mitch's door. Mitch gets in. One of the black guys comes over and taps on the window. Mitch rolls it down.

"Yo, lemme look inside."

One black head pokes into the window. Then another. There are five of them all together. Three on Mitch's side, two on Stuart's. They're all talking at once.

"This yo car?"

"Where you get a forty round here?"

"Whose ride is this?"

A hand slips inside. It opens the glove box.

"What the fuck," says Stuart. He slaps the hand away and closes the glove box.

"What you got in there?" says a voice. "Hey, you got any beer man? You got any dope?"

"No dope," says Mitch.

Stuart starts the car and gives it gas. The engine roars. The heads pull out.

"Hey!"

"Watch it."

"Easy there, whiteboy."

Stuart shifts into reverse and eases out of the parking lot. The black kids wave, hoot, one of them does a little robot dance in the headlights.

"Fuck, man," says Stuart, as he pulls away.

They drive. Mitch lights a cigarette. Stuart crosses the river and heads toward Gretchen's birthday party in Northwest–from the poorest neighborhood to the richest.

TWENTY SEVEN

Mitch gets out the flier and directs Stuart to the party. It's in the West Hills, just up from the expensive restaurants where Mitch used to deliver bakery stuff. They drive by the house. There are people standing outside, well-dressed men and women. Everyone looks rich, clean, artsy.

"What's this going to be like?" Stuart asks.

"Fuck if I know," says Mitch. The streets here are narrow. There's not much room to maneuver. At one point a Saab has to back up to let the Dodge Charger through.

"Well, fuck," says Stuart. "What do you think?"

"We're here. We might as well check it out."

They park. They get out. They approach the house. At the entrance, Stuart moves aside to let Mitch lead. Mitch makes his way through the front door. There are lots of people Mitch doesn't know. He moves through the large entry way.

"Jesus, man," whispers Stuart. "Beth isn't going to be at a party like this."

Mitch looks around. There are a couple cool dressed people but they're indie rock types. College students dressed like punk rockers. Rich kids dressed like slackers.

"Where to?" says Stuart.

Mitch picks a direction: straight. This leads him into the living room, here they see sliding glass doors and more people out on a wooden patio. They go outside. There's a keg there. And people smoking. They get in line at the keg. They get cups and pour themselves beers. Then they retreat to one corner of the patio. Mitch sits on the wooden railing. They drink their beers in the dark.

"Shit," says Stuart, suddenly turning his back to the crowd.

"What," says Mitch.

"It's the assholes who wear suits."

Mitch looks.

"It figures they'd be here."

Mitch sees them. They're in a line at the keg. There are only two of them. Maybe there are more inside.

Stuart keeps his back to them. Mitch lights a cigarette and smokes. When the suits get their beers they shy away from the other people just like Stuart and Mitch did. They end up standing right behind Stuart. One of them gets out a cigarette. He feels his pockets and then politely asks Mitch for a light.

Mitch politely gives him one. The guy nods at Mitch as he does. Mitch nods back. "What's up?" he says.

"Not much," says the suit. "How about you?"

"Just hanging out."

"Yeah, us too."

"Kind of a fancy crowd."

"It is."

Stuart slowly turns around. The suit with the cigarette sees him. "Oh, it's you," he says. "The Quest guys."

"I wish I was a Quest guy still," says Mitch, so that Stuart won't have to talk.

"Why's that?"

"I used to work there."

The suit nods. "How was that?"

"Great. Until I got fired."

"That sucks."

"Now I'm fucking broke."

"I hear that," says the suit.

Stuart looks him up and down. "If you're so broke why do you wear suits?"

"What do you care if I wear a suit?"

"I don't," says Stuart. "I'm just saying if you're broke maybe you should wear something cheaper."

"What do you mean?" says the suit. "This whole thing cost fourteen dollars."

"Yeah?" says Stuart.

"Yeah, you get them at Goodwill. They're dirt cheap."

"Hey, I'm into suits," says Mitch. "If they cost fourteen bucks."

"How much did that coat cost?" says the suit, pointing to Mitch's Stussy racing jacket.

"I don't know," says Mitch. "Like eighty bucks. I stole it."

"And you probably have to dry clean it."

"I don't have a problem with suits," Stuart tells the suit.

"Why are you always giving us shit about it then?"

"Because the way you wear them. You're like the suit gang or something."

"We're not a gang."

"Well, what are you?"

"We're nothing."

"Okay then, what do you do?" asks Stuart. "What's you're job?"

"I work at a restaurant."

"Doing what?"

"Washing dishes."

"Do you wear your suit?"

"What difference does that make?"

"*You* wear a parking garage uniform," Mitch says to Stuart.

"Yeah, but I *have* to wear that."

"So who cares what he wears when he's washing dishes?" says Mitch.

Stuart has no answer. They all drink their beers.

"What is this party anyway?" the suit asks Mitch.

"A bunch of fucking yuppies," says Stuart.

"Gretchen somebody," says Mitch.

The suit smokes. "Have you guys been to that new club across the river?"

"We were just there," says Stuart.

"Yeah? What's it like?"

Stuart looks at Mitch.

"It's pretty hip hop," says Mitch.

"What's that mean?"

"There's more real black people and that whole scene."

"Huh," says the suit.

"*More real black people*?" says the other suit. He hasn't spoken up until now. He's shorter than the first suit. His voice is loud and abrasive.

Mitch shrugs. "It looked all right. Our friend Dieter is DJing."

"You guys know Dieter?" says the first suit.

"Yeah, we hang out with him all the time."

"He DJed my graduation party."

"No shit."

"He's fucking awesome," says the suit.

"Totally."

"Fuck."

"Wow."

"All right."

Everybody nods. They all drink their beers.

"So what are you guys doing after this?" Mitch says.

"Maybe going to this other party in Southeast."

"What's that?"

"Just some party. Some bands are gonna play."

"Alpha Hydroxy is playing," says the shorter suit. "They're *awesome*."

"Huh," says Mitch.

"They're *the best*," says the shorter suit.

"Well, good for them," says Stuart, staring at him to make him shut up.

"Anyway," says the first suit. "We should probably get going. You guys should come to that party though."

"What's the address?" says Mitch.

The suit tells him. They leave.

"Fucking suits," mutters Stuart. He finishes his beer.

"It's a party though," says Mitch. "And it'll be better than this."

"It better be."

TWENTY EIGHT

It is. They can tell the minute they're out of the car. The people on the porch are real hipsters. Not posers. Inside a girl screams and laughs hysterically. Above them people are sitting in the window sills. From the basement they can feel the crashings of a band.

"This is more like it," Stuart whispers to Mitch.

Mitch isn't listening. He thinks he knows who that was screaming. It sounded like Tracy Richards.

But once inside he decides there's no rush. He goes into the kitchen. There's beer in the fridge, long neck bottles, he cracks one open and then–in case they run out–shoves another one down the front of his pants.

"What are you doing?" says a voice behind him. It's the short suit from Gretchen's party.

"Drinking a beer," says Mitch.

"Why'd you put one in your pants?"

"Because I felt like it."

"That's not cool, there's not that much beer."

"Do I know you?" says Mitch.

"We invited you to this party."

Stuart comes in. He gets a beer out of the fridge and twists it open.

"Why don't you take them all," says a short suit. "That's what your friend's doing."

Stuart looks at him. He looks at Mitch.

Mitch lifts his shirt, exposing the beer in his pants. "He thinks I'm stealing this. I get *my girlfriend* a beer and this guy accuses me of stealing."

"You stole your coat," says the suit. "I heard you say it."

Stuart looks down at the short suit. "Why are you talking?"

"Because I want to," says the short suit. He drinks his beer.

Stuart looks at him. He drinks his beer.

Mitch puts his shirt down and checks out the living room. Belinda and Jeanelle are sitting on the couch. The other suit from the Northwest party is standing with a girl by the stereo.

Then he hears that laugh again. Tracy. It's upstairs. Mitch's heart begins to pound. He finds the stairs. He climbs them. The second floor hallway is full of people. They're waiting for the bathroom. Mitch pretends he is too. He leans against the wall and waits for more laughter. He gets it. It's coming from the room at the end of the hall. But then the door opens. Out walks Erica, the guy in the trench coat, Tracy Richards.

Mitch takes a deep breath. He watches Tracy come toward him down the hall. Her hair is mussed. She looks drunk. Her fake fur coat is flapping open. She can barely walk on her platform clogs.

People move to let them by. Mitch isn't sure what to do. But Tracy takes care of that. "Oh, look!" she says with drunken exaggeration. She knocks into him. "It's Mitch!" she says.

"Hi," says Mitch, pressing back against the wall. Erica and the trench coat guy continue down the stairs.

"Mitchy-Mitch," says Tracy. She reaches up and grips his face. She squeezes his cheeks and wags his face back and forth. "Where's my little Amy? Huh?"

Mitch's hand shoots up. He grabs Tracy's face and pushes her back into the opposite wall. When her head hits, her mouth opens. Mitch is right on it with his own mouth. He kisses her. She pushes him away. She slaps him hard, a stinging flashing blow. But it doesn't really hurt. It feels good. And he's still got her pinned against the wall. So he kisses her again. This time she lets him. For one second. Then she kicks him in the shin with her clog.

"Ow! Fuck!" cries Mitch.

Tracy remains against the wall. Mitch lurches backward, clutching his shin. Tracy stares down at him. Her jacket hangs open, her chest heaves. The look on her face is savage. But Mitch can do nothing. He crouches on the floor beneath her, holding his leg. Tracy jerks her coat closed and runs down the stairs.

Mitch struggles to stand. One of the other guys in the hall kneels beside him. "Whoa, dude," he says. "What was that all about?"

Mitch gets himself upright. "Ahh, *fuck*!" he says.

The guy helps him. "Here man, have some beer."

But Mitch still has a beer. In his pants. It's jabbing him in the stomach. He pulls it out.

The guy watches in amazement. "Man, you really come prepared!"

Mitch tries to flex the ache out of his shin. He tries putting weight on it. It hurts. But he's standing.

"Man, check out your face," says the guy. "It's beet red."

Mitch touches his burning cheek. But he's now getting some vague idea he might catch Tracy. He limps down the hall and down the stairs to the main floor. He checks the living room. No Tracy. He tries the basement. No Tracy. He limps out to the front porch. He sees them. Tracy and Erica and the trench coat guy. They're in the street, walking toward Tracy's. Mitch hobbles down the stairs. He follows them half a block and stops.

"Tracy?" he says. His voice carries on the quiet residential street. All three of them stop and look back. But Tracy is the one Mitch is watching.

"What?" comes her reply.

"I want to talk to you."

"Why? So you can attack me?"

"I'm not going to attack you."

"What are you going to do then?"

"Nothing, I just want to talk."

Tracy is smoking. "About what?"

"About...this whole situation."

Tracy looks at her friends. Fortunately for Mitch, Erica and her friend are not particularly interested in this. They whisper among themselves and then start walking again. Tracy stays where she is. She smokes. Her coat hangs open. Mitch waits a minute, to let Erica get ahead. Then he cautiously limps forward.

TWENTY NINE

When Mitch catches up to her, Tracy turns and keeps walking. Mitch does too. He was preparing a little speech in his head but he senses immediately that Tracy doesn't want to talk. So he doesn't. They walk. It's strange. There is no tension between them. None whatsoever. It's like they understand each other completely. Like they are old friends, partners. Except that one of them is limping.

"How's your leg?" asks Tracy.

"It's okay."

"I didn't mean to kick you so hard."

"It's all right," says Mitch. Again they lapse into a pleasant silence. Mitch gets out a cigarette. He lights it and smokes as they walk.

But Tracy's house is just a couple of blocks away. Soon they are right in front of it.

"Now what do we do?" he says to her.

"What do you mean?"

"Can I come in?"

"I thought you just wanted to talk?"

"I do. But it's cold," Mitch is in a weird zone now. Like he wouldn't want to force anything on Tracy no matter what. He loves her too much for that. "Whatever," he finally says.

"You can come in," says Tracy.

"But what about Amy?"

"What about her?"

"I don't want to hurt her feelings."

"I don't either."

"What should we do?" says Mitch. He whispers this. They are right at the front steps now.

"Be quiet, I guess."

Mitch follows Tracy to the door. She's sobered up. Even wearing her clogs she is stealthy and sure of herself. Mitch follows her inside. Tracy carefully closes the door and slips off her clogs. She instantly goes from being two inches shorter than Mitch to six inches. Mitch feels an aching protectiveness form in his chest. He watches her put the clogs behind the stairwell. He watches the bounce of her black hair as she moves around. He feels like he's home. For the first time in his life he feels absolutely *home*.

Tracy doesn't look at him. She pads softly up the stairs. Mitch follows. He holds his breath as they pass Amy's door. The light is off in her room. Mitch thinks he hears music, something soft and bland. He feels a pang of pity for poor Amy. Which he forgets the moment he enters Tracy's room.

Mitch walks a few steps inside and stops. Tracy carefully shuts the door behind him. Mitch remembers the red light, and the rest of the layout. It looks different now though. Things are in different places. Mitch feels jealous of everything that's happened here, of everything Tracy has ever done.

Tracy goes to her closet. She takes off her coat and hangs it up. Then she unzips her dress. Mitch goes to the bed. He touches it. He sits on it. Tracy's dress drops to the floor. She steps out of it and puts on some sort of bathrobe. A kimono maybe. It looks like silk. Mitch tries not to watch. But he doesn't know what to do. He takes off his coat. He kicks off his shoes.

Tracy comes toward him from the closet. She stands in front of him and lifts his face. She touches his cheek, the side she slapped. "Did that hurt?" she whispers.

Mitch shakes his head.

Tracy caresses his cheek. She begins to comb his hair with her fingers. Mitch tentatively touches her body through the kimono: the sides of her legs, the curve of her hips. She's not wearing any underwear. Mitch pulls her closer. Her robe separates and he finds one of her breasts with his mouth. Tracy watches him suck her tit. Then she gently pushes him backward. He lays back and she crawls on top of him, straddling him. Her robe spreads more. He can see her black pubic hair, her small breasts. She pulls his shirt up.

"Should we put some music on?" whispers Mitch. "So Amy doesn't hear?"

Tracy doesn't answer. She touches his chest. Her eyes close as she presses her bare cunt against him. Mitch grips her ass in both his hands. She looks at him for a minute, flashes him a faint smile. Then her eyes close again. She scoots forward, onto his bare stomach. She presses down again. She twists slightly as she does. A rhythm has begun. Mitch squeezes her ass. He pulls her belly toward his face. He watches her cunt, her black pubic hair, the slow undulation of her torso. He pulls her more. He wants her in his face. All the way. She scoots forward, until she is straddling the very top of his chest. He can smell her now. It's a hard, salty smell. But he wants it. She wants it too. She lifts her cunt to his face, to his mouth. He licks it: one long lick from bottom to top.

"Ohhhh," says Tracy in a voice that's deeper than her speaking voice. Mitch tastes her. He licks her again. Tracy moves herself closer. Mitch grips both cheeks of her ass and presses his mouth against her.

"Mmmm," moans Tracy. Amy's going to hear her. They should have music on. But Mitch isn't going to stop. He gets his tongue inside her. Her hands suddenly grip the back of his head. She grabs his hair and holds his face against her cunt. She re-positions herself so she can rub harder. Then she begins to mash herself against him. All Mitch has to do is keep his mouth open, his tongue out. She does the rest.

"Uuunnnhhh," moans Tracy.

Mitch lifts his eyes and tries to see her face. He sees her tits, the bottom of them. He sees her head hanging forward, her face enclosed in a tent of hair. Her eyes are closed. Deeply closed. Mitch closes his own eyes. He savors the taste of her. He loses himself in the smell, the warmth, the wetness. Her thigh muscles begin to tighten and flex. Her butt cheeks clamp.

"Uuhhhh," she says. She moves faster. "Uh, uh..."

Mitch can tell her head has arched back. He can't see her face though. She's rubbing frantically against him and he's trying to keep his face in the right spot. Finally she begins to tremble. She grips his hair. She shakes and vibrates. He clutches her ass, and holds himself steady as she gets herself off.

When she's done, she releases his head. She crawls off him. Mitch doesn't move except to pick a pubic hair out of his mouth. Tracy gets her cigarettes off the bed stand. She lights one. She pulls her kimono closed and sits back against the head board.

She looks at Mitch. "Don't you want to take off your clothes?"

Mitch is still mostly dressed. He undoes his belt and pulls down his pants. He takes off his shirt. So all he's wearing are his boxers and socks.

"Don't you want to take off your socks?"

Mitch takes them off. He throws them on the floor and lays on his side next to her. He touches her thigh through her kimono.

Tracy smokes and watches his hand.

Mitch scoots closer and lays his head down. He closes his eyes. He breathes in her smell, feels the smoothness of her thigh.

When she's done with her cigarette, she scoots down beside him. They kiss. They touch each other. Mitch slips off his boxers and crawls on top of her. He gets between her legs, gets himself inside her. He begins to move back and forth.

She sighs as he does this. Mitch figures she's just going to let him fuck her, to get himself off, maybe she's not even into normal sex. But that doesn't last long. Soon they're thrashing against each other. They sweat and wrestle and pull each other's hair. She pushes him upright and they fuck sitting up. Then he turns her around and fucks her from behind. When he finally comes the pleasure is blinding. It's like his insides are being sucked right out of him.

Afterward, Mitch is nearly unconscious. Tracy unhooks herself from him and rolls onto her back so he can lie on top of her. He is grateful for this. It is the perfect end. His body spent. His brain soaked in pleasure. His head resting peacefully on the breast of the woman he loves.

THIRTY

An hour later Tracy makes him get up. They both move around in the darkness of her room. Mitch tries to kiss her on his way out but it doesn't really work. He tiptoes down the stairs, eases open the door and then hops down the steps to the street.

It's a long way home. But that's all right. He lights a cigarette. It feels good to be outside, alone, in the cool, wet air. He smokes and walks. He just fucked Tracy Richards. He smells his hands. He pulls another pubic hair out of his mouth.

When he turns toward downtown Mitch sees the dull orange-ish glow in the clouds above the city. He considers the bare winter trees all around him, the vein-like branches, how they reach into the sky. Their roots do basically the same thing in the other direction. Trees in fact are just big bundles of veins, half going up, half going down. And the streets: how straight they are when they're empty. And the buildings: all dark and lonely looking. All the human stuff is square and solid and straight and level. All the natural stuff is spindly, veiny, spooky, weird.

Mitch lights another cigarette. He is almost home now. But he is so wide awake he hardly feels like going there. He walks down Hawthorne to a 24 hour donut shop. He goes in and looks at the display menu above the counter. But when he gets out his wallet he doesn't have any money. Not even seventy-five cents to get a coffee. He goes back out. He'll look for a job today. He'll get some sleep and then start the job search.

But at home he can't sleep. He just fucked Tracy Richards. He lays in bed and stares at the ceiling. Then he gets up and goes downstairs and eats some cereal with Gillian's milk. Then he sneaks across the street and steals the neighbor's paper. It's December 9th. Mitch sits on the couch and studies the action photos on the sports page. He flips to the back, to the help wanteds. But the small print blurs before his eyes. It's six a.m. He reads the Living section instead. But it's all cheerful and fake. It's from a different world. An alien world. He shuts the paper. He stares at the wall. He just fucked Tracy Richards.

Mitch wakes up. It's mid-morning. He's on the couch downstairs, fully clothed, the stolen paper spread on the coffee table in front of him. He gathers it together, wads it up and takes it upstairs. He dumps it on the floor of his room. But he's still tired. He lays on his bed. He rolls onto his side, tucks his hands between his thighs, drifts off into a sweaty hallucinatory sleep.

Mitch wakes up at two in the afternoon. He goes downstairs and calls Stuart at the parking garage.

"Carlson's Parking."

"Hey, Stuart."

"Hey, Mitch. Whassup?"

"Not much."

"Just waking up?"

"Yeah, I had to walk home last night from the party."

"I looked around for you. Someone said you left with Tracy. Or you got in a fight with her or something."

"Yeah. We got into it a little upstairs."

"What happened? Where'd you go?"

"Over to her house."

"Yeah?"

"I fucked her Stuart."

"You did not."

"I did."

"No way."

"I fucked her."

"Whoa," laughs Stuart. "Well, good for you man."

"It fucking was. It was very good for me."

"Like what all did you do?"

"Fucking everything."

"Man."

"I fucked her."

"So what was the fight upstairs all about?"

"It was like, she was giving me shit about Amy, and I was like, fuck this, I'm fucking *you* tonight."

"No shit."

"Fuck yes. I grabbed her. I kissed her. She started slapping me and shit and I just said, fuck this."

"Well, there you go."

"I fucked her, that's all I know."

"You ought to be proud of yourself."

"I am dude. I am very fucking proud of myself."

But Mitch still needs a job. He drinks some coffee and then rides his bike downtown to the Wagon Wheel restaurant. They've had a help wanted sign up and Mitch knows a girl who used to work there. He fills out an application. The manager seems to like the look of him so they sit in a booth and go over his application. Mitch smiles pleasantly while she reads it.

"So you used to work at the Natural Bakery Company?"

"Yeah. It didn't work out though."

"Those are tough hours," says the woman, reading Mitch's handwritten explanation of the problem.

"I took it over from a friend. It was more like a favor. I should have known I couldn't hack the hours." Mitch looks out the window. It's cleared up for once. It's sunny and bright outside. People walk by. Everyone looks happy, relaxed. Mitch gets out a cigarette. He puts it in his mouth.

"Oh," says the manager. "We don't allow smoking in here."

"Oh, okay," says Mitch, nodding, smiling. But he leaves the cigarette in his mouth. He stares at a woman across the street. What a beautiful day.

"You can't smoke here," says the woman again.

Mitch refocuses on her face. She seems upset about something. Mitch takes the cigarette out of his mouth.

"If you really have to smoke, you can go outside."

Mitch does. He stands on the corner and lights his cigarette. It tastes great. And the sunshine, it couldn't be nicer out. After a while he turns and looks back at the door of the Wagon Wheel. He can survive a couple more days without a job. And this isn't the time to be dealing with it anyway. He unlocks his bike and pedals down the sidewalk. He coasts. The sunlight is brilliant. The air is crisp and cold.

Mitch can't stop grinning. He fucked Tracy Richards.

THIRTY ONE

"She's fucked everybody," says Dieter. They're playing pool at Hurley's. Mitch, Stuart, Dieter, the nice suit they met at Gretchen's party. "No offense," Dieter adds, when he sees the look on Mitch's face.

"No," says Mitch. "I don't give a shit."

"Who's she fucked?" says Stuart.

Dieter shrugs. "DJ Westy."

"Man," says the suit. His name is James. "That guy gets girls."

"He gets more than girls," says Dieter. "Have you seen that scar by his ear?"

Mitch looks at the pool table.

Dieter talks while he shoots. "He got that doing this club thing in L.A. Back in '96. Some gang thing got going. They trashed the platform. Wrecked all his stuff."

"Man."

"He's been in books and shit," says Dieter as he sinks a ball. "He's like forty years old."

"And he wears all those rings," says James the suit.

"Fuck that," says Stuart, watching from against the wall. "When I'm forty I won't be hanging around playing records at Quest."

Dieter lines up his shot. "What are you going to be doing instead?"

"Fuck if I know. Not that."

"But what about Tracy?" asks Mitch.

"What about her?" says Dieter. He shoots. He misses.

"Do you think she'll want to hang out?"

"With you? Are you crazy?" says Stuart, moving in to take his turn.

"What?" says Mitch. "She fucked me once. Why wouldn't she fuck me again?"

Stuart scoffs.

"She might," says Dieter. "But I wouldn't count on it."

"Well, what the fuck," says Mitch, staring at the table. "I got what I wanted. She's too fucked up anyway. Kicking me in the shin. Did I show you guys where she kicked me?"

"No man, let's see." They all gather around and Mitch pulls up his pant leg. The bruise is purple, green, there's a scab where it bled.

"Jesus Christ," says James.

"Wow," says Dieter.

"Fuck man," says Stuart, looking once and then going back to his shot. "She really wailed on you dude. She really kicked your ass."

"She didn't *kick my ass*," says Mitch.

"She kicked your leg," says James.

After that they all go to Quest. They go in the back. DJ Westy is on the DJ platform. The place is packed. And it's a good-looking crowd. They aren't three feet in the door when Mitch spots Tracy on the dance floor. She's with Erica, right in front, right beneath DJ Westy.

Mitch follows his friends to the bar. They get drinks. Mitch is broke. He orders a water. Then Jeanelle comes over and talks to Dieter. Then Gretchen shows up. She smiles at Mitch.

"What's up?" he says.

Gretchen lights a cigarette and settles in next to him. "So I heard about your little *encounter*," she says.

"Yeah?" says Mitch.

"With Tracy Richards? At the party?"

Mitch is surprised. "Yeah? What did you hear?"

"That she slapped you."

"She kicked me too," says Mitch. He starts to pull his pant leg up but thinks better of it.

"What's up with that?" asks Gretchen.

Mitch shrugs. "It just happened."

"You kissed her or something? That's what someone said."

Mitch nods. He wonders what else she knows. "Yeah. We were sort of goofing around."

"Is there something going on with you guys?"

"Like what?"

"Like maybe a sexual tension thing?" asks Gretchen.

Mitch smiles bashfully.

"I thought so," says Gretchen.

Mitch shouldn't talk about this. But he can't help himself. "All I know is she was drunk and I was drunk and before I knew it..."

"You had to have her?" says Gretchen, her eyes narrowing.

"I don't know if I *had to have her*," says Mitch.

"Don't you just love that? People think they can control what they want. But they can't. And then one little thing happens..."

Mitch says nothing.

"But I mean, Tracy, she's notorious for that sort of thing. I know this guy, he was going out with her, or sleeping with her or whatever..."

Mitch feels his face fall. He drinks his water.

"I don't know," says Gretchen. "It just seems like with some people there always has to be *drama*."

Mitch nods. But the thought of an endless string of guys before him...he doesn't want to talk about this anymore.

"Don't you think?" says Gretchen.

Mitch shrugs. "Do you have an extra cigarette?"

"Sure," says Gretchen. She opens her purse. She gives him one. "But whatever. You know. If that's what she's into."

Mitch lights the cigarette. He smokes. He watches the dance floor. He can't see Tracy anymore.

• • •

Gretchen wanders away. Mitch does the same. He circles around the dance floor. He's looking for Tracy but he's also just looking. The beautiful women are out tonight. Women he's never seen before. Thanks to DJ Westy.

He circles around the back booths. There's hipsters everywhere. Lots of hair dye, make-up, cigarette smoke. But no Tracy. Mitch cruises the bar. He checks out the two side rooms. He checks the coat check area and then swings through the video game room. That's where Tracy is. Playing pinball.

THIRTY TWO

Mitch watches Tracy for a moment before he approaches. She's playing the one old-style pinball machine, the one where an actual ball rolls around inside. She's pushing against it with her body, she bangs at the flipper buttons with her open palms. Erica is leaning against the machine, looking spaced out as usual. Tracy is focused on the ball. Her whole head moves to follow it.

Mitch takes a deep breath. He walks forward. He takes a place opposite Erica and watches the ball roll down through the obstacles, right down the center and between the flippers.

"Shit!" says Tracy, banging furiously.

"You missed it," says Mitch.

"*Duh,*" says Tracy.

Mitch smiles across at Erica. It's easier to deal with Tracy when she's being obnoxious. It eases the tension.

Tracy pulls back the silver lever and shoots another ball into play. She concentrates all her energy on the game. She rocks the table to the left to avoid an obstacle. When the ball gets to the bottom she whacks it back into play.

"So that DJ Westy really packs the place," says Mitch, taking out his cigarettes.

"Shit," says Tracy, when she almost misses the ball again. But she digs it out. It rolls slowly up one of the side ramps, then rolls gently back. She whacks it into play.

Mitch offers the pack across the machine to Erica. "Cigarette?"

"No thanks."

He holds it in the direction of Tracy.

"Get outta the way!" she says.

Mitch puts the pack in his pocket.

"Thank you," says Tracy.

He lights his cigarette.

Erica sees someone. She starts to leave.

"*Erica*?" says Tracy.

"What?"

"Where are you going?"

But Erica ignores her. She leaves. Tracy sighs. She doesn't want to be alone with him, thinks Mitch.

Tracy plays.

Mitch smokes.

"So what do you want?" says Tracy.

"Nothing."

"Then why are you standing here?"

"I don't know." Mitch takes a drag of his cigarette. "Just wondered what you're doing."

"I'm playing pinball."

"Okay. Whatever."

They both watch the pinball game, Mitch passively, Tracy actively.

"Listen, Mitch," says Tracy. "The other night was fun and everything but as far as I'm concerned, you're with Amy."

"What?"

"You're Amy's. She found you. You're with her."

"I'm not with anybody."

"I know. But you know what I mean." She blows her hair out of her eyes.

Mitch is captivated by the gesture. He stares at her face.

"But just so you know..." she says.

"What?"

"You and I, we're not going out."

"Did I say we're going out?"

"You're standing here aren't you?"

"So what? I watch Stuart play pinball. It doesn't mean I'm going out with him."

"You know what I mean."

"No, I *don't* know what you mean," says Mitch with a bite in his voice. He smokes. The ball is up in the top of the machine. It ricochets around, racking up points.

Tracy relaxes for a moment. "All I'm saying is, when people sleep together usually one of them wants to keep doing it."

Mitch says nothing.

"Right?" says Tracy.

"Sometimes."

"So that's all I'm saying."

Mitch shrugs. But he can't keep this up. He has to ask her. He smokes. He says it: "So why did you sleep with me anyway?"

"I don't know. Why did you sleep with Amy?"

Mitch stares down at the bright lights, at the silver ball.

"I mean, I think you're cute," says Tracy. "If that's what you mean."

Mitch's head has sunk slightly. He leans on the machine.

"And I was drunk," continues Tracy. "Would you mind not leaning on this?"

Mitch lifts up.

"And I felt bad because I kicked you. How's your leg?"

"Fine," says Mitch.

"And you know..." says Tracy. "I felt like it."

Mitch nods. Despite what he's hearing he's enjoying this. He likes talking to Tracy. No matter what they're talking about. He drops his cigarette on the cement floor and steps on it.

"But now," says Tracy. "I mean, three people have already asked me what happened with you at that party."

"I know," says Mitch, to the machine.

"I mean Jesus, get a life people."

"They're bored," says Mitch. "They need something to talk about."

"That Gretchen, what a little..."

"Yeah, she talked to me."

Tracy looks at Mitch. "Do you know about her? Do you know who she is?"

"No."

Tracy looks back at her game. "Her parents own Bitburg Beer. She's worth like twenty million dollars."

"Wow," says Mitch.

"And she comes down here and bums cigarettes off people."

"Actually, I just bummed a cigarette off her."

"Well, good," says Tracy. "Somebody should."

"But I think she was just bribing me."

"For what?"

"For more stories about our *encounter*."

"That bitch. I should kick *her* in the leg. *Shit*."

The last ball is gone. The game is over. Tracy's arms and shoulders go limp. "Well, that's that."

Mitch nods.

Tracy picks her coat up off the floor.

Mitch watches her. "What are you doing after this?"

"I have a date."

"With who?"

"DJ Westy."

Mitch nods. "Dieter says he's the best DJ on the West coast."

"I don't know anything about it," she says, putting on her coat.

"That's just what he said," says Mitch, casually. But she's leaving. He can't bear to be away from her.

"Okay then," she starts to walk out.

Mitch follows her. "So you don't want me to call you or anything?"

"I think you should call Amy."

"But I don't like Amy."

"Yes you do."

"No I don't."

"Well, then you don't. Whatever. Goodbye."

Mitch stops in the hall. He watches Tracy weave her way through the dance floor. Toward the front. Toward DJ Westy.

THIRTY THREE

Mitch stands in the doorway of the game room. His chest is starting to ache. He needs to get outside. He pushes through the crowd, past the bouncers, out the front door. But once outside he's unsure of where to go. Then he sees Stuart. He's across the street, standing behind a van. Mitch crosses over. Stuart is smoking pot with a tall black guy.

"Hey," says Mitch.

"Hey," says Stuart. He hands Mitch the pipe. Mitch takes a hit. He hands it to the black guy.

"Did you find Tracy?" says Stuart.

Mitch nods.

The black guy smokes. "I think it's cashed," he says.

"Here," says Stuart. He takes the pipe and slowly refills it. They all stand there in the cold waiting. Mitch sticks his hands in his pockets. The ache in his chest is spreading to his throat.

Stuart gets the pipe full. He lights it, takes a hit. "What did she say?" he says, his lungs full of pot smoke.

Mitch shakes his head. He kicks at something on the street.

"I told you," says Stuart, exhaling.

"Yeah, I know."

"What?" says the black guy.

"Nothing," says Stuart. "Just some chick."

• • •

When they're stoned Mitch and Stuart walk down the street to Magic Gardens. Mitch is too preoccupied to notice the bouncers. So they don't notice him. He follows Stuart inside without incident. The pool area is full so they sit near the stage. The waitress who helps them is the same woman who threw them out. Mitch barely notices. They order beers. But Mitch doesn't have any money.

"Fuck, man," says Stuart. "I can't keep paying for you."

Mitch nods.

The beers come. They drink. They watch the woman on stage.

Then a woman approaches them. It looks like Beth. But she's dressed differently. She's wearing normal clothes.

"Hi, Stuart," she says.

"Beth!" says Stuart. He practically spills his beer.

"What are you doing here?"

Stuart is so surprised he can barely talk. "I was just...we were just..."

"You mean you come here when I'm not dancing?" she jokes.

"No. I mean. Well, my friend here, we were just...oh uh, this is Mitch."

"I remember Mitch."

Mitch smiles sheepishly.

"Wow, I didn't even recognize you," says Stuart. "You look..."

"Like I'm not naked?"

"Yeah. No. I mean–"

"Actually," she interrupts. "I was just wondering. Do you have a car?"

"Yeah. Sure. Do you need a ride somewhere?"

"Would you mind? I just need to go back to my apartment."

"No, not at all. When do you want to go? Right now?"

"Oh, but you should finish your beers."

"Finish our beers?" says Stuart. "No problem."

Stuart drinks his beer in one chug. Mitch isn't as fast but he gets most of it down. Stuart puts his glass down on the table. "Are you ready?"

Beth is charmed. "Sure."

Stuart stands up. Mitch stands up. But he shouldn't come with them. He should leave Stuart alone with her.

"Oh, hey," he whispers to Stuart. "Go ahead. I'll go back to Quest."

Stuart nods. "Mitch here, he's going to take off," he tells Beth.

"No, no," says Beth. "We'll all go."

"But he doesn't want to," says Stuart.

"I don't," says Mitch.

"But I want him to. I just need you to drop me off. We'll all go," says Beth.

And so they do. Mitch and Stuart follow Beth as she leads them out. She doesn't know which car it is, so Stuart hurries ahead of her. Mitch lays back. He wonders if he should just sneak off. But that would be too weird.

Stuart unlocks the passenger door for Beth. She gets in. Stuart hurries around to his own side. Mitch crawls past him into the back seat.

"Wow," says Beth. "This is your car?"

Stuart nods. He starts the engine. He revs it a couple times. But not too much. He pulls into the street.

"You mind if I smoke?" asks Beth.

"No, go ahead," says Stuart.

"Want one?"

"No thanks."

"Mitch?"

"Sure," says Mitch. She smiles as she hands it to him. "Thanks," he says.

Mitch watches Beth light her cigarette. The Charger is drafty, she has to put her hand around the lighter flame as she lights it. The flame illuminates her face for a moment. Stuart too, looks over to watch this.

She gets it lit. She smokes. Mitch lights his own cigarette. They drive. Mitch looks out the window. It's starting to rain. Cars pass, their windshield wipers flapping.

"So, what were you doing at Gardens?" Stuart asks Beth.

"Picking up my check. And trying to get Sheila to switch shifts with me."

Stuart nods. He doesn't know what to say to her.

Mitch tries to help. He leans forward in the seat. "Do you know that girl Jeanelle?" he asks.

"Yeah, sure. Why?"

"Oh, nothing. We asked her if she knew you."

"You did? What did she say?"

"Oh, nothing," says Mitch. He doesn't know what to say now. He sits back and waits for Stuart to talk.

But Stuart can't think of anything to say either. And Beth isn't saying anything. Then she starts giving Stuart directions to her apartment. They pull up in front of her building.

"So this is where you live?" says Stuart.

"This is where I live," says Beth.

Mitch and Stuart both look at the apartment building. Stuart shifts into park and reaches for the ignition.

"Oh, that's all right," says Beth. "I'll just go."

"Oh," says Stuart.

"But thanks for the ride," she says. She opens her door.

"Yeah, sure, anytime," says Stuart.

She gets out. "You guys stay out of trouble."

"We will," says Stuart. For the first time his voice sounds natural. "Hey, I'm glad we ran into you."

"Me too," she says. "Bye."

She shuts the door. Mitch crawls over the seat into the front. Stuart shifts the Charger back into drive and eases away from the curb.

THIRTY FOUR

Stuart pulls into the street and punches the accelerator. The Dodge Charger lifts up and rockets forward. Mitch's head jerks back as Stuart runs it up to sixty. Then he eases off, and finally brakes hard to stop for a red light.

At the intersection Stuart stares out his side window. "Fuck, man. I fucking blew that."

"No, you didn't."

"I'm an idiot."

"It was all right."

"*Shit*!" says Stuart. He pounds the steering wheel with his open palm.

"That thing at the end, about being glad to run into her. That was slick."

"But all the rest of it. I couldn't think of anything to say. Fuck."

"It was fine," says Mitch.

"And what the fuck? She's not supposed to be there when she's not dancing."

"Yeah, but aren't you glad?"

"Of course I'm fucking glad. But fuck!"

"Dude," says Mitch, staring out ahead of them.

"It's too much," says Stuart. "Who is she going out with? She must have a boyfriend. We gotta talk to Jeanelle."

"Yeah."

"And what the fuck were you saying? About Jeanelle. *We asked her about you.* What was *that*?"

"I was trying to think of something to say," says Mitch.

"Well, think of something else to say next time."

Mitch looks out his window. Tracy is bleeding back into his thoughts. He gets out his cigarettes. He lights one.

"Fuck," says Stuart. "I can't believe we just ran into her like that."

"Do you think she was there to get heroin?"

"What?"

"Do you think she was scoring dope? You know, from one of the other strippers?"

"You saw her. Do you think junkies look that good?"

"I don't know. That's what Jeanelle said."

"Jeanelle's a fucking..."

Mitch smokes.

Stuart drives. "What was that about the car? What did she say about the car?"

"She liked it."

"Do you think?"

"Yeah. Totally."

"You don't think she was just saying that?"

"Not at all. She dug it."

"Her building was pretty nice."

"It was," says Mitch.

"She probably makes a ton of money stripping."

"It's definitely not the kind of place a junky would live."

"Would you stop with the junky shit?" says Stuart. "She's not a fucking junky."

"How do you know?"

"And who cares if she is?"

Mitch would care. Or maybe not. He tries to imagine Tracy as a junky.

Stuart looks around as he drives. "Well, whatever. It's a start.

She knows my name. I gave her a ride. I just wish I knew what to talk to her about."

"What did you talk about at the bar?"

"Nothing. At the bar she doesn't talk. She just smiles and smokes and drinks the fucking five dollar drink you just bought her."

"I told you."

"I know, and you were right so shut up." Stuart pulls into a Seven Eleven. They go in and buy forty-ounce Bitburgs. "So what happened with Tracy?" says Stuart, while they wait in line.

"Nothing."

"She doesn't want to hang out?"

"Doesn't sound like it."

"Well you figured that."

Mitch sighs. "She didn't even hesitate. She said shit about Amy too. That I was Amy's boyfriend. Which is bullshit."

"Maybe Amy said something to her. Girls do that. They set it up among themselves. *You take the one on the left. I got the one on the right.*"

"Yeah, whatever," says Mitch. He pulls a magazine out of the rack and flips through it while Stuart buys the beer.

They drive around. They drink. After a while they go to Hurley's and play pool. Mitch loses and sits by himself at a table. He watches the NBA highlights on ESPN. But he's bored. He decides to walk home.

But as soon as he's alone on the sidewalk the pain of losing Tracy floods his consciousness. He almost cries. She's the coolest girl in Portland and he had her and he lost her.

He lights a cigarette. He walks. He tries to see the up-side. At least he had her. That's more than most guys can say. He should try to use it. Turn it to his advantage. He's got to try for someone else. Someone on that same level.

He'll go after Erica. But she's always with the trench coat guy.

And he's old-school. Never talks. Probably has a motorcycle or something.

He'll ask out Gretchen. She seems into him. And she's rich. But she's too skinny. And her nose is too long. And she's got that weird old lady posture.

What about Jeanelle? But she's so inaccessible. And mysterious. And ice-cold. She's probably a lesbian.

What about Belinda? The one who thought junkies were gross. She's got nice tits. But she's a notch down from the Tracys and the Jeanelles. He might as well go out with Amy.

And then there's Carmen. But he already blew that.

And the Asian bartender at Pulsar.

And the girl at the airport. She was amazing.

And Tracy, god Tracy, the ache in his chest that is Tracy.

And then there's Brenda Collins, the last person Mitch would think of, if it weren't for the message taped to his door when he gets home. A message with "See what you were doing" and her name and phone number attached. Mitch reads it again. He shakes his head. Then he wads up the paper and shoots a twelve footer to the wastebasket. He banks it. He scores.

THIRTY FIVE

The next day, Mitch gets a call from Excel Temporary Services. Does he want to do a telemarketing shift? Six hours at six-fifty an hour?

Mitch does. He needs the money. He rides his bike downtown and goes to the assigned floor of the assigned building. He walks into a large room full of tiny cubicles with phones. A balding manager shows him to a cubicle. He gives Mitch a list of phone numbers and a stack of questionnaires. The job: call the numbers, ask the questions, fill in the answers. Mitch settles in. The girl in the next cubicle is a Goth. She has black hair, a black dress, black lipstick. Mitch tries to smile at her. She ignores him.

The shift begins. Mitch calls the first person on the list. "Hello," he says, reading off the sheet. "My name is Mitch and I'm calling to ask you about Easy Clean."

"Mommy," says the phone. "A man wants to axe you sumfin'."

"Hang up the phone sugar," Mitch hears someone say. Then there's a dial tone.

He calls the next number. "Hello, my name is Mitch. I'm calling to ask about Easy Clean."

Dial tone.

He calls the next number. "Hello, my name is–"

A loud grunting interrupts him.

"Hello?" says Mitch. "Uhm, my name is Mitch–"

It's not a grunting sound it's a wheezing sound. Then there's incoherent speech. It's very loud. It sounds like an old man.

"WHAA–!" shrieks the voice. He sounds like he's having a heart attack. Mitch hangs up.

He looks over at the Goth girl. "Man, this sucks."

This time she looks at him. He listens for a minute. She's not talking to anyone. She's listening to music on her phone. She's also filing her nails, which are black.

"Where do you get that music?" Mitch asks her.

She reaches over, hangs up his phone, then dials seven numbers. Mitch listens. A short message comes on, a beep, and then music.

"Wow," says Mitch.

The girl nods.

"My name's Mitch, by the way."

"Carrie."

"Man, how do you get any of these things filled out?"

She demonstrates. She takes one of the questionnaires, writes in a phone number, then goes down the line checking yes and no randomly. She slides the paper into the "complete" basket and gets a new one.

"And they don't figure that out?"

She shrugs.

Mitch nods. He writes a phone number on the top of his questionnaire. He goes down the line filling in yes's and no's. When he's done he slips it into the complete basket and gets a new one.

"But now what do you do?" he whispers to her.

She hands him an unfinished crossword puzzle.

Even with the music and the puzzle the first two hours seem like an eternity. And while the Goth girl isn't unfriendly, she's not particularly talkative either. Mitch ends up talking to the guy on his left. He's older. He's missing several teeth and might be drunk, or maybe drug damaged. He talks about the working conditions. He thinks there should be more breaks. He claims there's a law that requires them. He says he's going to quit. But since he never calls anyone or fills out a questionnaire, Mitch wonders who's going to care if he does.

At the first break, Mitch walks across the street to a convenience store. But he doesn't have any money. He steals a couple candy bars. He's going to have to call his parents. Get some money from Mom. Maybe borrow bus money from Gillian and go out there tonight. Or maybe Stuart would take him.

Back in his cubicle Mitch calls Stuart and then his parents. Nobody's home. He starts to call Tracy's number but stops. He considers calling Amy but what if Tracy picks up? He fills in a couple surveys. He works on the crossword puzzle.

At the end of his shift, Mitch has to stay and fill out a time sheet. He's the last one out. When he unlocks his bike he sees Carrie at the bus stop. She's kind of chunky. Especially around the legs. Also her face is kind of squished somehow. She has no chin. But the Goth stuff. It's kind of sexy. Mitch would fuck her.

"See you tomorrow," says Mitch, as he mounts the bike.

"See ya," says Carrie.

At home, Mitch is absolutely drained from the boredom of the job. And starving hungry. He immediately rummages through the pantry for something to eat. He finds some old pasta that is probably Gillian's. She won't notice it's gone. He looks for a pot. But then the phone rings. He runs for it. He doesn't want Gillian to come out of her room.

"Hello?"

"Hello? Is Mitch there?"

"This is Mitch."

"Hi, Mitch. This is Brenda."

"Brenda," says Mitch.

"How are you?"

"I'm fine Brenda. I'm kind of busy right now."

"What are you doing?"

"I'm trying to make something to eat." He's too hungry to deal with this. Whatever it is.

"Oh."

"Why? What are you calling for?"

"I'm bothering you aren't I?"

"No, I'm just really hungry and I'm trying to cook."

"What are you cooking?"

"Pasta. If I can find a pot."

"Do you want to get something to eat?"

"I can't. I'm totally broke."

"I could buy you something."

Mitch frowns. He looks back toward the kitchen.

"I mean, if you want," says Brenda.

"Well...where are you?"

"I'm at a pay phone. On Hawthorne and Twelfth."

That's less than ten blocks from Mitch's house. "Why are you downtown?"

"I just try to go out sometimes. And I thought I'd see if you were around."

Mitch is having trouble processing this. But he's starving. "You really want to buy me something?"

"Sure, I mean, I'm not really dressed or anything. But if you want to go to McDonald's..."

THIRTY SIX

They go to Burger King. Mitch gets a Double Whopper Deluxe Meal. They sit in a booth. Mitch wolfs down the burger. Brenda watches from the other side of the booth.

"Geez," says Brenda. "Look at you eat."

Mitch ignores her. He takes another huge bite.

"How come you don't have any money?" asks Brenda.

Mitch chokes down the bite and takes another. "Cash flow problems," he says through the mush of half-chewed burger.

Brenda nods.

Mitch eats.

At the booth next to them, two hipster girls are drinking milkshakes and talking about sex. Brenda watches them. Then she looks back at Mitch. "My mother's been bugging me to go out more. To try to meet people."

Mitch eats.

"I guess it's good advice," says Brenda.

Mitch chomps down the last of the burger. He licks his finger and attacks his large fries.

"It's just so hard now. I mean besides William. All my old girlfriends are moved away. Or else they have kids."

Mitch's head is beginning to clear. But he's eating too fast. He sits back. He drinks his large Coke.

One of the hipster girls looks over at him. She's wearing a

Suede jacket with fur around the neck. Mitch tries to make eye contact but she looks at Brenda and grins at her friend.

"What do you do at night?" says Brenda.

"Me?" says Mitch. He drinks more Coke. "Not much."

"That's what I told my mother. If you don't know anyone you can't just *go out*. You have to know people. I mean you can go to a movie by yourself or something like that. Or a bar maybe."

Mitch eats fries.

"Where do you go?"

"I don't know. Just wherever."

"Your mother said you used to work at a nightclub."

"Yeah."

"What was it called?"

"Oh," says Mitch. "I think it closed."

"That must have been fun though."

"It was just a dance place. It was dumb."

"So many places are like that. I try to tell my mother that. Of course she thinks it's my fault. Which it is I guess."

Mitch nods. He's avoided looking at Brenda but now he does. She's got brown hair. A round chubby face. Her sweater is a dull brown. She had nice tits in high school. But she's a mom now. Her baby probably sucks on them. The thought gives Mitch the creeps. He looks over at the hipster girls, who are leaving.

"Where do girls like that hang out?" whispers Brenda.

Mitch shrugs. "Dance clubs, probably."

When Mitch is done they leave Burger King. Mitch walks Brenda to her car. "You don't feel like having a drink do you?" says Brenda, as she gets her keys out.

Mitch doesn't answer. Then he belches. He wouldn't mind getting drunk. And he doesn't have anything better to do. "Yeah, all right," he says. He gets in her car.

He directs her to Popeye's, an old dive bar near his house. They go in and sit at a wobbly table. A waitress who is impressed by their relative youth brings them a large pitcher. Mitch pours himself a glass and takes a long drink. Brenda goes to the cigarette machine.

She brings back a pack of Camels. She lights one. Mitch watches her smoke. She offers him one. He takes it.

An old Motown song plays on the jukebox. Mitch drinks more beer. He drains his glass. He smiles bashfully as he fills it again. "I guess I was kind of thirsty too."

"Go ahead," says Brenda. "Drink up."

Mitch does. The beer begins to penetrate the Double Whopper and fries in his stomach.

He sits back and for a moment feels the peace of a full stomach. But it starts to get weird, the silence between them. "So," he says. "What's it like to have a baby?"

"It's all right," says Brenda.

Mitch nods. He looks at her tits. "Does it fuck up your body and all that?"

"Nah," says Brenda. She flicks an ash into the ashtray. "Not if you're young."

Mitch nods. He drinks his beer.

"My body came back pretty fast." She looks down at herself. "I mean, not that it was so great to begin with."

"What are you talking about?" says Mitch. "You were the first girl in junior high to have tits."

"I know. God. And a lot of good it did me."

"You always had a good body," says Mitch.

Brenda shrugs. She smokes. "Well, whatever. But thanks for saying it. You were always very sweet."

Mitch can't imagine that he was ever very sweet to Brenda Collins. But if she says so. He drinks.

When the first pitcher is gone they get another. They talk intermittently. Mostly about people from high school. It turns out to to be a pleasant two hours. Mitch enjoys it. He is reminded of the easy way Brenda has about her. He remembers drinking forties with her occasionally in the parking lot after school. She was always ready to party. She always had cigarettes.

When they leave, Mitch walks her to her car. They're near his house so he'll walk home.

"Thanks for the beer," he tells her, as she gets her keys.

"Maybe we can do it again," says Brenda.

"Yeah," says Mitch. He watches her dig through her purse. "Uhm, Brenda?" he says.

"Yeah?" she says, hopefully.

"Could you, uh," says Mitch. "Could you lend me ten bucks? I mean, I get my first check on Friday. But I don't–"

She's got her purse open already. She looks into her wallet. She frowns. "I only have a ten. That's all I got."

"Oh, well, fuck it. I'll get it from someone else."

Brenda continues to look at her wallet. She's thinking. She pulls out the ten. "Oh, just take it. Here. Take it."

"Oh, no," says Mitch. "That's all right."

"I'll just get more from my mom. It doesn't matter. I'm not going to need it between here and my house."

"Are you sure?"

"Yeah. Take it. You don't even have to pay me back. I'm glad to get out of the house."

"I'll pay you back. I will."

"Don't worry about it Mitch," says Brenda. She gives him a friendly hug. Mitch hugs her back. Her breasts feel good against his chest. They both hold the hug a beat longer as their bodies exchange warmth.

"I'll see you," says Brenda. She hurries to get into her car. She's avoiding looking at him. She's embarrassed now.

"Hey, Brenda," says Mitch as she gets in. "Thanks. Thanks a lot."

She waves. She starts the car. She drives away.

THIRTY SEVEN

The next day Mitch goes back to the telemarketing place. He gets the same cubicle. The old guy on his left is gone. A different guy is there, a college student. Carrie is still on his right. But when the shift starts, she spends the first hour talking to a friend on her phone. Mitch kills time on his own phone. He dials a sports line, a horoscope line, a celebrity scoop line. He listens to music. He eavesdrops on Carrie who is whining to her friend. Her social life sounds horrible. But the dress she's wearing, a black lacy thing, pushes her large breasts up in front. Mitch watches them when he can, and then, in the bathroom, jerks off in a stall imagining them cupped in his hands.

At the break he buys a frozen burrito at the convenience store. There are other people from Excel there also, so he has to wait for them to leave before he buys a quart of cheap beer. Then he's only got six minutes to drink it. He walks around the block to a park, chugging as he goes. He makes it back in time. And the beer buzz makes the time go by faster.

Near the end of his shift the balding manager guy starts walking around the room. Mitch is forced to look like he's working. He starts calling numbers off his sheet.

"Hello, my name is Mitch and I'd like to ask you about Easy Clean."

"I have told you people, that I don't want to be called during the dinner hour."

"Hello. My name is Mitch and I'd like–"

"Fuck you."

"Hello. My name is Mitch and I'd like to ask you–"

Dial tone.

"Hello. My name is Mitch and I'd like to ask you about Easy Clean."

"What about it, dude?" says a young male voice.

"Do you use it?"

"Do I use what?"

"This stuff called Easy Clean."

"No, I never heard of it."

Mitch skips forward to the first question on his sheet: "Would you use it if you knew it was non-toxic and didn't harm the environment?"

"Who is this?"

"Mitch."

"Mitch? Do I know you?"

"Probably not."

"What is this about again?"

"It's a survey. We're asking people about Easy Clean. It's this stuff you clean your kitchen with."

"Oh."

"I just ask you a few questions about it and you answer."

"That's like, your job?"

"Yeah."

"Dude. That sucks."

"Yeah, well, there's this Goth chick sitting right next to me with huge tits."

"Really?"

"I mean, it still sucks. But it could be worse."

"Dude, what's she doing?"

"Talking on the phone. Asking people about Easy Clean."

"Huh."

"So do you want to do this?"

"Do what?"

"Answer a couple questions."

"Yeah, all right."

"Would you use Easy Clean if you knew it was non-toxic and didn't harm the environment?"

"Yeah, sure, whatever."

Mitch checks yes.

"Like Goth," interrupts the voice. "That means, all dressed in black, right?"

"Yeah," says Mitch. "Are you into that?"

"Not really."

Mitch checks no on the survey. He looks for the manager guy. He's on the other side of the room. "How about chicks with big tits in general? Yes or no."

"Definitely yes."

Mitch checks yes.

"I mean, unless they're *mammoth*," clarifies the voice.

"All right," says Mitch. "How about big asses."

"Not into it."

Mitch checks no. "Blow jobs?"

"What do you think, dude?"

"I'll put down yes."

"Hey, wait a minute. You're not queer or something are you?"

"No."

"Are you sure?"

"Of course I'm sure."

"I think I'm going to bail on this."

"But it's almost done," pleads Mitch.

"Later dude."

"Man!" says Mitch. He looks over at the college kid who is finishing his fifth survey since the break. "So close!"

Friday is less fun. Mitch doesn't have money to buy beer for one thing. And Carrie isn't there. But when the shift is over he gets a check. Which he cashes. And then, when he gets home, there's a message from Stuart. Dieter is DJing at Quest. And then Jeanelle is having a party.

Mitch is psyched. He calls Stuart and waits for him outside. When the Dodge Charger pulls up, Mitch runs through the rain and gets in. Stuart hands him a pint of rum. Mitch takes a long drag. He lights a cigarette. Stuart pulls onto Hawthorne and floors it. The tires squeal. The Charger slides sideways, straightens, explodes forward. Mitch's body fills with a pleasant adrenaline rush. Now he's really psyched.

At Quest, Stuart and Mitch are on Dieter's guest list. Which means they have to wait in line, under the awning in front. But even this is fun. They sneak sips of rum. They watch cars pulling up, people walking up and down the line. At one point two girls come running across the street. One of them looks like Tracy Richards. Same type of coat. Same laugh. They squint in the rain as they run, then shake out their hair in the back of the line.

Inside, it's crowded. There's a nice buzz to the place. Mitch follows Stuart to the bar. Mitch buys the drinks. They cruise the back wall. Belinda, Gretchen and another girl are in the big booth. Mitch and Stuart pile in. "Hey, you guys."

"Hey, Mitch."

The girls go back to talking. Mitch lights a cigarette. Stuart drinks. Gretchen and another girl walk onto the dance floor. They start to dance. Belinda slides over to Mitch. "Hey, Mitch, you want to dance?"

"Nah, I never dance."

"Why not?"

"I used to work here."

"So?"

"If you work here you don't dance."

"You don't work here now."

"I know but still."

"C'mon. I really want to. And who am I going to ask?"

"Someone else?"

She gives him a cute, pouty look.

Mitch takes a drag of his cigarette. "Ah fuck, all right."

He follows Belinda onto the dance floor. He starts to dance. He feels awkward at first. But then he gets into it. It's fun. And Belinda's totally hot. She gives him the front-ways tit jiggle. The sideways profile. The from-behind ass wag. And she's not the only one. Mitch forgot what it's like on the dance floor. The heat. The light. The way the girls get off on it. It's just pure sex. Mitch smiles to himself while he dances. He's going to get laid tonight. He can feel it in his bones.

THIRTY EIGHT

Dancing is fun but the real event of the night is Jeanelle's party. Stuart offers Gretchen and Belinda a ride but when they go outside and Gretchen sees the Dodge Charger, she freaks out. She almost won't get in it. Mitch crawls in the back seat with Belinda. He's playing a little game with her where he grabs her wrist and she twists out of it. Gretchen finally gets in the front with Stuart. She's still afraid of the car. Stuart assures her it's safe. Then he floors it out of the parking lot. Both girls scream. Gretchen practically crawls under the dashboard. Mitch grabs Belinda's wrist, then her arm, then he gets her in a headlock.

They all calm down at Jeanelle's. This will undoubtedly be a very cool party. Nobody talks as they get out of the car. Stuart and Gretchen lead the way. Mitch lags back. He grabs Belinda's wrist but she twists free. She giggles and taunts him. Mitch will go home with her later. Unless something better comes along.

They've timed it perfectly. It's a little past midnight. The party is at its optimum groove. There are people dancing in the front room, people milling in the rooms beyond.

"Let's dance Mitch!" Belinda says, grabbing his arm. Mitch doesn't budge. She pulls on him. "C'mon!"

But Mitch has done his dancing for the night. He shakes his head.

Belinda grabs him around the waist. She whispers breathily in his ear: "Are you afraid?"

"I gotta get a drink," says Mitch. "You dance. I'll be back."

Belinda skips forward and joins the dancers. Mitch follows Stuart into the kitchen. There's a drink table. There's liquor, cups, ice.

"Score," says Stuart. They make drinks. Mitch lights a cigarette.

Just then the back door opens. A large group of people come in from the porch: James the suit. Erica. Her trench coat boyfriend. Tracy. Another guy. Amy Peterson.

Mitch looks into his drink. He's hoping they'll keep going but they seem to stall in the kitchen. Then Erica and her boyfriend come over to the drink table. Tracy comes too. Mitch and Stuart step away but there's not much room. Tracy ends up standing right in front of Mitch. He can't not say something. "Hey, Tracy," he says.

"Oh, hi, Mitch. What are you doing?"

"Not much."

Stuart moves away. Erica and her boyfriend move away.

Mitch smokes. Now it's just him and Tracy, there beside the table.

"You missed it," says Tracy. "People were smoking pot on the porch."

Mitch shrugs. "We got pot."

"Well, never mind then."

Mitch smokes. "So where's DJ Westy?"

"Working. At Pulsar."

Mitch nods. He looks around the room. "Where's Jeanelle?"

"Upstairs. Doing heroin."

"No, really."

"She is. They're smoking it. Out of a bong of all things."

"Wow," says Mitch.

Tracy tastes her drink. Mitch watches her. He loves her. He wants to take her drink, set it down, hug her.

"Have you ever done heroin?" says Mitch.

Tracy nods.

"Yeah?" says Mitch. "What's it like?"

"It makes you throw up."

"Wow."

"But then it's pretty great."

Mitch watches her face.

"Erica's boyfriend does it all the time," says Tracy, scanning the room for her friends.

"How about that girl Beth. Is she into it?"

"Probably. Everybody else is."

Mitch nods. This is good stuff to know. But it's deflating him. A second ago he was bragging about having pot.

"Tracy!" yells Erica, from across the room.

"Gotta go," says Tracy. She smiles at him.

Mitch smiles back. He takes a drag off his cigarette. He watches her go.

Stuart is on the back porch smoking pot with some girls. Mitch sits next to him on the step. He takes a hit when the pipe comes around. Then he leans forward and whispers to Stuart: "Jeanelle and those guys are doing heroin upstairs."

"Yeah? Right now?"

Mitch nods.

"Fuck."

"I know," says Mitch. "They're smoking it."

"Who told you?"

"Tracy."

"Man."

Mitch swirls his drink. "We gotta do that."

"Fuck," says Stuart.

The girl pot smokers get up and leave. Mitch sips his drink. "She said it makes you throw up and shit."

"Yeah, that's what I heard."

"Hey, Mitch," says a feminine voice.

Mitch thinks its Belinda. But it's not. It's Amy. She comes down the steps and stands above the two of them.

"Hey, Amy," says Mitch.

"I'll catch you later," says Stuart, getting up.

"Am I interrupting something?" asks Amy.

"Nah," says Mitch.

Amy moves to let Stuart by. She smiles at Mitch. "I just wanted to say hi."

"No, that's cool. Sit down."

She sits. "I haven't seen you in a while."

"Yeah, I know," says Mitch. Amy's wearing a new leather jacket. It's expensive looking, fancy. It's almost too cool for her. She's also wearing make-up. "Wow, look at you."

Amy smiles bashfully.

"Where'd you get that coat?"

"I bought it."

"It's slick. You look like...a model or something."

Amy smiles.

Mitch smiles. He lights a cigarette. Amy continues to smile. But she doesn't talk.

"So, what's up?" says Mitch, watching her.

"Nothing."

Mitch looks at their feet. "You know, actually, there's something I wanted to ask you."

"Yeah?"

"Did you tell Tracy that we were going out?"

Amy stops smiling. "No."

"Huh," says Mitch.

"Why? Did she say I did?"

"Well, not exactly."

Amy looks down. "Are you guys going out now?"

"No," says Mitch.

"You probably want to though," says Amy, staring at her shoes. "Every guy wants her."

"Yeah, well," says Mitch. He swirls his drink. "I guess they do."

"But I didn't say anything. About you and me. I mean, I never said you were my boyfriend or anything. She knew we got together a couple times. I did tell her that. But she knew that anyway."

"Yeah," says Mitch, "The problem is, well, I don't know if you know, but me and her..."

"Yeah, I know."

"Really?"

"I heard you."

"Oh," says Mitch. "Like through the wall?"

Amy nods.

"Oh," says Mitch. "Sorry."

"It doesn't matter," says Amy picking at her shoe lace. "And I heard she kicked you and slapped you and everything. Gretchen told me the whole story."

"Yeah," says Mitch. He grins slightly. He will forever be proud of being slapped by Tracy Richards.

"She's really into the drama," says Amy.

"It was stupid," says Mitch, trying to be humble.

"Yeah, I guess." Amy glances up at the porch. Her face brightens. "Hey! Hey, Brian!" she says.

Mitch looks up. Could Amy be with someone?

"There you are," says a male voice. "I thought you were dancing."

"I gotta go," Amy tells Mitch. She stands up.

"Oh," says Mitch. He starts to stand as she does. "All right, I'll...I guess I'll see you around."

Amy smiles politely. Then she runs up the steps.

THIRTY NINE

When she's gone Mitch wishes he'd gotten a better look at Brian. He was wearing a long coat. Maybe he's an indie-rocker. A college-student type. Or maybe he was tall and kind of forceful. Mitch didn't see. He drinks his drink. He gets up and goes to look for Belinda.

In the kitchen he runs into the short guy in the suit. The one he doesn't like. He's talking to some other suits. He's dominating the conversation. Mitch has to squeeze around him to get to the living room.

Belinda's there. But it's very hot. Mitch tries to "dance" his way through the crowd but it doesn't feel right. Then he tries to grab Belinda's wrist, but that doesn't feel right either. Belinda twists her wrist away. She smiles at him but it's a strained smile. She looks at the guy she's dancing with.

"Hey, you wanna get stoned?" he shouts into her ear. But he shouts it too loud. She cringes away from him.

"What?" she says.

"You wanna go out for a smoke?" says Mitch loudly. He's not dancing now. Neither is the guy Belinda's with.

"Not right now," is the answer.

"What?" says Mitch.

"NOT RIGHT NOW," she says.

Mitch nods. He backs out of the dance floor, stepping on someone as he does. Fuck. He goes back to the kitchen, squeezes around the short suit and makes himself a drink. Then he looks for Stuart.

He goes upstairs. He walks cautiously down the hall. One of the bedroom doors is open. He looks in. There's a bunch of people inside. Somebody's lighting a bong. The room is smoky and dark. Stuart is there. He's sitting on the floor, against one wall, talking to a girl.

Mitch steps over some people and sits next to him. Stuart doesn't acknowledge him. "Yeah," he tells the girl. "It breaks down a lot, but I know a guy who works on old cars."

"That sounds awesome," says the girl. "My friend has a '77 Matador."

Mitch watches the girl. She's sort of cute in a trashy East-side sort of way. She's wearing Dickies pants. Her boxer shorts are sticking out the top.

Mitch looks around at the rest of the room. This is where they were doing the heroin. He can tell just by the tone of it. The weird residual vibe. But who was doing it? The people nearest him, also sitting on the floor, are talking intently. The people with the bong are smoking pot. Of course. The real people are long gone. Maybe the guy on the bed, with his back to Mitch. He's not moving. His girlfriend, or whoever, is kinda leaning into him. They've got a cigarette. Mitch can't tell who's holding it, but neither smokes. They don't move. They're the ones.

More people come down the hall. They look in the room. They too can feel the weird vibe, but can't immediately identify it. But they want in. They enter and sit on the floor. Another girl looks in. "Hey, Patty," she says.

Stuart's girl looks up. "What?"

"Are we going to get Diane?"

"Why?" says Patty.

"Because we said we would?" says the girl, who is also sort of trashy looking.

Patty turns to Stuart. "But I want to see your car."

"Do you need a ride somewhere?"

"We're supposed to pick up my friend Diane."

"I'll drive you," says Stuart.

"Would you mind?"

"Not at all."

Now Stuart acknowledges Mitch. He turns quickly to him. "C'mon man, lets go for a ride."

They all go downstairs. Stuart and Patty continue talking. So much so that nobody introduces Mitch to the girl he's now with. When they get in the car this girl wants to sit in the front with Patty. But Patty won't let her, so she gets in the back with Mitch. She looks at him once. She doesn't say anything.

"My name's Mitch," says Mitch, as Stuart starts the car.

"I'm Lisa," says the girl, staring straight ahead.

Mitch checks her out. She's sort of cute, sort of trashy. Possibly fuckable. "How are you doing tonight?"

She gives him a skeptical look. "*Fine,*" she says.

Mitch shrugs. Stuart and Patty are talking intently about the Dodge Charger. "It's a '72," explains Stuart. "That was the best year for them."

"This is so awesome," says Patty.

Stuart drives. Mitch lights a cigarette. He doesn't offer one to Lisa, who immediately begins to wave at the smoke. Mitch rolls down his window slightly.

Patty tells Stuart where to go. She scoots closer to him and asks more questions about the car. Mitch watches as Stuart shifts in his seat. He's not very good with women. But that won't matter if Patty really wants him.

Mitch flicks an ash out the window. "So," he says to Lisa. "What did you guys do tonight?"

"Went to that stupid party," she says.

"Do you know Jeanelle?"

"We didn't know anyone. Somebody told us about it. We're supposed to be getting my friend Diane. She's getting off work."

"Where does she work?"

The question seems to irritate Lisa. "Domino's," she says.

A few minutes later they pull into a Domino's pizza place. Lisa gets out and runs to the door. She disappears inside.

Patty meanwhile is sitting very near to Stuart. Did she just kiss him? Mitch tries not to watch. He throws his cigarette out the window.

Lisa comes running back. "She's gone. She already left."

"Where'd she go?" says Patty.

"They didn't know," says Lisa.

"Well, get in," says Stuart.

Patty gives Stuart room as they pull back onto the main drag. "Maybe we should get some beer," says Stuart.

Patty agrees. Lisa looks annoyed. Mitch says nothing. They pull into a Seven Eleven and go inside. Lisa and Patty stop at the magazine rack. Mitch and Stuart proceed to the beer section.

"So what's up with your girl?" Stuart whispers to Mitch.

"She's not into it."

"Are you sure?"

"Yeah," says Mitch.

"Did you try to talk to her?"

"Yeah."

"And she wasn't into it at all?"

"Didn't seem to like it."

Stuart turns and casually looks across the store at the two girls. "She looks like she could be."

"I know. That's what I thought."

Stuart opens the glass door. "Cause the one I'm with. She's into it."

"Yeah, I know," says Mitch. "I saw."

"You sure there's no chance for you?"

"She won't even look at me."

"Maybe if we get them drunk."

"I don't think it's going to work. Maybe you should try to get yours alone."

"Fuck," says Stuart. "Do you think they'll separate?"

"I can't tell. They seem sort of stupid."

"Is that good or bad?" asks Stuart.

"I don't know. I can't tell."

"Maybe if we get them drunk," repeats Stuart.

"Maybe."

"Well, let's try it," says Stuart. He takes out a case of Bitburg. "And if it doesn't work, at least we'll be fucked up."

FORTY

When they take the beer up to the counter, Patty and Lisa are laughing about something. This seems like a good sign. They continue to giggle as they get in the car.

Patty and Stuart sit in the front. Mitch and Lisa sit in back. As soon as they're moving, Patty passes out beers. She takes a long drink of hers. Lisa, too, takes a long drink. Another good sign.

At first they just drive. Stuart plays his new Chemical Brothers tape. They all four talk, Lisa hangs over the seat and talks mostly to Patty but eventually she sits back and talks to Mitch.

"So what were you guys doing tonight?" she asks.

"Not much. We went to Quest earlier."

"What's Quest?"

"It's this club downtown. A dance club."

Lisa drinks her beer.

Mitch watches her. She's not that cute but she smells nice. Or at least she smells female. Not that Mitch is going to get laid. But maybe he can get a hand job or feel her tits or something.

"Yeah, I used to work there," says Mitch.

"Where?"

"At Quest."

"Oh," says Lisa. She drinks more.

Stuart pulls into a wooded park. They're back in Southeast, not far from Jeanelle's. Stuart parks. He turns down the stereo but it's still loud enough that Mitch and Lisa can't quite hear what's being said in the front seat. Mitch drinks his beer. Patty is sitting right next to Stuart. Their attention is directed at his lap. Patty suddenly laughs.

Mitch smiles awkwardly over at Lisa. She smiles awkwardly back. Mitch drinks his beer.

Patty leans over and pecks Stuart. She says something in his ear and he kisses her.

Mitch drinks more beer. He scoots closer to Lisa. "I think your friend is into my friend," he whispers.

She nods. Mitch stays where he is. Close enough to kiss her. He can't think of any way to do it, except to do it. So he does. He kisses her on the cheek.

She doesn't respond. She drinks her beer. Mitch scoots a little closer and kisses her again. She doesn't move. She's not into it. But she's not *not* into it. Mitch finishes his beer and sets the can above the seat by the back window. He pulls her hair away from her neck. She shies away from him slightly. But she doesn't stop him when he kisses her neck. He tries putting his hand on her thigh. But this she won't allow. She moves his hand away. He breathes in her ear and tries to touch her breast. She moves his hand away.

Mitch pulls back. Patty and Stuart are not kissing exactly. They are just sitting very close, and they are very focused on whatever's going on in Stuart's lap. Mitch looks over at Lisa. She stares straight ahead. And his beer is gone. And he doesn't want to ask Patty for another one.

"I gotta piss," he whispers to Lisa. He crawls over her and gets out. He walks into the woods. He pisses. But when he's done he can't quite bring himself to return to the car. There's a little path in the woods, which leads to the street on the other side of the park. He's not going to get anything off Lisa. And Stuart doesn't need him. And there might still be something going on at Jeanelle's. He starts walking.

It's late when he gets there. People are leaving. Mitch sees Amy on the porch. By herself. Maybe she can give him a ride home. The short suit is also there, he's standing with his buddies at the bottom of the steps. For the third time tonight, Mitch has to squeeze around him. But this time he knocks him hard as he passes.

"Excuse me," says the short suit as Mitch continues by.

Mitch ignores him. He mounts the steps to the porch. But then he's jerked backward. Someone's grabbed the back of his jacket. He throws a blind elbow at whoever it is and tries to yank free. But he can't. He misses with his elbow and the guy who's got him grips him harder. Mitch twists to see him. It's a big guy. Someone he's never seen before. The short suit talks: "What do you say when you knock into somebody?"

Mitch is not interested in this at all. He tries to jerk free of the guy holding him. "Let go of my fucking–"

"You say excuse me!" announces the short suit.

Mitch tries to kick him. But the guy holding him pulls him away. Mitch twists violently and throws another elbow. He doesn't hit anything but it turns him around enough to grab the big guy's coat. He swings him around. The two of them go spinning into the lawn. A third guy tries to grab them both. All three of them fall. The biggest one lands on Mitch's chest. He knocks the air out of Mitch's body.

For a moment the two big guys keep Mitch under them, pinned on the ground. But Mitch is not resisting. He's not fighting back. The big guy gets up. His friend gets up. Mitch remains on the ground. He can't breathe. He groans. He rolls onto his side.

Everyone stares down at him. The short suit is standing there too. "What did you do to him?"

"Nothing," says the big guy.

"I think we knocked the wind out of him," says his friend.

Mitch can't get air. His rib cage feels like it's collapsed. He rolls onto his other side. "Uuuuuu–"

"Mitch?" says a voice from the porch. It's Amy. She comes running into the yard. "Mitch? *Mitch*!"

"Uuuuuuuu."

"What's wrong with him?" Amy asks the short suit. "Should I

call an ambulance? Someone? Anyone? Should I call an ambulance?"

"He's friend's with that guy Stuart," says the short suit, still staring down at Mitch.

"That guy with the car?" says the big guy, suddenly worried.

The short suit nods.

"That guy's a fucking *psycho*."

"It wasn't your fault," says the friend. "He pulled you down."

The short suit backs away. The three of them turn and hurry off. Now it's just Mitch and Amy on the grass. Mitch finally gets a short gulp of air. Amy helps him sit up. "Are you all right? Do you need an ambulance?"

Mitch manages to shake his head no. He's breathing now. But painfully. Amy holds him up. Other people are watching this from the porch. No one approaches them.

Mitch's face is smeared with mud. "Does anybody have a towel? Can somebody help me here?" says Amy angrily now, to the people standing on the steps.

Tracy appears. She comes down the steps. She wants to see what happened. But then she sees it's Mitch. She turns around and goes back inside.

Amy helps Mitch stand up. He can't stand completely straight.

"Here," says Amy. "Come to my car. I'll take you home."

FORTY ONE

Mitch gets in the passenger side of Amy's Toyota. He's breathing now. Rasping and coughing but breathing. Amy gets in and starts the car. She pulls onto the street and drives.

For a while neither speaks. Mitch finally takes one long deep breath. It seems to clear his chest. He settles more comfortably into his seat and watches the street lights pass outside his window.

"You know that was your own fault," says Amy.

"Why was it my fault?"

"You walked right into that guy. I *saw* you Mitch. And then all you had to do was say excuse me."

"I hate that guy."

"You know, you're not very smart. And you're not very nice to people."

"That guy's a..." But he doesn't feel like talking about it. It doesn't matter anyway. Mitch is filled with a strange peacefulness. He doesn't care about the short suit. He's enjoying breathing. He's enjoying the oxygen buzz.

"Who was that guy you were with tonight?" he asks Amy.

"Brian? He's just a friend. We do stuff sometimes."

"Huh," says Mitch. A cigarette would be so good right now. He finds a pack in his coat. They're all crushed but he finds one that's intact. He lights it. He cracks the window.

They drive.

"So you guys aren't going out or anything," says Mitch.

"No. Why?"

"No reason."

Amy stares straight ahead. "Did you talk to Tracy tonight?"

"A little," says Mitch. He sighs. "I don't know what I was thinking with that. I never had a real chance with her."

Amy seems stunned by this admission. Stunned and happy.

Mitch smokes. "And she's just trouble anyway."

"But you wanted to go out with her. You were just saying tonight..."

"I'd rather be with you than her," says Mitch quietly.

Amy stares over at him. Then she looks at the road. "I don't believe that."

"I know you don't," says Mitch.

Amy drives.

Mitch smokes. He feels relaxed, at ease, at one with the world. Maybe this is what heroin is like. "So I heard Jeanelle and those guys were doing heroin upstairs."

"At the party?"

Mitch nods. "Everybody's getting into it now I guess."

Amy doesn't answer. Mitch likes how the word "heroin" sort of shuts people up. He thinks about that couple on the bed. Leaning into each other. They were cool. What would people think of him if he started doing it?

"So are you going to be all right?" says Amy. She's slowing. She turns onto Mitch's street.

"Yeah, I'm fine."

Amy pulls up in front of his house. "God, you scared me there for a minute. I thought you were turning blue."

"Nah," says Mitch. He starts to open the door and then stops. "You wouldn't want to...?"

"I don't think so Mitch."

Mitch looks at the door handle. "I don't mean sex or anything. Just come in and hang out while I clean myself up? To make sure I don't have a concussion or something?"

"You just said you were okay."

"Well, you know, if I lapse into a coma or whatever."

Amy smiles. "I'd like to. But I don't think I'd better."

Mitch stares at the door handle. "You know, it's not my fault that I'm attracted to you."

Amy looks into her lap.

"And I know you thought I was using you for sex or whatever," he turns toward her. "I'm just not very good at this. I never had lots of girlfriends. And when I did I always fucked it up. It's not like I know how to deal with this stuff."

Amy looks at him.

"And if you wanted to just be friends or whatever," says Mitch. "I mean, whatever level you want. I could live with it."

"But Mitch, you never call me."

"I don't call anyone."

"You'd call Tracy."

"Have I ever called Tracy?" says Mitch. "You live there. Have I ever called her?"

Amy shakes her head. "No, I guess not."

Mitch looks at the door handle. "Like right now," says Mitch. "I just don't want you to go."

Amy thinks about it. She sighs. "All right," she finally says. "But just for a little while."

Inside, they go upstairs to Mitch's room. Amy sits awkwardly on the bed while Mitch gets undressed. He goes into the bathroom and gets in the shower. The hot water feels incredible. He lets it run over his head, down his back. He picks the mud and grass out of his hair. It's weird that he feels no anger toward the short suit. He feels no anger toward anyone. What he does feel is the contentment of knowing he's going to sleep with Amy. He knew he was going to get laid tonight. And now he is.

When he comes back to his room Amy's taken off her coat. She's sitting on the bed reading the same *Bikini* magazine she read the first night she came here.

Mitch doesn't talk. He goes to his old dresser and puts on clean underwear and a T-shirt. He goes and sits down next to Amy. "That magazine's like four months old."

"I know," she says. Mitch leans toward her and smells her hair. He massages her neck, rubs his hands up and down her back.

She looks up from the magazine. She looks at his mouth. He kisses her gently on the lips. Her eyes close. His eyes close. Then he gets up and goes in the bathroom. He brushes his teeth. He puts a condom on. He turns off the light and returns to his room. Amy's pulling off her shoes. He sits next to her. He kisses her again and then they both lay back on the bed.

FORTY TWO

In the morning Mitch doesn't feel so good. He's sore. His chest hurts. It hurts to breathe. Still, Amy is there. She's naked. Her white skin is warm and soft. Mitch scoots closer to her and presses against her ass. He feels around, tries to find her cunt, tries to see if he can get inside her. He's interrupted by a soft knock on the door. "Mitch?" says a voice in the hall.

Amy shifts. Mitch lifts his head.

There's another knock. "Mitch?" It's his housemate Gillian. "There's a call for you. It's your dad. He says it's important."

Mitch gets up. He pulls on his pants. He thanks Gillian and creeps down the stairs to the phone.

"Hello?"

"Mitchell. It's Dad. I have some bad news. It's your grandmother. She's passed away."

Mitch stands up straight.

"Your mother and I are going to fly to San Diego this afternoon. We tried to call Irene Collins about feeding Brandy and Jake. She wasn't there but we left a message. We thought if you're driving the delivery truck you could stop in and check on them."

"How long are you going for?"

"Three days I think."

"What happened to Grandma?"

"She died in her sleep."

"Well, that's good I guess."

"Do you think you could come and check on Brandy and Jake?"

"Sure. I mean, I'm not driving the delivery truck anymore. But I can get over there. I got a friend who can drive me."

"Well, however you can arrange it."

"Okay," says Mitch. He wants to say more. But what? "Uhm, Dad?"

"Yes?"

"Sorry about Grandma."

His father breathes heavily. "She had a good life."

"And she was into stuff..." says Mitch, remembering her questions about Quest.

But Mitch's dad doesn't want to talk. "Well, stop in and check on the dogs if you can. I'm sure Irene can feed them. But they need to be walked."

"Yeah, sure Dad. I'll do it. No problem."

"All right."

They hang up.

Mitch goes upstairs and lays down across from Amy. He pulls the covers up around his neck. Amy lays with her back to him. When he doesn't scoot up against her, she rolls towards him, onto her back. "What was that?"

"My dad."

"What did he want?"

"My grandma died."

"Oh, Mitch," says Amy. She turns toward him, to console him. But he shakes his head, to keep her back. "It's not that big a deal," he tells her.

"Of course it is Mitch, it's your grandmother."

Mitch is staring blankly forward. His eyes are wide open. "She was like, seventy-five or something."

Amy reaches over and grips his hand.

"And she had a good life," says Mitch.

Amy's eyes fall. She looks like she's going to cry. Somehow

Mitch understands that he has to let her console him. Or else she'll be hurt. And there'll be more awkwardness to deal with. So he squeezes Amy's hand. She scoots closer and hugs him. Her body is warm. It seems to loosen his tongue, his emotions in general. "It's funny because I had a feeling this would happen," he says softly.

"I know."

"The thing about her was, she was sort of cool in a way. She bought me *License to Ill* for Christmas in junior high. My parents would never do something like that."

"I have an aunt like that," says Amy. "She always gives the best presents."

"And last Thanksgiving. She was asking me about Quest. And she really wanted to know about it. Because she was feeling old or whatever." This memory gets to Mitch. He suddenly feels a shortness of breath. Tears form in his eyes.

Amy holds him close. Mitch nestles into her. She kisses him once on the forehead as he settles his head down around her breasts. She strokes his hair.

Mitch closes his eyes. "I don't know how I should feel."

"Just be sad," says Amy. "And be happy for her if she had a good life."

"My life just seems so stupid," says Mitch. He doesn't know where that came from. Also, he's starting to cry. Amy can sense it. She hugs him, kisses him. Mitch struggles to control himself. But his eyes fill with tears.

"Your life isn't stupid."

"I don't even have a job," croaks Mitch.

"It's okay," breathes Amy. Mitch blinks the tears from his eyes. They sprinkle down his face and onto Amy's chest. She holds him tighter. They both rock slightly.

They lay like that. Mitch breathes, closes his eyes, clings to Amy. After a while the tears stop. The choking sensation subsides. As Mitch regains his composure he becomes aware of himself. He's got a throbbing hard-on, which he's been pressing into Amy's thigh this whole time. He finds Amy's cunt with his hand. She's as aroused as he is. Through some minor adjustments in their position, Mitch slips inside her. Amy says nothing. She continues to hold his head, to smooth his hair. Mitch simply lays there, his eyes closed, his dick safe inside her.

Eventually they begin to move. Very slightly at first, but then with more depth. But it's a different kind of sex. The dick-cunt part is almost secondary. It's more Amy's hands, her face, her soft hair and lips. When Mitch comes there's no groaning or thrashing around. His orgasm is barely noticeable. It's a gentle transference, an easy release.

Which is why Mitch is so surprised when he finally pulls away and sees that Amy has been silently crying.

FORTY THREE

When they finally get up it's afternoon. Mitch feels guilty and weird as he digs around for his underwear. Amy must feel the same way. She says nothing as she puts on her underwear, her skirt. She wads up her tights and stuffs them in the pocket of her new leather jacket.

"God," says Mitch, seeing the leather jacket. "Last night. It seems like a million years ago."

"I know," says Amy. She's avoiding looking at him. Mitch doesn't look at her either. "I should probably get going," says Amy.

Mitch buttons his shirt.

Amy now dares to look at him. But something deep and intense flashes between them. Mitch is momentarily speechless. Amy slings her purse over her shoulder. She turns to the door.

"Uhm," says Mitch, as she's about to leave.

Amy stops.

It's hard for Mitch to speak. But he gets out the words: "My parents need me to go to their house. They're going to the funeral in San Diego. Could you drive me out there?"

Amy nods, she releases the door handle and puts her hands in her pockets.

Mitch hurries to finish dressing.

In Amy's car they don't speak. They get on the freeway and drive deep into the suburbs. Mitch directs Amy into the development where his parents live. They pull into the cul-de-sac. "That's it," says Mitch, pointing at the house.

"That's what my parents' house looks like," says Amy.

"Yeah?" says Mitch. His father's car isn't in the driveway. They must already be gone.

"Do you need a ride back?" says Amy.

"Actually, I was thinking I'd just stay here while my parents are gone. They have a big screen TV. And it'll be easier anyway."

Amy nods.

"Maybe I'll call you though."

"You don't have to."

"I don't think I have your number with me."

Amy gets a piece of paper from the glove box and writes down her number. "If you need to, I could bring you back."

"That'd be cool," says Mitch. "Thanks."

Inside, the house is dark, messy, depressing. Mitch turns on lights. He turns on the big screen TV. He finds a college basketball game on cable. He makes himself a sandwich and watches it. All the commercials are about Christmas. It's one week away. He'd totally forgotten about it.

Mitch falls asleep on the couch. When he wakes up it's dark out. He's got to walk the dogs. He untangles their leashes and takes them down the street to the park. The neighborhood is aglow with Christmas lights and decorations.

In the park he releases the dogs to run. He lights a cigarette. He sits on a picnic bench. The dogs race furiously around on the grass. They disappear and reappear in the trees on the far side. They piss and shit. Mitch smokes a second cigarette. He wishes Amy were here. Not to talk. But just to sit here, opposite him on the picnic bench.

Later that night Mitch is watching TV when the doorbell rings. It's Mrs. Collins. She launches into a one-sided conversation: "I didn't know if you'd be here...I'm so sorry about your grandmother...I hope your parents are all right..."

Mitch says nothing.

"And Brenda said you two had fun the other night...I try to tell her to go out...you know, she's too young to be sitting around the house every night...should I send her over? Or are you still feeling bad about your grandmother?"

Mitch stares at her.

"Well, it's none of my business...now if there's anything we can do...and if you can't stay, I can feed the dogs...we're here if you need us..."

Mitch nods. Mrs. Collins leaves. Mitch goes back to the couch, to the big screen TV. *Saturday Night Live* is on.

The next day is Sunday. Mitch watches the Pittsburgh Steelers play the Houston Oilers. Pittsburgh wins by a field goal. Then he watches San Francisco play the Atlanta Falcons. It's twenty-eight to nothing at half-time. Mitch takes the dogs for another walk.

When he gets back he's bored. He goes down to the basement. He's got some stuff down here. He's been meaning to look through his old CDs and cassettes. He's had no money to buy new ones and he's sick of the ones he has.

But there's not much here. Stuff he listened to in high school. The Cult's first albums. A Nirvana tape. Metallica, U2, Motley Crüe. He finds the Beastie Boys' *Paul's Boutique* on tape. He looks through a different box for the twelve inch of *License to Ill*. He finds it. He looks at it. Old record covers are so much bigger than CDs. It's weird. Mitch puts it aside and digs through the cassettes. Most of these are his brother's: Elvis Costello. The Talking Heads. A Grateful Dead bootleg. It's strange how your family can be so different than you. That was the thing about Grandma. She was the closest one to Mitch. Like, if she was young right now she'd be into the same stuff he is.

The doorbell rings upstairs. Mitch puts the boxes away and

turns off the light. He climbs the stairs and answers the door. It's Brenda.

"Hi, Mitch," she says shyly.

"Hi, Brenda."

"I heard about your grandmother."

"Yeah," says Mitch.

Brenda can't quite look at him. "I brought you something," she says. She produces, from behind her back, a half-full bottle of scotch.

Mitch takes it. "Wow. Thanks."

"It's Dewar's. The real stuff."

"All right."

"It's my mom's. I didn't buy it or anything," she smiles bashfully.

"Thanks, thanks a lot." Mitch looks at the bottle. He looks at Brenda. "Wanna come in?"

FORTY FOUR

Brenda comes in. Mitch has the TNT Sunday night game on. Seattle at Denver. "I was just watching this," she says.

Mitch takes the scotch into the kitchen. He gets glasses and fills them with ice from the automatic ice maker. He pours in the scotch. It feels strangely adult to be operating out of his parent's kitchen.

He brings the drinks into the living room. He hands one to Brenda. She's sitting on the couch. Mitch sits in his dad's armchair. He tries the Dewar's. It's good. He watches the football game.

"I just wanted to say hi," says Brenda. "I won't stay."

Mitch rotates the chair to look at her. "It's all right."

"It's weird about your grandparents because sometimes people don't even know them. And other times they can be pretty close."

"Yeah," says Mitch.

"Were you close to your grandmother?"

"Not really. She lived in San Diego. I didn't see her much."

"Well. It's sad anyway."

"Yeah."

They watch TV.

"Can you smoke in here?" Brenda asks.

"No. But actually. Do you want to walk to the park with the dogs?"

"Sure," says Brenda.

They get the dogs and their drinks and walk down the street to the park. At the picnic table they smoke. And drink.

"How's your kid," Mitch asks her as the dogs race around.

"He's okay."

"What's his name again?"

"William."

"Huh."

"That was his father's name."

Mitch nods. "So, what's the father doing now?"

"He lives in Spokane. With his parents."

"Do you ever talk to him?"

"No."

"Doesn't he want to see his kid?"

"He doesn't seem to."

"Does it piss you off? That he's not around?"

"No. I mean, it sort of sucks. But it's hard to blame him."

"Huh."

"He was just young. And what's he going to do? Marry me? And get some terrible job? He's only twenty-two. I wouldn't do it if I was him."

"Yeah, I guess," says Mitch.

Brenda stares off into the park. "Do you have a girlfriend?"

"I think I might have just got one."

"What's her name?"

"Amy," says Mitch. "She's not really my girlfriend. We just hang out sometimes."

Brenda nods knowingly. "You still want to see other people."

"I don't know what I fucking want."

They both watch as the dogs come racing out of the trees. Jake chases Brandy around the swing set.

"I can't even imagine having a boyfriend now," says Brenda.

"Why not?" says Mitch.

"The baby. And just the way people are. Like whenever I go to a party or a bar it's so...I don't know. It's just this big pickup scene. And they're all trying to find someone to have sex with and eventually get married to and have kids. And the thing is, I'm already there. You know? I'm where they're all trying to be. And it's not that great."

Mitch smokes.

"And it's terrible to know something like that," says Brenda. "To look around a room and know something that everyone else is going to find out."

Mitch puts out his cigarette.

"I'm being depressing," laughs Brenda. "I'm sorry. My mother tells me not to be so drippy."

"You're not drippy."

Brenda smiles and drinks her scotch. "That's what's so funny about my mother. She doesn't think I know how to party. Or how to have fun. I'm like, *Mom, how do you think I got this baby*?"

Mitch smiles. The Dewar's is making him drunk. He looks at the small playground. At the jungle gym. "Do you remember when we were in third grade..."

"*Yes*," says Brenda, changing her tone. "And don't you dare say anything about that. God!"

"What?"

"God, how embarrassing. I can't believe you brought that up!"

"It was funny."

"It was sick!" says Brenda. "And my brother found out about it. He used to blackmail me." Brenda shakes her head. "I can't believe you remember that."

"Best sex I ever had," jokes Mitch.

Brenda laughs. "That wasn't sex. That was child abuse."

"Yeah, but who was abusing who?"

"*You* were abusing *me*."

"No way!" says Mitch. "It was your idea."

"My idea? You were playing pirates with that other kid. That creepy kid..."

"Chris. From Australia."

"Exactly," says Brenda. "He was the one who wanted to tie everyone up. And you went along with it. *I* was completely innocent."

"You were never innocent."

"I was *completely* innocent. It was Chris."

"I don't even remember him being a part of it," says Mitch.

"Well, blame it on him then. Because it wasn't my fault."

Mitch smiles. The dogs come back. Mitch scratches Jake's head. Brenda scratches Brandy. Mitch gets out the leashes. They walk back to the house.

Mitch puts the dogs away. Then he joins Brenda on the couch. They sit and watch ESPN. It's boring though. They switch to MTV. Then Mitch goes into the kitchen to make fresh drinks. Brenda follows him.

"So, did you ever," she starts. "I mean, as you got older. After the jungle gym thing. Did you ever get into..."

"Tying people up?" says Mitch.

Brenda nods.

"Not really."

Brenda watches Mitch put ice cubes in the glasses.

"Why? Did you?" asks Mitch.

"No. I mean, I kind of thought about it. Once I realized it was a big sexual thing."

"I guess I was never with someone long enough to get into something like that."

"Yeah," says Brenda. "And it would probably seem stupid to most people."

Mitch pours scotch into both their glasses. He hands one to Brenda. "I don't know. It might be fun. It was fun when we were pirates."

Brenda laughs loudly. She takes her drink.

"Don't you think?" says Mitch.

"Sure," says Brenda. She smiles bashfully, then lifts her drink. "To pirates," she says clinking her glass with Mitch's.

"To pirates."

FORTY FIVE

But the pirate game isn't as easy as they remember. The two most obvious problems: there's nothing to tie someone *to*, and there's nothing to tie someone *with*. Mitch looks for rope. He tries the garage, the basement. He finds an extension cord but Brenda says no. It's too thin. It'll hurt. They look in closets and cupboards. They finally find the belt from his mother's terry cloth robe. It's soft and thick. It's perfect. They get another strap from his father's raincoat. So that's two things.

Then they look for things to tie someone to. Mitch suggests one of the kitchen chairs. Brenda sits but it's an awkward position. And once she's tied to it, what are they going to do? Also, they're both very drunk by now. Brenda almost falls off the chair when she tries it out. They go into Mitch's parents' room. There's nothing on the bed to tie anyone to. And Mitch is having his doubts about the whole exercise anyway. There's something about Brenda. Something unfeminine. Or else he's just known her too long. She's too much like a sister. And it's not like they've made out or anything. They haven't even touched each other. And what about the mommy factor? What's she going to look like naked?

"Do you even want to do this?" says Brenda, as they stand looking at the bed.

"I don't know," says Mitch. "I'm pretty drunk."

"Me too," says Brenda. She stands there. Mitch stands there. "You know what I think?" says Brenda.

"What?"

"I think we just have to do it." She takes the straps from him. "Here, go lay down."

Mitch takes off his coat. He kicks off his shoes. He flops on the bed. But it feels good to lay down. He closes his eyes. He's more tired than he knows.

Brenda turns off the light. She crawls onto the bed. "Turn over."

Mitch rolls onto his stomach. Brenda takes his two hands and ties them together behind his back. Amy immediately appears in his mind. Not in a guilty way. Not in a disapproving way. She's just there. In her new leather jacket.

"Now roll onto your back," says Brenda.

Mitch does. But this is uncomfortable. He's squishing his own hands. Also, he's unnerved by the sight of Brenda undoing his belt. His dick isn't even hard. And her hands are cold. He watches as she separates his underwear from his jeans. She's going to leave his underpants on. Which he's thankful for. When she gets his pants off, she rolls him onto his stomach. Now what? Mitch feels his body shiver.

"Are you nervous?" says Brenda.

Mitch shakes his head.

"Are you cold?"

"A little," says Mitch. He feels her tying his ankles together. Then she unties it and ties his legs together just above the knees. For some reason that does something to him. His dick suddenly swells.

"Does that hurt?" says Brenda.

Mitch shakes his head. He's starting to enjoy this. He closes his eyes as Brenda begins to caress the back of his legs: a feather touch from the back of his knees up to his butt. Mitch hopes she isn't going to do something weird. Like stick something up his ass. But whatever. It feels good.

After a while, Brenda rolls him over again. His dick is thick and hard in his underpants. He watches as it springs free when she pulls down his briefs. When they're down around his mid thighs, she scoots down on the bed and takes his dick in her hands. At first she just caresses it. Then she licks the top. Then she puts it in her mouth.

Mitch strains against the straps around his wrist and knees. Brenda is sucking him, she's licking him, she's holding his balls. She looks up. "Do you want me to take off my shirt?"

Mitch nods yes.

Brenda sits up. She gathers her sweater and lifts it over her head. She's a little flabby around the waist but her tits are big in her bra cups. She sticks them out as she reaches behind her to unfasten the back strap. Her bra falls away. Her breasts are big, full. She leans over him, so they touch his cock. Mitch moans at the sight of it. He watches her work his dick, suck it, hold it against her tits. Then she combines the two: his dick in her mouth, her tits on his balls. He strains against the restraints when he comes. It's a smooth, deep coming which she sucks in and swallows.

When it's over Mitch lets his head fall back against the bed. And again, Amy appears in his mind's eye. She's not doing anything. She's just standing there. It's strange for her to be there. But Mitch doesn't fight it. Mitch leaves her where she is. He needs the company.

Mitch is worried Brenda is going to want to continue with the bondage thing. But she seems to know he's had enough. In fact, she's completely cool about it. They joke around as she unties him. She also remembers to put the belts back in his mother's bathrobe and his father's raincoat. Mitch would have forgotten. Then she volunteers to go. Mitch pecks her once on the cheek and promises to do the same for her sometime. She leaves.

Mitch is relieved when she's gone. He puts ESPN back on the TV and takes a bath with the door open, listening to the sports chatter, letting his brain empty. Afterward, he watches a bad action adventure movie on HBO. He's hoping he'll doze off on the couch. He doesn't. So he turns off the TV and goes to his old room. He undresses and gets in the bed. He pulls the covers up. But his eyes stay open. This is what he was afraid of. The quiet. The dark. The aloneness. He lies in the bed and stares at the wall, like he used to do at Christmas when he was a kid, his grandparents snoring on the hide-a-bed in the living room. But it's not just that. It's everything. Amy comforting him this morning. Brenda leaving just now. His own life. His parents' lives. The dogs running around in circles. What's the point of any of it?

Were he less drunk, less drained of bodily fluids, Mitch might cry. But the day has taken its toll. Mitch is exhausted. He drifts slowly but inevitably into a deep, dry, emotionless sleep.

FORTY SIX

The next morning Mitch wakes up with a start. His parents are home. They're in the house. They weren't supposed to be back until tomorrow. Mitch gets out of bed. He pulls on his pants.

He creeps down the hall. His father doesn't speak to him when he passes through the living room. In the kitchen his mother is cleaning up Mitch's mess. When she sees him, she holds up the empty Dewar's bottle. "Having a little party?"

"No," say Mitch. "That was–"

She throws it in the trash. Mitch goes back to the living room. His dad is going out. He's got his coat. His parents are fighting. Mitch retreats down the hall to his parents' bedroom. He's got to get out of here. He calls Amy. She's not there. He calls Stuart. He's home. He'll come get him. Thank god.

Mitch waits on the curb outside his house. When the Charger appears he walks into the street to meet it. He gets in and immediately lights a cigarette. Stuart runs it up to sixty on the road back to the freeway. Mitch breathes a low sigh of relief.

Neither has eaten though, so they stop at the McDonald's by the freeway. They get Big Mac meals and sit in a booth.

"So your grandmother died," says Stuart.

"Yeah."

"That sucks."

"Yeah," says Mitch. He eats.

Stuart eats.

Mitch drinks his coke. "So what happened with Patty?"

"Hand job," says Stuart.

"Yeah?"

"She didn't do it right though. It kinda hurt."

"Huh."

Stuart shrugs. He eats.

Mitch eats.

"So what happened to you at Jeanelle's?" asks Stuart. "James said you got beat up."

"Nah. I just fell. I got the wind knocked out of me."

"Well, fuck."

"I was trying to grab this guy but he fell on me."

"The short guy?"

"A different guy."

"What was the short guy doing?"

"Nothing. Mouthing off."

"He started it?"

"I sorta bumped into him."

"But he still started it."

"Yeah, I guess."

"So the next time we see him we pound his little face into the concrete?"

"Fuck, I guess," says Mitch.

"We got to," says Stuart. "Come on. That guy's a prick. And he's fucking four feet tall. We might as well."

"Whatever," says Mitch.

They both lapse into silence. Mitch considers saying something about Brenda. He decides against it.

"So anyway," says Stuart, finally. "There's some good news too."

Mitch drinks his coke.

"On Saturday I went down to Magic Gardens," says Stuart.

"Yeah?"

"I talked to Beth."

"What about?" asks Mitch.

"What do you think?"

"I don't know."

Stuart looks around the McDonald's. "*Heroin,*" he whispers.

Mitch stares across at him.

"She's going to get us some," says Stuart.

"Jesus Christ," says Mitch, sitting up.

"I know."

"Fuck," says Mitch. "When's she getting it?"

"Like right now. I'm supposed to call her tonight."

They've still got the afternoon to kill. They go to Hurley's and drink cheap happy hour pitchers. They play pool. At six they go to Mitch's. But Gillian is on the phone. They go upstairs to Mitch's room. There's a phone message from Amy. Mitch pulls it down and stuffs it in his pocket.

"Hey, that's no way to treat your girlfriend," says Stuart.

"She's not my girlfriend," says Mitch

"You better make her your girlfriend."

"Why?"

"She'll stop fucking you."

"No she won't," says Mitch. He checks to see if Gillian's off the phone. He's not thinking of Amy now. He's thinking about the heroin. "So what exactly is the deal with this?"

"Beth's going to get us some dope."

"But like, then what do we do?"

"Nothing. We get fucked up."

"But like, we don't know how."

"She's going to show us."

"We don't have to shoot it with needles right?"

"Nah. We just snort it. Or smoke it. Why?" says Stuart. He looks at Mitch. "Don't you want to? I thought you wanted to?"

"Of course I want to," says Mitch. He looks downstairs. Gillian's off the phone.

They hurry down to the living room. They sit on the couch. Stuart sets the phone on his lap and dials Beth's number. He puts the phone to his ear and waits. And waits. And waits.

"Fuck," says Stuart.

"Now what do we do?" says Mitch.

"Shhhh," says Stuart, then into the phone: "Hey Beth. It's Stuart. I'm at Mitch's. Give us a call." He tells her the number and hangs up.

"Fuck," says Mitch.

"Hey, if you don't want to do this, it's a little late now."

"No, I want to. I totally want to. Did I say I didn't want to?"

Stuart puts the phone back on the coffee table.

Mitch lights a cigarette.

Stuart stares at the TV against the wall in front of them. "What if we OD?"

"We won't OD," says Mitch. "You have to shoot it to OD."

"How do you know?"

"Have you heard of anyone ODing from smoking it?"

"I didn't know you *could* smoke it until a week ago."

Mitch stares at the TV.

"Fuck," says Stuart. "I don't want to look stupid in front of Beth."

"Nah. She'll be cool."

They both stare at the TV.

"What if we become junkies?" says Stuart.

"We won't."

"But what if we do?"

"We're too smart to become junkies," says Mitch. He stands up and turns on the TV.

"That's probably what everybody thinks."

"Yeah, well, whatever," says Mitch, sitting back down. "We'll deal with that problem when we get to it."

FORTY SEVEN

They watch TV. An hour goes by. Then the phone rings. Stuart grabs it. "Hello?" But it's not Beth. It's Amy. He hands the phone to Mitch.

"Amy," says Mitch.

"Hi, Mitch."

"What's up?"

"Nothing," she says. "What are you doing?"

"Nothing. Watching TV," says Mitch. Stuart waves for him to get off the phone.

"How was your parents'?" says Amy.

"It was okay."

"That's good." She pauses. "How are you feeling?"

"Fine, fine," says Mitch.

"Are you hanging out with Stuart tonight?" asks Amy.

"Yeah. Sort of."

"Because I was going to invite you to come over if you want," says Amy, her voice lowering slightly.

"Oh," says Mitch. Stuart is staring at him. He shifts the phone to his other ear. "That sounds fun."

"Do you think you'd want to?"

"I don't know. We're trying to get a hold of someone."

"Oh."

"A friend of Stuart's. She's getting us drugs."

"What kind of drugs?"

"Just, you know...pot."

"Oh."

"So we gotta deal with that."

"Huh."

"But I'd like to come over," says Mitch.

"How long is it going to take?"

Mitch looks over at Stuart who is shaking his head. Then to Amy: "It might take a while actually. How late will you be up?"

"I don't know. Not too late."

Stuart is shaking his head wildly. Mitch puts his hand over the phone. "*What*?" he says to Stuart.

"You can't hang out with her tonight," he hisses. "We're gonna be totally fucked up."

"You know what?" Mitch tells Amy. "Maybe we should try for tomorrow night."

"Do you want to go to a movie or something?" says Amy, hopefully.

"Well...whatever. We'll do something."

"Will you call me?"

"I'll call you."

"All right."

"All right."

"Mitch?"

"What?"

"Did you get my message?"

"What message?"

"From when I called earlier."

"Oh, yeah. I did get it."

"But you didn't call me back."

"I was running out the door. We're trying to get this...pot."

"Because Mitch?"

"Yeah?"

"I never know if I'm bothering you. And if you call me then I know you really want to do something."

"Okay. I'll call you."

"You know?"

"Yeah."

"If you don't want to hang out..."

"I do want to."

"Well, then you have to take some initiative."

"Right, right," says Mitch. Stuart is giving him the hurry up sign. "I really gotta go."

"Okay," says Amy.

Mitch hangs up. Stuart tries Beth again. This time she answers. Can they come over? Yes.

They run to the car. They speed across town to her apartment building. They find her name on the directory: Beth Sinclair. Stuart pushes the buzzer. They wait. Beth comes on the intercom. They identify themselves. She buzzes them in.

They walk quickly through the apartment building. They run up the stairs to the third floor. They find Beth's apartment number. They pause for a moment to catch their breath. Stuart knocks.

The door opens. Beth appears. "Hey, you guys," she says.

"Hey," says Stuart.

"What's up?" says Mitch.

Beth lets them in. The room is dimly lit. There's a strange smell to it. Mitch follows Stuart inside.

"That was fast," says Beth.

"Yeah, well..." says Stuart.

Beth walks toward the kitchen. "Do you guys want a beer?"

"Sure," says Stuart.

They both watch Beth go into the kitchen. She's dressed in shiny black bell-bottoms, a black turtleneck with a baby blue sweater. Her blonde hair is stuck up with pins. She looks strange without make-up. She has no eyebrows, no lips. But she's graceful. And confident. She's beautiful in a way Mitch didn't see before. He sees it now.

Stuart sees it too. He runs his hand through his hair. Beth

comes back and hands them each a Bitburg. "Did you guys run all the way over here?" she says.

Stuart laughs nervously, "Yeah, pretty much."

"Yeah," adds Mitch, pointlessly.

"Well, let me show you what I got," says Beth. She leads them to her kitchen table. They remain standing while she sits and opens a small cigar box. She pulls out a tiny ziplock bag of brownish powder. She lays it on the table in front of Stuart. Stuart nods. He looks at it. He picks it up. "Great, thanks," he says.

"You can't do it here though because a friend of mine is coming over."

Stuart continues to nod. Mitch takes a swig off his beer.

"But here, sit down..." says Beth.

They sit.

"I can show you what to do."

Mitch and Stuart scoot close around the table.

"Have you ever done coke?" says Beth.

Mitch and Stuart stare at her.

"Is that a yes?"

"Yeah," says Stuart.

"Yeah, sure," says Mitch. "Lots of times."

"Okay," says Beth. "You scoop out a little. Not as much as a coke line." She's got a mirror out and she's dumping a bit of the powder onto it. "And you make a little bullet line...like this."

Mitch and Stuart stare at the mirror. Mitch is also looking at her face. The combination of her beauty and the way she's doing this: explaining it to them, being so patient and friendly. What did they do to deserve this?

"About that much," she says. "And then you just snort it up like a coke line."

"Man," says Stuart.

"Wow," says Mitch.

They both watch her scoop the small line back into the ziplock. Mitch sips his beer. Stuart sips his.

"And then what happens?" says Stuart.

Beth smiles. It's like they're all back in junior high, teaching each other how to smoke. "Well, you might get sick."

"Huh," says Stuart.

"I've heard that," says Mitch.

"If you've never done it you probably will," says Beth.

"Can I drive on it?" says Stuart.

"Not really. I mean, you probably won't want to."

Stuart nods. Mitch drinks his beer.

"I heard it's like Valium or something, I mean in how you feel," says Mitch.

"Kind of," says Beth. "But more."

Mitch nods. He watches Beth's face. He watches her hands. He has a revelation: Beth is the coolest girl. Not Tracy. Not Jeanelle. Beth. And Mitch is partying with her. Right here. Right now. Mitch is *scoring dope* from the coolest girl. It might be the high point of his life. So far.

FORTY EIGHT

Back outside, they get in the Dodge Charger. Stuart revs the engine and eases onto the street.

"Where are we going?" says Mitch.

"Where should we go?"

"We can't go to my house. Gillian will freak out."

"We can't go to my dad's house," says Stuart. He slows for a red light. As they sit at the intersection he pulls the ziplock out of his coat pocket. He looks at it.

"Let me see," says Mitch.

Stuart fingers the ziplock.

"C'mon, lemme see," says Mitch.

Stuart doesn't want to give it up.

"C'mon."

Stuart hands it to him. "Keep it down."

"Nobody can see what it is," says Mitch.

"Just keep it down."

Mitch holds it in the light. He can't really see it. But he can feel the power of it. It's heroin. It's the most bad-assed, hardcore drug in the world.

"Keep it *down,*" says Stuart.

"Nobody can fucking see it," says Mitch, handing it back.

Stuart slides it into his pocket. "So where should we go?"

Mitch watches the street ahead. "I don't know."

"Fuck. And we don't have a mirror."

"We don't have a fucking straw either."

They drive. "Maybe we should just park somewhere," says Stuart.

"Where?"

"Forest Park. The back part."

"But she said we shouldn't drive."

"Well, where else is there?"

"Fuck."

Stuart pulls around and heads back toward Forest Park. Mitch doesn't have a better idea, so he busies himself looking for something to chop with, and something flat to snort off.

Ten minutes later Stuart steers through the back entrance to Forest Park. He turns onto a maintenance road and drives deep into the woods. When the road ends he backs up between two heavy evergreen trees, so that they are almost completely hidden in the dark forest. He kills the engine and turns on the overhead light.

"We need a CD case or something," Mitch reports. He's leaning into the back seat, still looking for a flat surface.

"Here, use the back of this," says Stuart, pulling the Chemical Brothers cassette case out from under his seat.

"We don't have a razor blade," says Mitch.

"Do we need one?"

"Beth had one."

"Shit."

"Do you gotta knife or something?" says Mitch, looking in the glove box.

"Fuck it," says Stuart. "We'll just do it."

Once the ziplock is out they calm down. Mitch holds the tiny cassette case while Stuart sprinkles some of the powder on it. Stuart uses a bank card to straighten it into lines. He rolls a dollar bill into a straw. But he hesitates. He looks at Mitch. "Do you think we'll throw up?"

"Fuck if I know."

They both stare at the two lines on the cassette case. The forest around them is quiet and damp. One of the tree branches above them is dripping water on the roof.

"Go for it," says Mitch.

Stuart snorts up the line. Then he sits back, holds his nose, stretches his face.

"What's it feel like?" says Mitch.

Stuart shrugs. "Nothing."

"Here, hold it," says Mitch.

Stuart takes the cassette case and Mitch snorts up his line. Stuart's right, it doesn't really feel like anything.

"Well?" says Stuart.

Mitch shrugs. He takes the cassette case back. He sets it carefully on the dashboard.

Stuart turns off the overhead light and rolls down his window. Mitch rolls his window down too. He lights a cigarette. But when he inhales the smoke feels funny in his chest. It tastes different. It's stronger. It almost chokes him. Mitch tosses it out the window.

"Dude!" says Stuart. He grins at Mitch.

"Fuck!" says Mitch. "We just did fucking heroin!"

They high five each other. Mitch lights another cigarette. But this one tastes even stranger than the first one. He throws it out the window.

"Why'd you throw your cigarette out the window?" says Stuart.

"I don't know," says Mitch, grinning.

Stuart grins too. They both stare out the front of the Dodge Charger. It's drizzling. The trees in front of them are dripping wet. "God, I love this fucking car," says Stuart.

"It's rad," says Mitch.

They sit.

"I think I feel sick," says Stuart. He opens the heavy door and goes outside.

Mitch watches him walk back into the trees. He gets out another cigarette. He lights it. He smokes. This time he can handle the nicotine rush. But just barely. A cigarette never felt like this before.

It's like it's hitting some direct pleasure center in his brain. His whole body fills with a dreamy joy.

He opens his door and throws up on the wet ground. He shuts the door. He smokes. He focuses on the dashboard. Stuart's right. This car is awesome. Then he throws his cigarette out the window. He's too high.

He gets out of the car. The woods are deep and dark and saturated with rain water. Mitch wobbles back into the trees. "Stuart?" he says. Stuart is there. He's sitting against one of the trees. Mitch sits on the ground by his feet. But he wants to lay down. So he crawls to a different tree. He leans back against it. The forest is full of sound. Creaking, mushing, dripping, absorbing.

Mitch hears Stuart throw up. He loves Stuart. He throws up himself. He's all wet. How long has he been sitting here? He decides to stand up. But he can't. He crawls across the mud soaked grass and settles against a different tree. It's more exposed here. He can see the sky. It's grey and black and strangely luminous. A tiny swirling rain drop finds its way through the branches and alights on his grinning face.

Then his dead grandmother is there. In the woods somewhere. She wants to say something to him but then doesn't. She's there though. Mitch waits for her to communicate with him. She seems just about to. But then she recedes, in that humble way she has. It's all right though. Mitch loves her. Mitch understands. And anyway other presences have begun to reveal themselves. The forest is crowded with auras and spirits. The trees for one. They live. They breathe. And smaller forces. The grass. The rain. The soggy earth. It all melds into one single dream of pleasure and love and life force. Mitch's head tips forward. His eyes close. But he does not sleep. He simply observes through the top of his skull. He can see deeper into the forest this way. Deeper and clearer and with an infinite comprehension...

FORTY NINE

Mitch wakes up. He's in his bed. At home. He looks at his clock radio. It's two in the afternoon. He sits up. His clothes are strewn around the room. His suede Vans are covered with mud. So are his pants and coat.

He gets out of bed. He scratches his head. He looks down at his body, his arms and legs. He's all there. He's in one piece.

There are some less dirty clothes in his laundry box. He puts those on. He goes downstairs. Gillian and David are at work. Mitch stands in the living room. He's having trouble focusing. He needs some coffee. In the kitchen, there's half a cup in Gillian's coffee maker. Mitch drinks it in one gulp. He goes to the phone. He calls Stuart. No one's home. He calls the parking garage. Stuart isn't there. He called in sick.

Mitch hangs up. He needs more coffee. He needs it bad. He also wants company. He can't stand how quiet the house is. He calls Amy.

She's home. "Hi, Mitch!" she says.

"Hey," says Mitch. "What's up?"

"Nothing. What are you doing?"

"Nothing."

"I was going to go Christmas shopping later."

"Yeah?" says Mitch.

"Did you get your pot?"

"Uh, well, sort of. What I really need is coffee. Have you had coffee yet?"

"Yeah. But I could have more. Do you want to go out for coffee?"

"Yeah. But could you come, like, right now?"

"If you want. Why? Are you all right?"

"Yeah, yeah," says Mitch. "I'm fine."

She's there ten minutes later. Mitch is relieved to be out of his house. But it's weird being in the car with Amy. He cracks his window and lights a cigarette. It hits him a little harder than usual. But at least it tastes normal. The world in general is back to normal. Except that it's so bright. Even the grey overcast is hurting his eyes.

They go downtown. Amy parks in the garage beneath the Pioneer Mall. There are Christmas shoppers everywhere. They ride a crowded escalator up to the main level and then proceed to Starbucks. Mitch waits at a table while Amy gets them coffees. Amy looks good. She's wearing her new leather jacket. Mitch studies himself in the glass. He looks puffy, pale, half-asleep.

Amy brings the coffees to the table. Mitch gulps his. Amy sips hers. "So did you guys get your pot?" Amy asks.

"We didn't get pot," says Mitch.

"Oh?" says Amy. "What happened?"

"We got heroin."

"Oh," says Amy.

Mitch drinks more coffee.

"You mentioned that the other night."

Mitch nods.

"And you did it?"

"Yeah."

"Wow," says Amy. She thinks for a moment. "How did you get it?"

"That girl Beth. Jeanelle's friend."

Amy doesn't know what to say. "What was it like?"

"It was intense."

Amy nods. She's out of her league on this. A fact Mitch is enjoying.

"I don't think I could do something like that," says Amy. "I don't even like pot."

"It's not really for beginners."

"I don't even like to get drunk."

Mitch says nothing.

Amy drinks her coffee. Then she brightens. "That reminds me. I heard Jeanelle is going out with DJ Westy now."

"Really?" says Mitch.

"That's what Erica said. I guess Tracy was freaking out about it."

"Huh," says Mitch. He finishes his coffee. But he likes that thought: Tracy freaking out. Jeanelle stealing DJ Westy. Still, they should get back to the important subject: Mitch doing heroin.

But the Starbucks is packed. And a yuppie couple want to share their table. Amy finishes her coffee. They leave.

They walk around the crowded mall. Amy buys an Offspring CD for her younger brother for Christmas. She also looks at sweaters for her mom. Mitch walks along behind her. The weird tension he felt when he woke up is gone. Now he just feels spaced out. Pleasantly fogged. It's kind of fun. Also there are cute girls everywhere in the mall. And Amy looks good in her leather jacket. Mitch enjoys drifting off from her, checking out the other girls, and then having her reappear.

"Aren't you getting anyone a Christmas present?" says Amy as they stroll past the Gap.

"Nah."

"Don't you have a brother?"

"Yeah, but he lives in Tacoma."

"What about Stuart?"

"Stuart?" says Mitch. "Are you serious?"

"I guess guys don't get each other presents?"

"Do you get your friends presents?"

"*Sometimes,*" she says. She kind of bumps him. She's grinning.

"What?"

"Nothing."

"Don't get me a present," warns Mitch.

She stops, backs away from him. "Why not?"

"Because."

"Because you don't want to get me something?"

Mitch is suddenly irritated. They've been in the mall for almost an hour. He needs a cigarette. "Just don't," he tells her.

"But what if I already bought it?"

"Take it back."

"But you haven't even seen it yet."

"I don't want to see it."

"But it looks so good on me."

It does look good on her. It's lingerie–a teddy, with stockings, panties, a garter belt, the whole thing. They're back at Amy's. Mitch sits on her bed while she models it for him. When she approaches him, Mitch kisses the space between her breasts. He touches the sheer material of the stockings. But as things progress Mitch gets frustrated. He's never dealt with this stuff before. He doesn't know how to get it off. He wants to lose the teddy but keep the stockings. But he feels stupid trying to explain this. Finally, he just lays her down on the bed. He spreads her legs and gets inside her. That's all he really wants. He positions himself and gives her a long steady fuck. In the midst of which he happens to look at the wall above her head. She's gotten rid of the Counting Crows poster. Now it's Elastica. Rockstar girls in black leather pants. He looks at the lead singer, stares at her face and tits. Then he shuts his eyes and comes inside Amy.

FIFTY

After sex, they lay in bed for a while. But Mitch gets bored so they go downstairs and watch TV. They watch Letterman and then Conan O'Brien. Then Tracy comes home.

Amy, who had been slouched beside Mitch on the couch, sits up when she walks in. "Hi, Tracy," she says.

Tracy doesn't answer. She's looking at the mail. "Hi," she finally says. She sees Mitch. "Hey, Mitch."

"Hey," says Mitch.

Tracy comes over and sits in the armchair beside them. "Are you still alive?" she asks him. "Last time I saw you you were lying in the lawn at Jeanelle's house."

"Yeah, I'm still here," says Mitch.

"Well, thank god for that," she stands up. "I think I'm going to have a drink. Would anyone like one?"

Amy shakes her head no.

"What do you got?" says Mitch.

"Vodka. Jim Beam."

"I'll have that."

Amy watches anxiously as Tracy goes into the kitchen. Mitch continues to stare at the TV. When Tracy comes back with the drinks she hands one to Mitch. She sits back on the armchair. "What are you guys watching?" she asks Amy.

"Conan," says Amy.

Tracy sips her drink. Mitch looks over at her. She smiles at him.

"Maybe I should make some popcorn," says Amy, who can't get comfortable now.

"That sounds good," says Tracy. Amy gets up and goes into the kitchen.

Mitch continues to stare at the TV. He's playing it cool with Tracy now. He can afford to. Now that he's hanging out with Beth and doing heroin.

In the kitchen the microwave oven goes on.

"Are you having a nice Christmas, Mitch?" says Tracy.

"I didn't even know it was Christmas."

"How could you not know?" says Tracy, watching the TV.

Mitch looks at her. She's wearing her fake fur jacket, her white go-go boots. Her thick black hair curls forward along her jaw.

Amy comes out of the kitchen while the popcorn cooks. She doesn't sit down. She stands behind the couch, with her arms crossed, watching the TV. She's guarding him, thinks Mitch. She goes back into the kitchen.

"So you haven't done anything?" Tracy asks Mitch.

"Not for Christmas," he says. He wasn't going to say anything about his recent exploits. He shouldn't have to. But he can't help himself. "But we did find Beth."

"Why were you looking for her?"

"We were trying to score drugs."

"What kind of drugs?"

Mitch looks at the TV. "Just, you know..."

Tracy nods. "I see."

Mitch brought it up to impress her. But now he just wants to talk to her about it. That's the thing about Tracy. He always wants to talk to her. "Yeah, it was rad," he says. "At one point I was trying to smoke a cigarette..."

But Amy comes back. She's got popcorn. In a bowl. "Oh, look at that," says Tracy. "Amy, you'd make such a good wife."

Amy smiles painfully. She offers the bowl around. Tracy takes a big handful, dropping several kernels on the floor as Amy sits back on the couch. She places the bowl in front of her and eats them one at a time.

"So, you tried to smoke a cigarette..." says Tracy.

Mitch avoids looking at Amy. "Yeah. But I couldn't hold it down. It was like I'd never smoked before."

"Did you throw up?"

"Yeah."

"I threw up," says Tracy. "The first time. Not after I did it a couple of times." She's watching the TV now. "Oh my God! Look!" she says. "Sonic Youth!"

Sonic Youth is on Conan. Mitch shifts awkwardly on the couch. They all watch Sonic Youth.

"I love Kim Gordon," says Tracy.

"I have their new CD," says Amy. "You can borrow it if you want."

Tracy doesn't answer.

"So how's Jeanelle?" says Mitch.

But Tracy isn't paying attention. She's watching the TV. She reaches over and takes another handful of popcorn, spilling most of it down her front as she sits back. She eats it, watching the TV. Then she picks the fallen kernels off her fur coat.

"I think I'm going to get a pop," says Amy. "Does anybody want anything?"

"Vodka and grapefruit juice," says Tracy, handing Amy her empty glass. "Thanks."

Amy goes into the kitchen.

"What was that, about Jeanelle?" asks Tracy, when Amy's gone.

"I asked how she was," says Mitch.

"Why did you ask that?"

Mitch finishes his own drink. "Amy said she was hanging out with DJ Westy."

"What do you care who she's hanging out with?"

"I don't."

"DJ Westy is a pathetic limp-dick asshole anyway. She can have him."

Mitch smiles. Amy comes back. She gives Tracy her drink. She's also got a fizzing coke for herself. On the TV, Sonic Youth are squeezing the last bits of feedback from the end of their song. Tracy watches intently. When it's over, she takes her drink and gets up. "Well, I'll leave you kids alone," she says.

"Goodnight," says Amy.

"See you," says Mitch. He watches her stand up. He watches her walk to the stairwell. When she's gone he stares at the TV.

Later that night Mitch and Amy have sex again. This time without the lingerie. Mitch fucks her from behind. "Oh," groans Amy, a little louder than necessary. "Oh, *Mitch*!"

It's almost like she's doing it right to the wall. So that Tracy will be sure to hear. Mitch tries not to think about it. He stares at the Elastica poster.

"Oh, *yesss*!" says Amy loudly.

Something stirs in Tracy's room. Then her bedroom door opens. It slams shut. Mitch pauses for a moment to listen. Amy too pauses. Footsteps march down the hall. They go down the stairs. The front door slams. Silence.

Amy disconnects herself from Mitch and turns over. She smiles up at him. His bare cock, wet with moisture, bobs in front of her.

"Oh, Mitch," says Amy, quieter now. She reaches up and holds his dick. She guides it between her legs and inside her. "I'm so glad you're here."

Mitch begins to move inside her.

"I'm so glad you're with me tonight."

But Mitch wishes she would stop talking. He just wants to fuck in peace.

FIFTY ONE

Amy drops Mitch off at home the next day. There's a message from Excel. Does he want to do a telemarketing shift today? He has nothing better to do. And he needs the money. He goes downtown.

Carrie is there. In her usual cubicle. She's wearing a lacy Victorian dress, her creamy white breasts fit snug inside it. But Mitch got laid twice last night and once this morning. He still stares, but it's more an aesthetic attraction than a sexual one.

Mitch starts the day by calling around for Stuart. He tries Stuart's house, the parking garage, the auto repair shop where he used to work and often hangs out. But he can't find him anywhere.

So he dials up some music and does the daily Jumble with Carrie. They pass it back and forth. Mitch stares openly at her tits. Carrie doesn't seem to mind. Maybe she wants him. "So where do you hang out at night?" Mitch asks her as they work on the Jumble.

"Around."

"Do you ever go to Quest?"

"The dance place? *No*. Yuck."

"What's wrong with it?"

"All that rave stuff? That is *sooo* over."

"But where else is there to go?"

She smiles at him and hands him the Jumble.

He studies it. "No, really, is there some Goth club somewhere?"

"I don't go out," says Carrie. "I hate people."

"But you still gotta get drunk somewhere. Don't you?"

"I do my drugs in the privacy of my own home."

Mitch considers telling her about doing heroin. But she's probably done it. He hands her back the Jumble.

An hour later he calls Stuart again. This time Stuart answers.

"Stuart! What's up?"

"Nothing, what's up with you?"

Mitch scoots his chair forward. "I'm at work," he whispers. "I've been trying to call you. How come you're not at the parking garage?"

"I'm blowing it off."

"Where were you yesterday? Did you do some more of the stuff?"

"Yeah, actually I did."

"By yourself?"

"No."

"Who with?"

"Beth."

"Beth?"

"Yeah. And Jeanelle."

"Are you serious?"

"Yeah, Beth called and invited me over. It was weird. And then Jeanelle came over."

"Fuck," says Mitch, switching the phone to his other ear.

"And we did it up."

"Dude!"

"But fuck," says Stuart. "I'm so spaced out."

"Drink some coffee."

"I have been."

"So what did Jeanelle...what were they doing?"

"They were just hanging out."

"And they did all your heroin," says Mitch.

"Well, yeah."

"Fuck. We gotta get some more."

"I don't know. I am so spaced out. And I can't shit. And my stomach, it feels really weird."

"Well, fuck, but we could hang out with them more."

"I don't know. Beth isn't really into me. She just wants to be friends."

"So be friends with her," says Mitch. "And then work on her. I mean, look how far you've already gotten."

"I just want to take a shit."

"Maybe I can scam on Jeanelle."

"I don't think so."

"Why not?"

"Have you ever talked to her? She is harsh. She was saying shit about DJ Westy. How his dick is too small. How he can't fuck when he's high."

"You're supposed to be able to fuck on that?"

"I guess. I'd be happy if I could take a shit."

"God, maybe they'd want to have an orgy or something."

"I kind of doubt it."

"Why?"

"They're too much. Like when we were hanging out. It was like they were talking right around me. You know? Like I didn't even understand what they were talking about."

"Well, they're the raddest girls. They probably do that to everyone. They're the shit now."

"What about Tracy Richards? I thought she was the shit."

"She was. But now they are. And we can hang out with them. We could be the top."

"The top of what?"

"Of everything."

"I don't know, man. And how are we going to score more dope? I'm totally broke now."

"Fuck. So am I. Maybe you should call Beth. Maybe they'll want to return the favor and get us high. Since we got them."

"*I* got them. And it was *my* dope. You didn't pay for it."

"You know what I mean," says Mitch, checking on Carrie in the next cubicle.

"And anyway what about Amy?"

"Amy?"

"If you don't watch it she's going to dump you."

Mitch scoffs. "You worry about Beth. I'll worry about Amy."

Stuart picks Mitch up after work. Carrie is waiting at the bus stop when Stuart pulls up. "What's up with the Goth chick?"

"She's an idiot," says Mitch.

"Should we give her a ride?"

"No."

"Nice tits."

"Wave to her," says Mitch, waving at Carrie. "That's right. You're too cool for Quest but you're not too cool to ride the bus."

Stuart pulls into the street. "Is that where we're going? Quest?"

"I guess," says Mitch. He lights a cigarette. "So did you call Beth?"

"No."

"Are you going to?"

"I don't know."

"I don't understand this," says Mitch, "You were so into this girl. And now you're backing off."

"I'm not backing off. It's just not going to work. They're too hardcore. And not just the drugs."

Mitch scoffs. He smokes.

"Besides, I think Jeanelle is into chicks. The way she was talking."

"Ah, fuck that shit," says Mitch. He rolls down the window and flicks out an ash.

"I'm telling you. It's a whole different level," says Stuart. "And the way they talk about guys. It is harsh."

"They're just trying to shock you. They're just fucking with you."

"Yeah, well, it worked."

"Don't let it work. We gotta hang out with them. We can do dope with them. We can scam on them."

"I don't think you understand what we're dealing with here," says Stuart. But they're at Quest. Stuart finds a spot across the street. He parallel parks.

Mitch stares straight ahead, thinking.

FIFTY TWO

Quest looks pretty quiet. They walk toward the front but the door girl is new. So they go around back. But it's the fat bouncer. The one who wouldn't let Mitch in the other time. They go back to the front. Mitch talks to the new door girl. "Hey," he says.

The girl smiles a tight, bored smile.

Mitch looks behind her. All he needs is one person who knows who he is. But the security guy is also new.

Mitch smiles at the door girl. "My name's Mitch. I used to work here."

"Uh-huh," says the girl, like she's heard that before.

"No, I did. I used to work with Vince. On Sundays."

"I'm sorry. I just started here. I don't know Vince."

"He was a bartender."

"Oh."

"So I usually get in for free."

"Usually?"

"Yeah."

"Does the manager know that?"

"No, just, you know."

"No, I *don't* know."

"It's just like, part of the deal."

"Part of what deal?"

Mitch sighs. "We're friends with Dieter."

"Yeah?"

"And DJ Westy."

"Sounds like you have a lot of friends," says the girl. She smiles at him.

Mitch is going to say something back but Stuart crowds in. "We're sort of broke," says Stuart.

The security guard walks away. But being alone just makes the girl snottier. "That's too bad," she says. "Because if you don't have five dollars, I can't let you in."

"But I used to *work* here," says Mitch.

"Sounds like you should start *working* somewhere else," says the girl.

Mitch is losing his temper but Stuart pushes him away. "Can you just cut us a deal? Two for five or something? It's a slow night anyway, right?"

"I have an idea," says the girl. "Why don't you give me ten dollars. And then you can both come in."

"You're really funny," says Mitch, from behind Stuart.

"I know," says the girl.

"You're a fucking cunt," says Mitch.

"Oh am I?" says the girl.

"Yeah and you can fucking–"

But the bouncer comes back. And Stuart is pulling him away. Mitch tears loose of Stuart's grip and glares back at the grinning girl. But he stays with Stuart. He follows him back to the car.

They go to Hurley's. Dieter is there. With James the suit. And some other guys. Nobody looks particularly happy to see Stuart and Mitch. They continue to play pool while Mitch and Stuart combine their money and buy a cheap pitcher. Nobody says anything when they sit down across from the pool table.

Stuart puts up quarters and eventually plays pool with Dieter. James, who lost, comes over and sits in the booth with Mitch. "So, I heard some guy fell on you at Jeanelle's."

Mitch feels around for his cigarettes.

"Patrick was telling me about it. You were wrestling around and some guy accidentally fell on you?"

"Who's Patrick?"

"The short guy. With the suit."

Mitch finds his cigarettes. He lights one.

"Is that what happened?" says James. "Somebody fell on you?"

Mitch looks at him. "Whatever. I don't give a shit."

"Because Patrick felt bad about it."

"Yeah, he'll feel even worse when I break his fucking head."

James watches the pool game. "Patrick is like a Golden Gloves guy."

"What's that?" says Mitch.

"He's a boxer."

"So?"

"He wasn't trying to cause you guys any trouble."

"Yeah, well, why did that other guy grab me?"

"I don't know. I wasn't there. I just want you to know. They didn't mean it. If I were you I'd forget about it."

"I already did forget about it, until you brought it up."

James gets up and goes to the bar. When he comes back he sits at a different table.

Dieter beats Stuart. Stuart comes and sits with Mitch. "What's up with James?"

"He's trying to weasel out of that thing with the short suit. *Patrick* is his name."

Stuart drinks his beer. "Yeah. That's what I thought."

"Do you still think we should kick his ass?"

Stuart shrugs. "Maybe not."

"Yeah?"

"I mean, James is cool."

"He said Patrick is a Golden Gloves guy."

"Well, whatever. I mean, those guys are all right. They can be fun to hang out with."

Mitch sneers. "You just did heroin with Beth and Jeanelle and now you're worried about a bunch of losers in suits?"

Stuart watches Dieter shoot. "I don't know what you think you're going to get out of Beth and Jeanelle."

"They're fucking *rad*. They've got balls for one. Not like these fucking losers," says Mitch, waving dismissively at the Hurley's crowd.

Stuart looks back at Mitch. "You gotta chill out. That was not cool with the door girl at Quest."

"She fucking deserved it."

"Where's Amy? Get her to give you some money."

"Fuck Amy."

"Where is she?"

"I don't fucking know."

Stuart watches the pool table. "I don't understand why you're not into her."

Mitch stubs out the cigarette he's smoking.

"She's not going to fuck with you," says Stuart. "She's got a job. And a car. And she's cute."

"She's got a fucking Elastica poster over her bed."

"So what? She's got a hot body. And she's into you. What do you fucking want?"

Mitch stares at the wall.

"You want Jeanelle? You want a fucking junky dyke?"

"I want Tracy Richards."

"You're not going to get Tracy Richards."

"That's what you said before. And you were wrong."

"I was wrong for one night."

"Yeah, well, that's all it takes. I fucked her. And I don't fucking back off a chick because she's a little bit bad-assed."

Stuart stares at him. "What's wrong with you anyway? What are you all bent about?"

"You were so into Beth and now you're backing off."

"I'm not backing off," says Stuart. "The situation changed. And I'm dealing with it."

"Yeah, well, I don't let the situation deal with me. I deal with the situation."

"Yeah, sure you do tough guy," says Stuart, standing up. "Sure you do."

FIFTY THREE

The next day Excel calls. They want Mitch to do a shift at a different telemarketing place. It's outside of town. On the west side. Mitch will have to take the bus. But he needs the money. He agrees.

He rides the 57 bus through downtown. The streets are decorated with Christmas ornaments. A man selling flowers is dressed like Santa Claus. Mitch watches it all through the rain blurred windows. The bus is freezing. He shivers and pulls his jacket tight.

As the bus climbs the hill to the west side, Mitch thinks about Brenda. He should call her. This time, he'll tie her up. Maybe spank her or something. Whip her. If she's into it. Could Amy do something like that? It wouldn't be the same with her. With Amy everything means something. Every time you fuck her you're in a little deeper. More relationship. More commitment. More connection to the scene in general.

Mitch has had enough of the scene: everyone telling him how cool he is, who he can fuck, what *level* he's on. Fuck that shit. He'll fuck Brenda Collins. He'll tie her to the bed and do all sorts of kinky shit to her. And nobody will even know.

The set up at the new place is the same as the downtown office. Mitch takes his script and questionnaire sheets into a cubicle. He dials up the weather and then a local sports line. He pokes his pencil into a hole someone else has worn into one of his cubicle walls.

He fucks the hole with his pencil. Amy comes to mind. He imagines being with her. Tying her up. But then it's back to Brenda. Brenda who's easy. Brenda who doesn't care. Brenda who puts her tits on your balls while she's sucking your dick. The thought of it is giving him a hard-on. Mitch calls information and gets Brenda's number.

Mrs. Collins answers the phone. "Hello, Mitchell."

"Hi, Mrs. Collins. Is Brenda there?"

"Just a minute–" she covers the phone and yells, "*Brenda*!" Then she talks to Mitch. "She's coming. So, Mitchell, are you having a nice Christmas?"

"Yeah, it's been okay."

"It can be so stressful this time of year."

"Yeah."

"Are you going to be spending the day with your family?"

"Yeah, probably."

"Brenda's so happy you called. Here she is. Bye now."

Mitch waits. Brenda picks up the phone. "Hello?"

"Brenda?"

"Mitch. Hi. What are you doing?"

"Not much," says Mitch. "I'm at work. But I was thinking maybe later, when I get off, we could go get a drink."

"Oh."

"I mean, if you're up for it."

"Uhm, well, William has an ear infection."

"Huh."

"But I guess I could...what time?"

"I get off at nine."

"Let me ask my mother."

Mitch waits. He can hear muffled talking. Then the baby crying. The baby is very loud. Brenda must be holding it right next to the phone.

"Mitch?" says Brenda. The baby is now shrieking in the background.

"Yeah?" says Mitch, loudly.

"I can go. But just for a little while. Where are you? Do you want me to pick you up?"

Mitch does. He gives her the address. He hangs up. Then all he has to do is sit in his cubicle for five hours.

When his work day is over, Mitch stands in front of the office. It's raining. He stands under an awning with his co-workers, the ones who have rides. Brenda is one of the last people to show up. It's almost nine-thirty when she finally arrives. "I'm sorry I'm so late," she says as Mitch gets in. "We had to give William ear drops. It's really awful."

Mitch nods. He immediately lights a cigarette. He gives one to Brenda. She lights it and smokes as they drive. "Where do you want to go?" she says.

"I don't care."

"Actually, I know a place. It's right near here."

"Okay," says Mitch. But it's not really okay. He was hoping they could go straight to his house. And get right into the kinky sex. But maybe it'd be better to get drunk first.

They go to Brenda's bar. It's a bright, suburban brew pub. It has a dart board and pool tables and a lot of bland looking locals. They get pints of micro-beer and sit in a booth. Jethro Tull plays on the jukebox.

It's then that Mitch sees the zit on Brenda's chin. It's huge. And her hair is so dirty it looks wet around her temples. Her whole face is shiny. It looks swollen. She lights another cigarette. "God, I can't stand my mother," she says.

Mitch looks down into his beer. He drinks it. This isn't going to work. Why did he even call her?

"And William, I mean, it's not his fault. But sometimes I swear..."

Mitch nods sympathetically. He's got to get out of here.

"So what were you doing today," says Brenda.

"Telemarketing."

"I did that."

"Yeah?" says Mitch. Jethro Tull goes off. Garth Brooks comes on. Mitch drinks his beer.

*"Hello, my name is Brenda and I'm calling to ask you about...*whatever crap they're trying to sell."

Mitch tries to smile at her joke. But it's a strained, fake smile. He drinks his beer.

FIFTY FOUR

When they finish their beers a waitress comes by. Brenda is going to have another, but when she sees Mitch's expression she hesitates. "Do you want to go?" she asks him.

"Actually, I sort of need to sleep. I didn't realize how tired I was."

Brenda nods. But she's obviously disappointed.

"Do you mind?"

"No, no, it's fine," says Brenda. He's hurt her feelings. But what can he do?

They leave. Brenda drives him downtown. She passes Third Street, where Hurley's is and heads toward the bridge to Mitch's house.

"Actually, I should probably just get out here," says Mitch, looking back at Hurley's.

"I thought you..."

"I gotta find this guy who owes me money. You know, for Christmas presents."

Brenda slows down abruptly. She pulls over.

"Yeah, this is cool," says Mitch.

She looks over at him but he's already out the door.

"Thanks for the ride," he says. He shuts the door and walks back toward Third Street.

• • •

Hurley's is packed. Partly because it's a Thursday and partly because it's now the night before Christmas Eve. Mitch picks his way through the crowd. He can see Stuart's Fuct cap above the other heads in the back. He's playing pool. Mitch squeezes into the pool area. Everyone is here. Stuart, Dieter, James the suit, Patrick the short suit, some other suits, the big guy who fell on Mitch at Jeanelle's.

"Hey," says Mitch to Dieter as he approaches.

"Hey."

"Whassup?" Mitch asks Stuart. But Stuart doesn't answer. He's intent on the game. Mitch looks around at the other people. No one will meet his eye. He looks back at the pool table. Stuart, who never beats Dieter, is actually winning.

Mitch stands off to the side. He doesn't have any money. He looks for a pitcher to bum a glass of beer from.

The big guy who fell on him at Jeanelle's approaches him. "Hey, are you Mitch?"

"Yeah."

"Sorry about the other night. I didn't mean to land on you like that."

Mitch looks at him. He doesn't mean it. But then the guy glances over at Stuart. That's what it is. These guys are afraid of Stuart. But whatever. Mitch isn't looking for trouble. "Yeah, sure, no problem," says Mitch.

Patrick, the short suit, is standing against the far wall. He looks over at Mitch. Then he looks back at the pool table. Stuart makes a tough shot. "All right," says someone. Everybody is apparently rooting for Stuart.

Mitch lights a cigarette. He needs a beer. He picks up an empty glass off the side board. He looks around for a pitcher.

"Yes!" says someone when Stuart sinks the last solid. Now all he's got left is the eight ball. He lines it up. He shoots. It drops. Everyone cheers. Dieter is cool about it. Of course. Patrick is next. He'll play Stuart. People shift around. Mitch wanders over to the other wall and pours himself half a glass of somebody's beer.

"Hey, what are you doing?"

Mitch knows that voice. He turns around slowly.

"That's my pitcher," says Patrick, the short suit.

"Oh," says Mitch.

"Why are you drinking my beer?"

"I didn't know. I thought it was Stuart's."

"It's not Stuart's. It's mine."

Mitch glances once at Stuart. He's chalking his cue. He's not looking at either one of them.

"Sorry," says Mitch.

"Put it back."

"Put it back in the pitcher?" says Mitch.

"I said, put it back!" Patrick comes tearing around the pool table toward him. He drops his cue and reaches for the glass in Mitch's hand.

Mitch throws it in his face. Patrick grabs Mitch and drives him back against the wall. He punches Mitch in the chest. He punches him in the head. Mitch is bigger than him, taller, but he can't seem to hold him off.

Then there's a whipping sound and a crack. Patrick suddenly staggers backward into the pool table. Stuart is standing behind him, the pool cue still in his hand. He just hit Patrick across the back with it.

The big guy makes a move toward Stuart but stops when Stuart turns toward him. Everyone freezes. Nobody's going to fuck with Stuart.

Then the bartender pushes into the room. "What's going on back here?" he wants to know. Stuart lowers the pool cue and holds it as if he were considering his next shot. Mitch straightens up. Patrick, who has his back to the bartender, remains where he is, grimacing, leaning against the pool table.

"What's going on here?" repeats the bartender. He looks around for a responsive face. He finds Dieter. "What just happened?"

Dieter looks at him. "I lost."

"So?"

"I never lose."

"Oh, yeah?" says the bartender. He looks Dieter up and down. Then he looks at the other people, most of whom are staring guiltily at the ground. "Well, don't give me no problems here. It's Christmas, for chrissakes."

The bartender leaves. When he's safely gone, everyone looks at Mitch. Stuart especially. "Maybe you better leave," he says.

"Me?" says Mitch.

"Yeah, you."

Mitch straightens up. But then Patrick springs forward. He punches Mitch in the jaw, turning his head. Mitch falls back against the wall. Again Stuart tries to stop Patrick but this time the big guy grabs him. Mitch gets pinned against the wall. Patrick pounds him with fists.

Then Dieter grabs Patrick. He pulls him back. Mitch picks up a chair and hits both of them with it. He grabs a pool cue and takes a wild swing at Patrick. He hits Dieter. Stuart, meanwhile, has wrestled the big guy to the ground. But then someone else jumps on Stuart's back. All the suits are getting involved now. One of them tries to pull Dieter off Patrick. Another gets tangled in the extension cord attached to the big neon Budweiser sign in the window. The sign pops loose, falls, shatters on the floor.

Patrick twists away from Dieter and attacks Mitch again. But this time Mitch attacks back. He slams into Patrick with his shoulder. He grabs his tie. Patrick goes down. Mitch goes down. On the floor, they scramble for the advantage. But Mitch gets it: he gets Patrick in a headlock. He immediately rolls on top of him and uses his full weight to grind Patrick's face into the coarse carpet.

Then the bartender's back. With a small army of regulars. These are grown men. Big, thick, strong. They grab Mitch. They grab Dieter. They grab Patrick. Stuart is the only one they can't control. But Stuart's done. He raises his hands to indicate he'll go peacefully.

FIFTY FIVE

Apparently the damage is bad enough that the police have been called. Mitch and Stuart and the others are brought to the front and then taken out to the sidewalk by the regulars. But once they're outside, the regulars are unsure of their role. They don't want to wait for the police. It's not their problem. And it's cold. And they're thirsty. Nobody really does anything when Mitch walks down the street a few steps. He's bent over, as if in pain. Stuart goes to help him. The two wander a little further toward the corner. Then they're around it. Then they're sprinting down the street.

"This way!" says Stuart. Mitch falls in behind him. They run to Stuart's car. Stuart gets in, Mitch gets in. They both check in every direction as Stuart pulls onto the street. They ease down Second Street. They've gone two blocks when they see a white flash on the sidewalk. It's Dieter. He's running. And a little bit ahead of him is Patrick. Also sprinting, his tie trailing off behind him.

Mitch rolls down his window. "Dieter! *Dieter*!"

Dieter looks over his shoulder. He sees the car. He angles into the street. Mitch scoots over. Without stopping completely, Mitch pops the door and Dieter jumps in.

"Get Patrick," says Stuart, checking his rear view mirror.

"What?" says Mitch.

"Get Patrick!"

"Patrick!" shouts Dieter. "Patrick!"

Patrick has already seen them. But he hasn't stopped running. Now he does. He looks at the car. He looks around the street.

"C'mon!" says Stuart. Dieter waves for him to come.

Patrick runs toward the car.

"Get in the back you guys! Get in the back!" says Stuart.

Dieter and Mitch tumble over the seat. Patrick jumps in the front.

"Now, everybody get down!" says Stuart.

Mitch and Dieter are already down. They're tangled on the floor in the back. Patrick lays across the front seat. Stuart slowly turns the corner and eases over the bridge. He steers the Dodge Charger carefully onto the freeway entrance ramp on the other side. Then he punches it. Everyone remains down as the car accelerates onto the freeway. Ten minutes later they are fifteen miles out of town.

Mitch is the first to raise his head. Then Dieter sits up. Then Patrick.

Stuart is just driving now. He's cruising at eighty down the Interstate. For a moment they all stare forward as the freeway hurtles by.

Stuart looks over at Patrick. "Are you all right?"

Patrick stares forward. "Yeah."

"How about you, Dieter?" says Stuart into the rear view mirror.

"Yeah," says Dieter. "Except for my arm. Where Mitch hit me with a pool cue."

"What?" says Stuart.

Dieter clears his throat. "Mitch hit me with a pool cue."

"Sorry, dude," Mitch says to Dieter. "I didn't mean to."

"Yeah, you were trying to hit *me*," says Patrick, but he doesn't seem particularly upset about it.

"Fuck," says Stuart. "We fucking trashed that place."

"Where are we going to play pool now?" says Dieter.

"Magic Gardens," says Stuart.

"It costs a dollar a game," says Dieter.

"I know," says Mitch. "That's what I tried to tell him. That place is too expensive."

Stuart turns to Patrick. "You ever go to Magic Gardens?"

Patrick shakes his head.

"Fuck," says Stuart to the car in general. "I could use a beer. Maybe we should go there right now."

No one answers.

"Feel like a beer?" Stuart asks Patrick.

Patrick shrugs. "Not really."

The car settles into silence.

"My face hurts," says Mitch.

Stuart looks over at Patrick. "So you did Golden Gloves?"

Patrick nods.

"What weight were you at?"

"One twenty-five."

"I tried to do that. But I'm so big. You know, I had to go against these huge black guys."

Patrick stares forward.

"But I guess the little guys," says Stuart. "They're probably pretty quick."

"They're faster'n shit," says Patrick. "I lost the regionals to a Mexican kid that went to the Olympics."

"Wow," says Stuart. He nods. The Dodge Charger cruises easily at eighty-five. "Hey dude, sorry I hit you with the pool cue. It was kind of a cheap shot."

Patrick doesn't answer. And then: "I've been hit harder."

"I bet," says Stuart. "I bet."

After a while they turn around. Stuart gives Patrick and Dieter a ride home. Then Mitch and Stuart go to the twenty-four hour supermarket on Hawthorne. They go to the beer display. Mitch studies his swollen face in the glass. "Man, did you hear that. I fought a guy who almost went to the Olympics. And I practically kicked his ass."

Stuart scoffs. "You're lucky he didn't kill you."

"Yeah, well, you practically kissed his ass to death. *Oh, you're in the Golden Gloves. Oh, you must be really quick.* Why didn't you just go home with the guy?"

"Yeah, yeah," says Stuart.

"Did you check out how scared Dieter was when he got in the car?" says Mitch, checking his profile.

Stuart tries to stuff a forty down his pants. "Yeah, after you hit him with a pool cue."

"Hey, it was the heat of battle." Mitch stops looking at himself and opens the beer display. He grabs a sixteen ounce tall boy and stuffs it in his pants. Stuart is having trouble with the forty. It won't fit. He puts it back and goes for a tall boy. It fits easily. He goes for two. Mitch goes for two. They leave.

They drive around. They drink their beers. Mitch keeps opening and shutting his mouth. He can feel the place where his jaw is swollen. Finally, he lights a cigarette. "So, I think I'm going to hang out with Amy over Christmas."

"Yeah?"

"I might as well."

Stuart drives. "I should get a girlfriend."

"Or someone to get laid with occasionally," says Mitch.

"It's good for your health, I saw this thing on TV."

"Sure. It calms you down."

"But how do you get one?" asks Stuart.

"Don't ask me. I don't even know why Amy likes me."

"Because she can't get you."

"You think?" says Mitch.

"Probably."

Mitch smokes. "But if she gets me," he says. "Then what happens?"

"She gets bored with you," says Stuart. "And she starts doing someone else."

Mitch thinks about this. "So this is the best part then. Right now."

"Probably."

Mitch looks out the window. "I know I got her. But she doesn't know if she's got me. It kind of sucks for her though."

"Yeah, but they don't mind. They're into all that intrigue and wondering about everything."

"You think?"

"Sure," says Stuart. "They're women. They love that shit."

FIFTY SIX

The next day Mitch wakes up at noon. He feels weirdly calm and at ease with himself. He lays in bed for an hour and just thinks about things. Then he gets up and goes downstairs and pours himself half the coffee left in Gillian's coffee maker.

It's Christmas Eve. Mitch looks out the window. It's overcast, grey, wet. He takes his coffee and sits on the couch. He looks at the phone. He should call Amy. He'll hang out with her tonight. If she's around. Maybe she'll have to do something with her family. Mitch notices there's been no call from his own parents.

He lights a cigarette. Maybe he should get Amy a Christmas present. He's only got a couple of bucks but he could probably find something. Or steal something, if need be. He should at least check it out. And he doesn't have anything else to do today.

The streets are crowded downtown. Mitch is on his bike. He weaves his way through the pedestrians and eventually walks his bike when it's impossible to ride further. At the Pioneer Mall it's the same: so crowded Mitch can barely maneuver. He tries weaving his way through the throngs but he keeps crashing into people. He finally submits to the natural crowd flow and then ducks into a bookstore.

Here he looks for something for Amy. He looks at cards. He likes one in particular but when he flips it over it's three dollars. He glances around the store, hoping he can slip it in his jacket. But there's no way. There are store employees everywhere. He puts it back on the stand.

He gives up on the present. It doesn't matter. Amy knows he's broke. He ventures back into the mall. This time he doesn't hurry. He just walks along with everyone else. It's strangely pleasing. Like a narcotic: the masses of people, the gentle flow of humanity. He gets a cheap coffee and leans against the railing in the center of the mall. He stares down into the atrium. Below him people flow like water: around an espresso cart, a bench, an exercise machine display. He watches a middle-aged couple, arm in arm, as they point into a jewelry store. Three young boys chase each other through the crowd. Two teenage girls walk slowly with ice cream cones. Mitch becomes aware of an ache in his chest. It's in his throat too. Like when his grandmother died. Like when Tracy rejected him. Except this feeling is more general. More total. And it doesn't seem to have any cause. Mitch looks behind him. He looks at the other people perched on the railing around him. It's nothing. He drinks his coffee and settles against the railing. But he should get back. He's got to call Amy.

Outside the sky is dark and heavy. Raindrops are beginning to fall. He unlocks his bike and rides across the river. He heads first toward his own house. But Amy's is closer. And it's really raining now. He steers toward Amy's. He rides hard, pedaling all the way, but he's still soaked when he gets there. He hauls his bike onto her porch and looks in the window. There's a light on in the kitchen. She should be home, her car is in the street. He knocks. He sees someone move. It's Tracy. She comes towards the door.

FIFTY SEVEN

"Hello, Mitch," says Tracy, opening the door.

"Hi," says Mitch.

She smiles at him. "You're all wet."

"I know."

"Are you looking for Amy?"

"Yeah."

"She's not here."

"Her car's here," says Mitch, pointing behind him.

"I think Brian picked her up."

"Oh."

Tracy looks at him. "I don't know what their plans are. They might come back. Or they might not."

"Huh," says Mitch.

"Do you want to come in?"

"Nah, that's all right."

"Are you sure?"

Mitch isn't.

"Come in," says Tracy. "I'm trying to make a cake. It's not working though. Do you know how to bake stuff?"

Mitch moves forward. "Not really."

"Didn't you used to work at the Natural Bakery Company?"

"Yeah, but I don't know how to make anything."

Mitch is inside. Tracy shuts the door. Mitch unzips his Stussy racing jacket. He hangs it on the stair railing to dry.

"Come in here," says Tracy.

Mitch follows her into the kitchen. There's cooking stuff everywhere. Flower, sugar, butter. Measuring cups. Tracy puts on a huge cooking mitt and opens the oven door and looks in. "See?" she says.

Mitch looks in.

"Is that the most pathetic thing you have ever seen?"

Mitch laughs. "Yeah, I guess it is."

"Don't laugh!" says Tracy.

Mitch backs away from the oven and sits at the kitchen table. "Why are you making a cake anyway?"

"Isn't that what you do at Christmas?"

"I thought you made a turkey."

"You don't *make* a turkey. A turkey already *exists*."

"Cakes are more for birthdays," says Mitch, getting out his cigarettes.

"Well, I don't care. This is a Christmas cake."

Mitch lights a cigarette. Tracy stares into the oven. "I don't think you're supposed to keep opening the door," says Mitch.

"Maybe that's the problem," says Tracy. She slams the door shut and sits across from him at the table. She pulls off the mitt and throws it into the sink. Mitch gives her a cigarette and lights it for her.

Tracy slouches in her chair. She puts her feet up on a third chair. She smokes. "So do you and Amy have plans?"

Mitch shakes his head no. "I guess I sort of assumed she'd be around."

"You know what?" says Tracy. "I think she said something to Brian about going to church."

"Church? Like, with her parents?"

"I don't know."

Mitch looks at his cigarette. "They're just friends though, right?"

"As far as I know," says Tracy.

Mitch thinks about it. He frowns.

"You should have called her," says Tracy. "You can't just assume people are going to be around."

"Yeah," sighs Mitch.

Tracy puts her cigarette in the ashtray and stands up again. She gets the mitt out of the sink and opens the oven. She reaches inside. "Ouch!" she says. She's trying to get the cake out.

Mitch watches her.

Tracy tries again, burns herself again. "Shit!" she says. She glares at Mitch. "You could help out a little."

"I could," says Mitch. "But it's not my cake."

Tracy gets it out. She drops it on the stove. Then she tears the mitt off and throws it back in the sink. She comes back to the table and takes a drag off her cigarette.

The cake is burned. It's filling the kitchen with smoke. "So I guess Jeanelle isn't going out with DJ Westy anymore," says Mitch.

Tracy says nothing.

"Stuart was hanging out with her and Beth. He said Jeanelle was ripping on everybody."

"I used to be like that," says Tracy. She puts out her cigarette. "And now I make cakes."

Mitch stares at a band poster on the wall. "That Beth though. She's so cool. And she's *nice*. That's what's so weird. How could someone that cool be so *nice*?"

"Is she nicer than Amy?"

Mitch glares at her. "Why do you always have to bring up Amy?"

Tracy shrugs. "You just seem like a good match."

"Why do you always say that?" says Mitch, sitting up. "And why are we such a good match?"

"You have sex don't you?"

"So what? Anybody can have sex. What the fuck difference does sex make?" But Mitch is raising his voice. He calms himself. He sits back. He smokes.

"Is there someone you think would be better?" asks Tracy.

Mitch doesn't answer. He looks at the band poster on the wall.

Tracy goes back to her cake. She pokes one of the burned parts with a fork. "Mitch? Is there someone else?"

"Well, yeah, obviously."

"Who?"

"Who do you think?" says Mitch.

"Beth?"

"No."

Tracy turns toward him. "You don't mean *me*?" she says.

"Well, who the fuck else would I mean?"

Tracy sighs. She goes back to stabbing the cake. "Oh, Mitch," she says. "Oh Mitch, oh Mitch, oh Mitch."

Mitch stares at the wall.

"I mean, I'm very flattered."

"Ah, fuck you," says Mitch.

"And you know I like you as a friend."

"Did I say fuck you? What I really meant was *fuck you*."

"I'm sorry. I can't help how I feel."

"Well, neither can I."

"You're like a little brother or something. I can talk to you."

"But that's the thing," says Mitch. "Look at this. Look at what we're doing *right now*. I can fuck any girl. But you're the only one..."

"What are we doing right now?" asks Tracy.

"We're..." says Mitch, helplessly. "We're..."

Tracy is still holding the fork. She watches him.

"Ah, fuck it," says Mitch. "Never mind."

Tracy pokes the cake.

Mitch stubs out his cigarette. "You just love this don't you? You live for this."

"Live for what?"

Mitch doesn't answer.

"What do I live for?"

"I gotta go," says Mitch.

"You don't have to."

"Yeah, I do." Mitch gets up. "Will you tell Amy I came by?"

"Of course."

Mitch walks through the living room. He grabs his coat off the stair railing. He opens the door. He glances once behind him on the way out. But Tracy has not followed. She's still in the kitchen. Mitch closes the door and goes out.

FIFTY EIGHT

It's dark outside. Dark and wet. Mitch rides his bike slowly back to his house. He lugs it up the stairs to the porch and locks it up. Inside, the house is dark. Everyone's gone. He turns on the lights and goes upstairs. He showers, changes into dry clothes and finds some stale Rice Krispies in the kitchen. He pours some in a bowl with some of Gillian's milk and takes it into the living room. He turns on the TV. There's not much on. A singing choir. Some sort of Christmas cartoon. A re-run of *Married With Children*. He watches that. Then the beginning of a movie. He gets more Rice Krispies. The phone rings.

"Hello?'

"Mitch!"

"Amy. What's up?"

"I just got home. Tracy said you were looking for me."

"Yeah. I stopped by."

"What were you doing?"

"Nothing. What are you doing?"

Amy hesitates a beat. "Nothing," she says. There's something sweet in her voice. Mitch feels a warm shiver pass through his body, a pleasant feeling of familiarity, of connection.

"I was going to midnight mass with Brian. But if you want to do something."

"Well...if you already have plans."

"But I don't. I mean I'll change them. I want to be with you tonight. If you want to."

"Oh," says Mitch. "I don't know what we could do."

"You can come over here. Tracy made a cake. And Erica's coming over with her boyfriend. And Gretchen is maybe coming too."

"Maybe I should invite Stuart."

"If you want to. We got a movie. *Earth Girls Are Easy*. Have you ever seen that?"

"No. But I just...I think Tracy's kind of sick of me."

"She's not sick of you. And who cares if she is? Just a sec—" Amy covers the phone and talks. Then back to Mitch: "She's not sick of you. She wants you to come over. She says you have to eat some of her cake."

"All right," says Mitch. "All right."

Mitch calls Stuart. He's not there but he leaves a message. Then he hauls his bike back off the porch. He pedals to Hawthorne and coasts down the hill, slaloming through the traffic lines. He lowers his head and bombs straight downhill for the last fifty yards. He's flying when he gets to Amy's street. He just makes the corner and then lets his momentum take him two blocks before he pedals the rest of the way to the house.

Inside, Amy immediately gives him a hug. She holds him, resting her head on his chest for a moment. "I'm so glad you came!"

Mitch smiles at her. She looks good. She's wearing her leather jacket. They go into the kitchen where Erica and her boyfriend are watching Tracy frost the cake.

"Hey, you guys," says Amy as they all crowd into the kitchen. The doorbell rings. "That's probably Gretchen," says Amy. She runs to the door. Mitch watches from the kitchen while she opens it. But it's not Gretchen. It's Stuart. And he's got a date. Beth Sinclair.

FIFTY NINE

Mitch pulls back into the kitchen but he can hear Amy greet them.

"I hope it's okay," says Stuart. "Mitch said to come over."

"Of course," says Amy, cheerfully. "Come in. We're all in the kitchen. Tracy's baking a cake."

Stuart and Beth follow Amy into the kitchen. Amy introduces everybody. They all know Stuart but nobody really knows Beth. Amy is gushingly nice to her. Erica says very little. Tracy is polite and asks her how her Christmas is going.

"Okay, you know," says Beth. She looks stunning. Her face is made up. Her blonde hair is messily pinned, bits of hair fall down around her face.

Stuart comes over to Mitch. "Is there any beer?"

Amy gets him a beer from the refrigerator. She gets one for Mitch. And then Erica's boyfriend wants one too.

"Bitburg Beer, on Christmas Eve?" says Tracy. "Well, we know Gretchen will have a nice Christmas."

Everyone laughs. Mitch wanders into the living room to check the stereo. Amy yells for him to put something on. Stuart comes over to help. They stand over the stereo. "Fuck, man," whispers Mitch, "Where did Beth come from?"

"She called me."

"What for?"

"I don't know. She wanted to hang out. I think she wants to get dope."

"Jesus Christ," says Mitch, looking back toward the kitchen. "I thought you weren't going to hang out with her."

"I didn't think she wanted to hang out with me!"

"Dude!" says Mitch.

"I know."

"She just called you up?"

"She just called me up."

"What did she say?"

"She asked if I was doing anything. And I wasn't. And she said she was going to meet some guy. And maybe score dope."

"That's why she called you," says Mitch. "You got a car."

"Well, yeah, but look at her."

"She looks amazing," says Mitch.

"I know. That's the thing. She's all dressed up," Stuart looks behind him. "Do you think that means something?"

"Like what?"

"Do you think she wants to get laid?"

"With you?"

"Well, *yeah*," says Stuart.

"I doubt it."

"But she called me."

"Maybe she does," says Mitch, looking back to the kitchen.

"I can't fucking blow this," says Stuart, staring down at the stereo. "I always blow it in situations like this."

Amy comes over to them. Mitch picks through the CDs.

"Finding anything?" she asks.

"Nah," says Mitch.

Amy puts her arm through Mitch's and looks too. Mitch doesn't like this joining of arms. He gently unhooks himself and reaches for his beer.

Amy puts on the Elastica CD. Then she looks at Mitch as if it has some special meaning for the two of them.

"Do you like Elastica?" says Amy.

"Yeah, they're cute," says Mitch. He drinks his beer. They go back to the kitchen. Erica is now sitting on the counter. Beth is standing off to the side. Tracy is doing her best to make conversation. "Actually, my first cake attempt was earlier today," she tells Beth.

Beth smiles.

"Do you make stuff?" Tracy asks her.

"Not really."

"I never did either. But since it was Christmas," she says. "What are you and Stuart doing tonight?"

"We're going to see a friend of mine," says Beth. "But he won't be back until eleven."

"Well, that's nice," says Tracy.

Mitch and Stuart squeeze into the kitchen. It's crowded with all of them in there.

"Maybe we should go in the living room," suggests Amy. "And put the movie in?"

No one seems to want to.

"What are you guys doing tonight?" Stuart asks Erica and her boyfriend.

She shrugs.

"Has anybody been up to Cutter's Ridge?" says Tracy. "To see the Christmas lights?"

"I know that place," says Amy. "I love it there!"

"Christmas lights, oh boy!" says Mitch sarcastically.

Amy hits him in the shoulder. "Boys have no comprehension of the meaning of Christmas," she tells Tracy.

"Boys have no comprehension, period," says Tracy.

"Let's go up there," says Amy.

"Maybe we should," says Tracy.

"You want to," Amy tells Mitch. "I know you do."

"I don't fucking care," says Mitch.

"We can take my car," says Amy.

"We should take Stuart's car," says Mitch.

Stuart asks Beth. She doesn't mind. "But then we gotta take off," says Stuart. "We gotta be somewhere at eleven."

SIXTY

It's decided. They're going to Cutter's Ridge. Amy gets a scarf. Tracy goes upstairs. Erica and her boyfriend talk among themselves. Mitch and Stuart finish their beers.

They regroup in the living room. Amy wraps her scarf around her neck. Tracy comes down the stairs in her fur coat. Amy starts to slip her hand around Mitch's arm. Then she stops: "Oh, sorry," she says. "You don't like that."

Erica and her boyfriend come out of the kitchen. "We have to go to my parents for a little while. We'll try to come back later."

"All right, Erica," says Tracy. She hugs her. "Merry Christmas, if we don't see you."

It's cold outside. There's a wet fog in the air. Mitch pulls the collar of his jacket up around his neck. Amy taps his arm. "Look," she says. She points to a glowing yellow halo formed by the fog and the street light. It's positioned perfectly above the Dodge Charger.

Stuart unlocks his door. He holds his seat forward while Amy gets in. Mitch follows and then Tracy. When they're all seated Mitch has Tracy on his left, Amy on his right. Amy taps his arm. She whispers in his ear: "*Can I hold your hand*?"

Mitch shrugs.

Amy takes his hand.

"Brrrrr," says Tracy.

Stuart starts the car. He revs it a couple of times. He turns the heater on. Mitch settles back against the seat. Amy squeezes his hand. She's also gripping his elbow with her other hand. She leans over and whispers: *"I'm going to make you sooo happy later."*

Mitch smiles bashfully. He sneaks a look at Tracy. She's holding her coat tight around her. Mitch looks forward. He lays his head against the top of the seat. They've begun to move. Stuart is steering slowly through the residential streets. It's hard to see in the fog.

"This looks more like Halloween than Christmas," says Beth.

Stuart turns right onto Hawthorne. He accelerates up the hill. Mitch and the two girls are pressed back into the seat.

"Please don't drive like a maniac," Tracy tells Stuart.

"Stuart, drive like a maniac?" jokes Mitch. "Never."

Stuart responds by accelerating more. But a red light appears in the fog. He slows and stops.

"So what's the deal with Erica and that guy?" Mitch asks Tracy.

"What do you mean?"

"Are they going out?"

"I would hope so. Since they live together."

Mitch nods. He doesn't really care. He just likes talking to Tracy. Even not talking is fun. Just sitting here is fun. Mitch feels a gentle calm spreading over him.

The light turns green. Stuart eases the Dodge Charger forward. It's getting warmer in the car. Mitch looks outside the window on Tracy's side. The fog is thickening. He can barely make out the Natural Baking Co. sign as they pass it.

Stuart veers slightly to avoid something. Mitch enjoys the sensation of rocking back and forth between the two women. He looks over at Tracy again. He watches her hand where it rests on her leg.

"I love Christmas lights," says Amy, when they pass a glittering store front.

"Yeah," says Mitch, his head back, his eyes half-closed.

"Yellow, yellow!" Beth says suddenly.

Mitch doesn't have to move his head. He can see the yellow light ahead of them turn red. He hears Stuart's foot push down on the accelerator. The Dodge Charger lifts up and speeds toward the empty intersection.

Then he sees the headlights from the right. It's a large sedan. It's moving at the exact wrong speed, from the exact wrong distance. Beth screams. Amy burrows her head into Mitch's side. Mitch sucks in his breath.

But then there's another sound. It's Stuart: letting off the gas and slamming it down again. The Dodge Charger lifts higher, revs harder, explodes forward. Mitch's head jerks back. The car interior fills with light all around him. There's a shrieking of horns, of tires, and then...they're through the intersection. They're alone in the fog. They're alive.

Stuart drives. Beth slowly lifts her head. Amy tentatively sits up. Mitch lets out his breath. Otherwise, he hasn't moved. Except for his hand. He's got them both now. Amy and Tracy. One in each hand.

Blake Nelson is the author of the novels *Girl* – now a major motion picture – and *Exile*. His writing has appeared in *Details, Jane* and *The New York Observer,* among others. He lives in New York City.